TARRAGON ACADEMY

Book One of the Tarragon Series

Elizabeth James

Thrall of Darkness

ISBN-13: 978-1-9449-6900-4
ISBN-10: 1-9449-6900-4

THE TARRAGON SERIES

CONTENTS

PROLOGUE

Jamie lay in his bed and waited for his father to come home. The room around him was familiar but without his father's presence, everything seemed slightly off. The shadows didn't quite fall the way they usually did; the clock ticked a little slower than usual. A strange aura of chaos infiltrated the floorboards and they creaked at the slightest breeze from his open window, startling him from his drowsing sleep.

Ever since Jamie's mom died when he was a child, it had just been him and his dad and they became the best of friends. His mom earned the big salary so after she died, his dad had to work long hours to keep them in Jamie's childhood home and make sure Jamie had healthy food and clean clothes, but Jamie never minded his dad's constant working. It just made their moments together that much more precious.

In three years from now, as soon as Jamie turned sixteen, he planned on getting a job to help out. He already babysat for the neighbors and made enough so that his dad didn't have to pay him an allowance, but he wanted to help with the bigger bills, too. He hoped that someday, before he went off to college, he and his father could live like they did before his mother's death and not have to worry so much about money.

He was tired of having to scrounge for coupons and buy food that he had to hide when his friends came over for fear that they would ridicule him. Not that he had many friends. He tended to be a loner after his mother died; for a long time he had avoided contact with his friends out of grief, and by the time he was ready for relationships again no one accepted him. Except his father. His father was always there to talk and comfort him, and make the house more livable.

When they were together, it was like his mother was alive again and the family was complete. He wanted that feeling to last forever. The whole house was different: brighter, happier, with a brilliant glow that vibrated with laughter and emitted heavenly scents of chicken dumpling soup when his father could be persuaded to cook. His mother's presence was in everything and when he and his dad played together, talked together, laughed together, the world was complete and Jamie knew deep down in his heart that everything was well.

But when his dad was gone late like this, working as always, the house began to take on a sinister feel. The rocking chair where his parents had taught him to read, where just last week his dad had sat while Jamie awkwardly came out to him and admitted that he liked guys, where he himself frequently sat while doing homework, began to fill his mind with terror. What if it started rocking by itself, with no one in it? What if he looked over and saw his mother, long dead, or his dad, cold and white like his mother had been when Jamie last saw her in the coffin?

The normally reassuring creaks of the stairs were hideous now, because they reminded Jamie that he was all alone in the house, without a father to protect him. And the shadows, always the shadows, growing twice as long on nights when his father had to work late, stretching up his bed as if to strangle him in his sleep. On nights like this he missed his old live-in nanny, who was now married and expecting a child of her own.

A pounding on the door below set his heart racing and he leapt up, gasping and sweating. A burglar? Should he stay here or run for help? The pounding continued and someone called his name. Ice crawled into his heart. Once, one of his friends said that her father always came home too drunk to unlock the door. Jamie's father had never been drunk, at least not that Jamie could tell. Why would he start now? Jamie slid out of bed and went downstairs. There were blue and red flashing lights outside and he peeked out the window and spotted a police car. He froze.

The pounding continued. In a daze, Jamie opened the door, hoping to see his father. Even if his father was in handcuffs and had committed some horrible crime, Jamie wanted to see him. Needed to see him. Because he knew, was afraid but knew, what the officer on the other side of the door would say. He couldn't bear to hear it or admit it, but in his heart he already knew.

His father was dead.

CHAPTER ONE

Desire

The class stretched on forever as Jamie stared at the clock overhead. Mr. Ferrin droned on about some medieval cult and he shook his head to keep awake. He was nineteen-years-old now and shouldn't be waiting for the minute hand to finish its slow arc like some first-grader. But he couldn't focus on college today, even though they were nearing exams. He couldn't even focus on how unusual the exam preparation was becoming. The strange thing about the exams was that no one told them what the exam was over or what it would be like. The teachers just kept saying it would test everything they'd learned in and out of the classroom, and the same exam would count for every class.

But it didn't matter. All that mattered was Scott. A dreamy smile flitted across Jamie's lips before he could stop it. He glanced around to see if anyone had noticed. No one had. The others were busy taking notes on the history of the ancient cult his teacher was obsessed with. The Drakonens, a tribe of dragon worshippers from ancient England. Sounded made up to Jamie, but then again he was in this Academy to learn about lost cultures. When he heard that there was an entire university dedicated to uncovering and studying lost civilizations and languages, he knew he had to attend. There were plenty of other perks as well, not to mention the fact that they were giving him a full ride and a stipend for expenses. He should be repaying their kindness by listening to the lecture, but it was hard today, with thoughts of Scott on his mind.

A few other students were staring off into space like him and he wondered if they were in love. His cheeks felt hot and he knew he was blushing. Love. It couldn't be, not after such a short time. He'd only met Scott last month after class. He still wasn't sure why the upperclassman had been hanging around the younger students and he couldn't imagine why the muscular, dark-haired man had taken an interest in Jamie, but he had.

Scott was tall, dark, and handsome, and now Jamie understood why girls always squealed over that combination. Scott wore his hair a little shaggy so that it always looked perfectly mussed, and he was just tall enough that Jamie would have to stand on tiptoe if they kissed. Not if, Jamie thought to himself. When. He was determined to make it happen, to call that beautiful face his and to kiss that finely planed nose and chiseled cheeks, straight out of a catalogue, and to know that those sparkling grey eyes belonged to him and no one else.

When he had left class and seen Scott out in the hall for the first time, his stomach flipped and he felt dizzy. It was as if fate had decided to stop being subtle and instead had thrown out huge neon signs announcing that this was the man he would spend the rest of his life with. The only problem was that Jamie hadn't told anyone that he was gay, and he didn't know if Scott was gay. So he played it as cool as he could and introduced himself to the handsome upperclassman. They talked about the class he had just left and Scott – what a beautiful name, he had thought – offered to walk him back to the dorms. Another sign from fate, he figured. He almost felt as though Scott had been placed in that hallway just for him, because while Scott had talked to other students, he only offered to walk with Jamie.

Jamie had smoothed down his hair and nervously rubbed his jeans. He was in his favorite black t-shirt with dragon patterns on the front and black slacks, and he suddenly felt too goth to be next to the immaculate senior. He was a loner and back in high school the only clique that accepted him dressed all in black, so he had gotten used to it. He knew the color made too much of a contrast with his pale skin and often made him look ghostly, and walking beside Scott, he realized for the first time that he actually cared what someone else thought about his appearance. He didn't have many color tops but after that initial encounter, he tried to wear colors on the days he knew he would run into Scott.

It was getting to be every day, he thought with a pleased smile. He had been to Scott's apartment on campus a few times to hang out, and already he considered Scott one of his good friends. But he still wasn't sure about Scott's sexuality, and until today he had been too frightened of the fallout to announce his own sexuality publicly. The only person he had ever come out to was his father, and his father was dead. As much as he knew it didn't make sense, he equated coming out with death and he was terrified that if he told anyone, something terrible would happen.

The bell shattered through his skull and he jumped, much to the amusement of the class. Mr. Ferrin harrumphed and went about picking up his books, not even seeming to care that half the class was already out the door or laughing hysterically. Jamie felt a little bad for the teacher, but not too much.

Just two days ago after class, the handsome Mr. Ferrin had placed his hand on Jamie's shoulder and pulled him a little too close, asking how he was doing and if there was anything he could do to help. Jamie had pulled away and Mr. Ferrin looked disappointed. Maybe he was trying to be a father figure, since everyone knew Jamie's father died years ago in a mysterious fire, but it felt more like a come on and Jamie couldn't think of any- thing creepier, even though Mr. Ferrin was only a few years older than his students and pretty hot.

In fact, the teacher's hotness was the only redeeming quality of the class for many of the students, even though it was an all- boys university. There were numerous gay guys on campus but if anything, it made Jamie long to hide even further in the closet because he felt so inadequate next to their slim physiques and tawny good looks. He couldn't imagine why Mr. Ferrin would hit on him when there were so many other attractive guys around who would love that kind of attention from the history teacher.

Jamie wasn't out to anyone at school because he never had a reason stronger than his fears, but now that he was falling for Scott, he knew he needed to at least tell his roommate. Jamie was determined to make something happen between him and Scott, preferably today. Those neon signs from fate were too hard to miss and he couldn't deny his own feelings any longer.

Jamie's roommate and best friend Amar was waiting for Jamie to compose himself and head to their fencing meet together. He didn't know Jamie was planning on skipping and asking Scott out. Jamie had been planning it in careful detail for days now. He would find Scott near the campus rose garden and they would walk alone together while Jamie spilled his heart. Scott would listen carefully, then confess his own love and passionately kiss him again and again even while Jamie protested that someone would see. Jamie wouldn't care if anyone saw, though, because for once he wouldn't be ashamed of being gay. Normally he tried to hide to his identity, but with Scott, he wouldn't care. People could stare all they liked. Scott meant everything to him.

Blushing and realizing Amar was still waiting for him, he hesitated. This was his first step in coming out. Once he told Amar, he was determined to finally become the person he had always been inside: a gay man. But what would be the fallout from that decision? He had come out to his father, and his father had died. Ever since then he had never told anyone. It was irrational to think that being gay led to his father's death, but he still blamed himself and couldn't shake the feeling that if he allowed himself to come out to his friends, something would happen to them. But he was gay, and there was nothing anyone could do to change it. It was time to tell Amar that he was gay. And very much enthralled by a certain upperclassman.

Well, no time like the present, Jamie thought. After checking to make sure they were alone, Jamie took a deep breath and pulled Amar into the seat next to him.

"I met this guy, an upperclassman. I think I really like him."

4

He waited as the words dangled in the room like bait for his playful friend to snatch and rip him to shreds with. He'd seen Amar with one of the girls at the sister campus nearby; hell, he'd seen tons of freshmen with girls. It wasn't like being gay was normal, even though an unusual amount of guys here were, and he had carefully decided to keep it to himself until he had a good reason to share. Like Scott. He smiled. Scott was a very good reason to come out.

He rubbed his palms against his pants. He hadn't expected to get this nervous. If he was this nervous with Amar, would he have the courage to tell Scott? Yes, he told himself. He would just gather his courage, blurt it out, and let the chips fall where they may. Fate had given him the signs and Scott could pick up the pieces.

"Oh, um," Amar stumbled. "Well, I don't know how to say this but I kind of knew. I mean, that's why I like you as my wing-man. The girls love you and you don't love them, you know? And you're not like, well, the way I imagined guys like you would be so I always thought you were kind of cool."

Jamie laughed. A wingman? He had never thought of it like that, probably because he wasn't interested in the girls. But it was true: although he didn't have many female friends, he always attracted female attention when they went out. And he'd always noticed that the girls he shared a few drinks and laughs with always ended up with Amar. He'd just never put it all together before.

"So this guy," Amar continued. "Wow, this is weird. But I guess I talk to you about girls, right? So does this guy even know you exist?"

"Yeah, actually he does," Jamie said. He blushed. "We met a month ago and hung out for a while, just talked and stuff after one of my classes. I see him every day and we've gotten to hang out a couple of times since then."

"Okay, don't tell me if I don't want to know, but what does hang out mean?"

"You know, like we do. Talk. Play video games. We ordered a

pizza last week and played video games."

"So he's a nerd."

"No, not really, I mean I think he would have rather watched football or something but he has a lot of interests."

"Are these dates? I mean, is that how it works? Cuz if I had my ideal date, it would be pizza and a video game. That chick would rock."

"No. He doesn't know how I feel. It's just – hanging out."

"You know what you have to do, right?"

"Yeah, and today's the day. I'm going to tell him."

Jamie nodded, more to give himself courage than to assure Amar of anything.

"Wait, is he even gay?"

Jamie ducked his head. He'd been wondering the same thing for a while. People didn't just take an interest in other people like this, not unless they were interested. Friendships didn't start like this, did they? No, friendships were more casual. Scott seemed to be actively finding him after his classes and asking him over to his place to hang. There had to be more to it.

Amar whistled. "Well, just tell him that if he hurts you, I'm gonna beat him up."

"Thanks, buddy."

"Good luck."

Amar headed off to fencing practice and Jamie sat in the desk a little longer. He felt reassured. Amar had reacted well, and nothing disastrous was happening yet. Maybe the world wouldn't fall apart if he allowed himself to be happy for once. He shut his eyes and Scott's face floated in his mind. With a smile, he stood up and prepared himself to tell Scott about his true feelings.

CHAPTER TWO

Confrontation

Scott nearly walked in on Jamie and Amar and slid back into the hallway before they noticed him. What were they talking about? It was tempting to listen, but he respected Jamie's privacy too much. He noticed another man leaning against the doorframe; Mike Ferrin had no such qualms. Scott knew more than enough about Mike's character from when they were students together to know that the newly hired teacher had been eavesdropping since class ended. Only four years ago Scott had been a freshman and Mike had been a senior and what Scott had assumed was an innocent crush turned into rape. He knew Mike's tactics now and he wasn't about to let the same thing happen to Jamie.

Mike was watching Scott with a smirk, as if he knew how badly Scott wanted to hear what Jamie was saying and he knew Scott would never ask Mike what had already been said. There was also a possessive gleam in his eyes that worried Scott. He knew firsthand how dangerous the man could be, and since Mike was Jamie's teacher he was afraid Jamie might be intimidated into something he would later regret. Scott had felt pressured into sex by the situation and the fact that Mike was so much older than him; Jamie would feel doubly intimidated.

Grabbing Mike's shirt, he dragged the man away from the room and ignored the startled looks from the freshman who were shocked to see their teacher manhandled. Well, he wasn't a teacher in Scott's eyes. He was nothing but a lecherous creep. Mike allowed himself to be dragged and appeared amused by

Scott's anger. Once they were a safe distance away, Mike broke his grip and turned the tables, slamming him against the wall. He was too surprised to fight for a moment and the man's handsome red-blond locks brushed against his cheek as Mike leaned in to whisper in his ear.

"Jealous?"

Mike pressed his body against Scott's fully for a moment and he went rigid, all too aware of the students in the hallway staring. He hoped it looked like a fight from their point of view, and not the sexual advance that it was. The feel of Mike's body against his brought back his memory of the rape vividly: Mike had brought him here, to this hallway, when he was a freshman like Jamie. It was after hours, when everyone was gone, and Mike had forced him against this very wall while he stroked and kissed and pushed against Scott. Scott fought at first, but Mike's persistence and skilled hands did things to Scott's body that were incredible and when Scott's attempts to fight began to grow desperate and violent, Mike had overpowered him. Scott eventually surrendered with a wail that brought one of the teachers. The teacher had simply stared at the two of them locked in only partially consensual sex, then turned his back.

At the time, Scott had felt raped twice, once by Mike and again by the teacher who knew but let it happen. He didn't know then about the exam, or the consequences of taking it as a virgin. He didn't know that the upperclassmen, including Mike at the time, were assigned freshmen to seduce in an attempt to reduce the inevitable casualties that took place at the exam. All he knew was that a teacher had seen Mike forcing his way into him while Scott cried and tried to say no, and the teacher had done nothing.

This year, very few of the students were virgins and all but one had been taken care of already. All but Jamie. He had resisted everyone's efforts, including one physical assault by an overzealous senior in the locker room. It didn't help that everyone assumed he was straight until quite recently. The council who ran the exam had sent dozens of girls after him and he had skillfully deflected them, just as he was deflecting the men they were now sending.

Scott had been watching the situation closely because he saw himself in Jamie's attempts to be free. Jamie just wanted to do things at his own pace, just like Scott had wanted, but at this school you either had sex or died. It was a cruel fate and sometime Scott wondered why Jamie had even been allowed into the school.

Scott had never taken part in what he considered the rape of the underclassmen, but when he saw that the council was seriously considering sending men like Mike after the boy, he had approached them and asked if he could try. The old men had been practically salivating at the thought that Scott was finally obeying their commands and participating in their ridiculous, corrupt practices. He hid his disdain, though, because he honestly wanted to be the one to take Jamie and angering them would injure the boy.

The council didn't let him go easy, though. He had to agree to be on their list of upperclassmen they could call for difficult cases like Jamie in future semesters. The council could call him back to the school until he turned twenty-five: three more years. It was worth it, he decided, to be able to woo Jamie the way the boy deserved. And he was having results. He and Jamie had already developed a friendship, and he had seen Jamie looking at him with a hint of fire in his eyes.

The boy seemed so fragile, but Scott was willing to be that under the surface was a passionate, outgoing man just waiting to burst out of the protective shell he had built over the years. He ached for the pain and hardship the boy had been through: losing both parents and having to live in an emotionally abusive home the past few years. The scars ran deep in Jamie and Scott just wanted to hold the boy and fill those scars with kisses and love, but Scott also had a time limit. The first year exam was in two weeks and if Jamie was still a virgin, he would be unable to form the kind of emotional attachment necessary to survive.

Scott tried to accustom the boy to physical contact frequently, but Jamie was still hesitant. He tried subtle gestures, since larger gestures seemed to frighten Jamie: bumping against him in the hallways, brushing hands while passing him a slice of pizza, gripping his shoulder and gazing into his eyes when he said something important or funny.

Slowly, Jamie was coming out of his shell in a way he hadn't with any other upperclassman and Scott was finding himself entranced by the gentle, sweet boy. He wished he could push back the exam, but no human could do that. Jamie deserved proper wooing, and the council was giving them no time. Only two weeks to the exam and Jamie hadn't even admitted he was gay, but perhaps this conversation with Amar was a sign that Jamie was becoming more comfortable with the thought of intimacy.

"Thinking about Jamie?" Mike asked.

Scott had nearly forgotten he was there. Mike had backed off a few feet and the jealousy in his eyes was clear as he continued.

"Everyone is allowed to go after him, you know," Mike continued. "Not just you. And I have a proven track record for my ability to break difficult men."

He stroked Scott's cheek and Scott shivered. Scott had also been considered a difficult case, like Jamie, until Mike was assigned to him. The council preferred to avoid rape, but would allow it as a last resort. Scott had been raped two days before the exam and as much as he hated Mike for what he had done, he knew it had saved his life. Students needed to have the ability to form an intimate, physical relationship with another creature during the exam, and as the council always pointed out, the best way to do that was to form a sexual relationship beforehand as practice. It was a cruel truth and Scott knew that Mike's actions were absolutely necessary in his case. But they wouldn't be necessary for Jamie. Scott would see to that.

"I'm taking care of it, Mike," Scott said. "You don't need to get involved."

"Yeah, I think you might be right, based on what he was saying in there. But if this falls through, I'll be waiting. Everyone else has given up. They think he's incapable of new relationships after his father was killed. But I won't let one of my students go into the exam unprepared."

"How noble of you," Scott said under his breath.

He wondered if Mike had taken any other students to bed, and if the young teacher had bothered to get permission from the council first. Mike was only three years older than him and six years older than his students, so age wasn't that much of an issue, but the power of his position should have made Mike unable to pursue the students. The idea of a teacher and student together was unpleasant, to say the least. There was no way a student could fully consent in that relationship and Scott was quite sensitive to the pain of nonconsensual encounters.

"If you haven't finished the job in a week, I'll take over," Mike warned. "The council wanted me to warn you."

"I have two weeks," Scott said, alarmed at having his time cut in half. Two weeks he could manage, but not one. Not with a boy as sensitive and nervous about intimacy as Jamie. "I'll be there in two weeks, and well on my way in one."

"The council says one week," Mike said with a shrug. "They want to be safe and I don't blame them. It's not too late to expel him, after all. He doesn't know anything about us."

"No. He'll take the exam and he'll get through it. And I'll be the one to help him."

Mike sighed. "I believe you. Like I said, I think he has potential and I haven't given up on him. But the council has. You have one week and then he's expelled. Better expelled than, well, you know."

Scott thought of the corpses that littered the ground after each of the exams. No matter what the council did, how many students they weeded out during the first few months, there were always casualties. There was just no way to truly determine who would live and who would die once the exam started and the eggs began to hatch.

He felt the familiar brush of another voice on his consciousness reaffirming his belief that Jamie would survive and he nodded. Mike must have taken that as agreement to the one week because he left, but Scott didn't care. Whatever happened, Jamie would take the exam and he would live through it. He had to. Narné had never been wrong before and was far more perceptive than many of his kin, and Narné predicted that Jamie would not only pass the exam, he would take the most prized egg of all: the Queen's.

Inwardly he cursed the council for their interference and wondered if he could get out of his side of the agreement since they had changed theirs. Probably not. They did what they wanted and no one could say otherwise. They had become corrupt and only someone with a Queen egg had any chance of overthrowing them. If Jamie managed to survive the exam and bond with a Queen, he would be equal to the council and he could put an end to the rapes and bribery that went on behind the scenes at the council's command. The council only saw Jamie as a weakling, but Narné saw him as the man who would bring about a new era at Tarragon Academy. As long as Scott could get him there.

CHAPTER THREE

Confession

Jamie found Scott disturbingly close to the classroom where he and Amar had been talking and immediately he wondered if Scott had been eavesdropping. But Scott's smile was surprised and he seemed as happy as ever to see Jamie, so Jamie pushed the thought aside. It was ridiculous, after all. He was a bit disappointed that they wouldn't meet in the rose garden, but not all fantasies could come true. As he drew closer to Scott, he couldn't help but inhale the fine scent of cloves and leather that always lingered near the man's strong form.

Like a cowboy from the old days, he thought, except real cowboys had almost certainly smelled terrible. Not like Scott, although Scott would have made a fine cowboy nonetheless. Jamie shut his eyes for a moment and pictured Scott on a horse, the two magnificent creatures working together to tame the herd into submission, Scott's pelvis providing the only direction needed by the well trained horse as his hands threw the lasso and perfectly hooked a stray cattle to pull it aside for special attention. He would love Scott's special attention, and he would love to be the horse underneath Scott, obeying his every command without need for words, two beings united by passion and communicating through their flesh.

"Hey, Jamie, you okay?"

"What?"

Jamie felt himself going red again. He was glad for his baggy jeans because he was a little hard, but he didn't think anyone could notice. Thinking of Scott as a cowboy was far too sexy for the school hallway. He needed to keep that image for nighttime as he worked through his lust privately.

"Yeah, I'm fine. How are you?"

"Great. Want to do something tonight?"

"Let's do something right now," Jamie said, determined to go through with his plan.

Without thinking, he took Scott's hand and started pulling him towards the school exit. A few students looked at him oddly. Then he realized that they were holding hands and he stopped, embarrassed.

"Oh, I know what's wrong," Scott said with a dark chuckle. He gripped Jamie's hand more firmly and led them both out.

Jamie's mind swarmed with worries. What did that mean? Did he know that Jamie was gay and now he was being rejected? But then why were they still holding hands? Why was Scott taking him to – wait, Scott was taking him to football field! The freshmen jocks were out there and they frequently beat up gay freshmen no matter how many times the academy punished them.

"What are you doing? I don't- let me go," he said, pulling against the stronger man's grip. Damn Scott's strength. Even if it was part of what made him sexy.

"I'm not taking you to the field, you idiot," Scott said. "I'll get beat up too if the freshmen jocks catch us holding hands. I'm taking you somewhere else. You do want to talk to me privately, don't you?"

"Um, yes?"

Jamie walked freely now, surprised how much he was willing to trust the other man. He didn't really think Scott would get beat up but it was reassuring to know that Scott understood what he was thinking. He felt himself bouncing on the balls of his feet as they walked. Scott knew, he had to know, he had just admitted holding hands meant they were both gay and could get beat up, and he knew Jamie wanted to talk to him, and he still wanted to talk so the answer must be yes. A smile stretched across his face as he followed Scott.

Scott led him behind the field into the forest. Jamie had heard there was a forest near campus that was a make out spot but had never dreamed of going there. He wasn't a monk by any means – his sheets were proof of that – but he had never met the guy that he was willing to come out for until now, so he had no experience at all. He eyed Scott's tall figure. Scott probably knew all sorts of things and had tons of experience. Would he be disappointed to learn how inexperienced Jamie was? Jamie hadn't even kissed anyone yet and he was already nineteen. That was pretty pathetic, according to Amar.

A clearing opened up before them, a small hollow with soft green grass about ankle high and flowers scattered throughout. A hill at one end provided elevation and Jamie could imagine snuggling together while lying against the hill. He imagined Scott turning towards him, leaning over him until the weight of his body rubbed him in the most delightful way and he would have to clutch Scott and beg for relief. That might happen sooner than later, he thought with a shiver. He wasn't quite sure how he felt about such physical intimacy yet. He wanted it desperately, but he was afraid that Scott was planning on using him and then dumping him. He needed something real, something he could hold on to. He needed love.

"Are you cold?" Scott asked, wrapping an arm around his shoulders.

"No," Jamie said. Scott hesitated and started to remove his arm but Jamie grabbed it and kept it in place. "It's okay. I don't have to be cold for you to hold me."

He took a deep breath, then faced Scott. With Scott's arm around his shoulder, they were face-to-face, close enough to kiss.

"I, um, wanted to tell you that, well, I'm kind of interested in you," he said softly, unable to meet Scott's eyes.

Rejection at this point would be too much. Was Scott just playing along, toying with him so that he could dash his hopes even further? Tears welled up at the thought and he shut his eyes. He remembered his mother's body, cold and white, and his father's ashes in the urn at his aunt's house. He thought of his aunt and her children, and how she had ignored him unless she had chores for him to do. He was just another responsibility, she frequently told him. Just someone she promised her damn brother-in-law she would look after, and now that her brother-in-law kicked the bucket she was stuck honoring that promise. No one in that family loved him, he knew. The cousins saw him as a toy or someone to do their homework for them, and his aunt saw him as a useless body she had to feed.

Sometimes he wished he could move to a foster family, but he doubted it would be any better. No one would care for him after his father died. No one could care for him. He was lost and unlovable. The touch of a hand on his chin brought him back to the present and he stared up at Scott.

"I was hoping you'd say that," Scott said to Jamie's surprise, "because I've been kind of interested in you since you first came here."

"I – wait, what? School started three months ago! We only met one month ago. What happened before that?"

He felt a pout on his lips but couldn't stop it. Was he unlovable? Had Scott seen him and dismissed him at first, because of something Jamie had done? Scott had known about him for two months and done nothing. Two months they could have been sneaking out to the forest like this, two months they could have been kissing or perhaps even more. What had changed in that time to make Scott approach him?

Perhaps in two months Scott would have persuaded Jamie to strip for him, and they would have laid down together and Scott would have stroked his body and kissed him while Jamie whimpered in pleasure. Perhaps Jamie would have cried out while Scott pierced him for the first time, while Jamie gasped at the pleasure he knew he felt only an echo of at night by himself.

Scott trailed his finger along Jamie's jaw and he leaned into the caress.

"I wanted to make sure you had friends your own age at this

school. Besides, I wasn't sure if you'd be interested in me. You're a little hard to read."

"Yeah," Jamie said and gulped. It was his fault. He had been so busy avoiding people that he had almost lost out on the man he was already thinking of giving his virginity to. It warmed his heart a little that Scott was still pursuing him after all this time, and that Scott had his best interests at heart. But the question still remained: now that he was out to Amar and Scott, would something terrible happen to them?

Jamie shrugged. "I don't really want everyone knowing. Until now, I guess. Now I don't care."

"Good," Scott said, pulling him into a hug and tucking Jamie's head underneath his. Because of Scott's height, he fit perfectly in the crook of Scott's neck and he could feel Scott's throat hum as he continued speaking.

"Because I'm very possessive and I want everyone to know that you're mine."

Jamie flushed and knew he was red from head to toe. His hands, which had been at his sides until then, now traveled hesitantly upward until they rested on Scott's hips.

"I know why I want you, but, well, why do you want me?"

Scott laughed, the sound reverberating against Jamie's head as he lay tucked against the man's body. "Haven't you seen yourself, little angel? And you're so intelligent and witty, too. I can't believe I'm the first person to pursue you."

"You're hardly pursuing me," Jamie said, reluctantly pulling back so that he could see Scott's eyes glittering in amusement. It was true; Jamie was doing most of the pursuing in this conversation. He had initiated it, after all. He was the one exposing all of his secrets and laying his heart out for Scott to trample or cherish. His chest was heavy and happy at being called 'angel' even as he worried that he couldn't live up to Scott's standards.

"I've been pursuing you from the moment you set foot on this campus, even if you didn't know it, sweetheart. And I'm not the only one. I'm just the only one you've noticed."

Jamie's thoughts flew to Mr. Ferrin, then to a senior who had approached him in the shower one day. He had been so embarrassed that he had assumed it was a prank, not a come on. The other boy had tried to get in the shower with him and had seen him naked. Jamie didn't like to think about that – his body was shameful and the thought that anyone had seen him naked was humiliating. Even in his fantasies of Scott, he was always at least partially dressed to cover the pale scars criss-crossing his shoulders and thighs where he used to cut himself after his father died. No one was supposed to know about those scars, and except for the upperclassman in the shower, no one did. They were shameful, his body was shameful. But maybe Scott would be able to accept him despite his flaws.

Jamie shut his eyes. "I don't want anyone else. Just you."

"Good," Scott whispered, clasping him to his breast again. "You have no idea how happy that makes me."

Jamie smiled tremulously and pushed all of the negative thoughts out of his head. This was not the time to worry, this was the time to be in the moment with the man he was falling in love with. Every word out of Scott's mouth melted Jamie's heart a little more and as he pulled back to study Scott, his smile became firm and his stomach gave a tiny flip. It felt like electricity between them and Jamie knew this was what it was like to be in love.

CHAPTER FOUR

First Kiss

After a few moments holding each other, Scott reached down to cup Jamie's face. His lips moved closer and Jamie panicked, tensing immediately. He wasn't ready for his first kiss yet; he had barely started thinking about what he was going to do or how it would work or which way to turn his head or any of that. His fantasies were just that: fantasies. He never imagined the details of the kissing, just the intense pleasure he would get from it. But now that he was faced with two lips headed his way, he realized he was vastly unprepared and he pulled back.

"What's wrong? Did I do something?"

Ashamed, Jamie hung his head. "It's not you, it's just that I've – well, I've never kissed anyone before. Like that. I don't want to mess up."

"You won't. Just relax and let me guide you."

Scott cupped his face again and Jamie shut his eyes. The press of lips against his was nothing exciting at first, just flesh against flesh. Failure. Was this a kiss? How disappointing. He was doing something wrong, he knew he was. Kisses should be like – Lightning! Scott had pressed closer to him and the lightning was there, sparking his nerve endings and nearly making him jump out of the kiss. But one of Scott's hands went to his waist and pulled him close, until their groins touched. Jamie moaned. Instantly, Scott was inside his mouth. Incredible. It was everything he'd dreamed it would be and he clung to Scott's tongue, trying to imitate what the other man was doing even as he felt himself growing hard.

He knew Scott could feel his arousal and that just made him harder until he whimpered and Scott shifted slightly against him, giving him a little friction. All the time his mouth was being explored and claimed and his body went limp in Scott's strong, capable hands as he reached up and clung to Scott's shoulders, unable to think as he tried to pull Scott closer.

He opened his eyes and for a moment, thought he saw a second face beside Scott's face, an alien, reptile face that was strangely reassuring. It seemed to be crooning in time with his heartbeat and his knees went weak. The reptile's long tongue flicked out to his neck just as Scott began giving little kisses to his cheek, his jaw, then mouthed his way down Jamie's neck as Jamie moaned in sheer pleasure and wrapped his hands in Scott's hair. With Scott's face lowered the creature was now exposed and even though desire was Jamie's primary concern, he was also intensely curious.

The creature looked like a giant, winged dinosaur, a tyrannosaur with larger front limbs, perhaps, although it was hard to tell because the creature was the same dark emerald as the forest and its folded wings were tipped in sienna right where they intercepted tree trunks. Was it camouflage or was the creature invisible? The creature stared at him with single-minded intensity and he gave a start as he recognized hunger in the eyes, the same hunger he felt in Scott's mouth as the man kissed and nibbled along his collarbone, pulling his shirt away to expose his pale flesh and kiss even more.

At Jamie's motion, Scott stopped and stood straight to look down at him, concern reflected in those grey eyes.

"What's wrong, baby?"

Without a word, Jamie pointed to the creature but as soon as he did, the creature was gone. He blinked in surprise. Scott turned.

"Did you see something?" he asked. He didn't sound patronizing, just confused.

"A- an animal was there. I guess it left," Jamie said, feeling silly and disappointed at ending their first intimate moment so abruptly.

"What kind of animal?"

Jamie tried to laugh in a husky, seductive way. "You must be a good kisser because I was seeing things. It looked like a dinosaur with wings but it must have been a deer or something."

Scott was completely silent and he stared at the forest where the creature had been. After a few seconds, Jamie shifted uncomfortably. He had tried to turn the situation into a chance for a compliment and another kiss and it had just made him look like an idiot. Great. Long, impatient moments went by while Scott stared into space, clearly trying to figure out what to say next.

"I've seen that too, sometimes," he finally said.

It was not what Jamie expected.

"You have?"

"Yeah," Scott said. "You know Tarragon Academy is named after the mountain these woods border. Mount Tarragon. Do you know what tarragon is?"

"It's an herb, right?"

"Dragon's herb."

Jamie grinned. "So I saw the ghost of a dragon who once roamed this mountain? I suppose the locals have some cool stories about dragons and that's why we aren't allowed out, so we don't get freaked out by the tales and want to go to school somewhere less haunted."

"You laugh, but it's a serious concern."

Scott wasn't looking at him and sounded uncomfortable. Did the other man believe in ghosts and dragons? Everyone knew there weren't dragons, at least not the ones in stories, the ones like the creature he had just imagined. But then again, he had imagined it. Why?

"I'm sorry," Jamie said. "I didn't mean to say something wrong, and I certainly didn't mean to make you stop. I was just startled because I thought I saw something. Maybe we could go back to the whole kissing thing? I was kind of liking that."

"Kind of?" Scott laughed. "You kind of like a lot of things."

Jamie shrugged in fake nonchalance, pleased that the older man's strange mood was broken and they seemed headed on a better path in the conversation. His lips ached and he wanted to feel Scott's pressed against them again. He had never imagined that kissing could feel so good.

"I'll keep my eyes closed this time," Jamie promised, wrapping his arms around Scott's shoulders and tilting his head up.

A small frown played around Scott's beautiful lips. "It might be better if you don't. But you're too beautiful for this conversation. I just want to kiss you, sweetheart, so that's what you get."

Jamie grinned in victory and let his eyes flutter shut as Scott plundered his mouth a second time. It was even more incredible than the first. Scott's tongue darted around his with a skill that had his knees weak and trembling in seconds and he would have collapsed if Scott's strong arms weren't holding him up. His body vibrated with pleasure and Scott's thumbs made smalls circles against his flesh that made him moan and squirm in the stronger man's grasp, but Scott held him tight as his breath and love were stolen by the dark, handsome man kissing him. Jamie gave himself entirely to the experience, shutting out everything in the world beyond this moment, this passion, this kiss.

They finally broke away when Jamie began to feel lightheaded. He was surprised to see that Scott appeared truly breathless as well. He had seemed so in control during the first kiss but now he gasped for air with the same abandon as Jamie.

"I," he began, "have never felt that with anyone."

"Me neither," Jamie said, then laughed with Scott until the laughter petered out and Scott clasped him again.

"I'm so glad I could give you your first real kiss," he whispered.

"I hope you give me more firsts," Jamie said without thinking, his body aching against the strong muscles of the older, taller and, in his opinion, more beautiful man.

Scott laughed again. "In time, sweetheart. I don't want to rush you and you have that exam to prepare for. I don't want to take away from your studies."

Jamie felt the need in his groin and knew there would be no studying tonight, if he even knew what to study for. But the thought of the upcoming exam cooled his lust a little and he knew Scott was right. It was already starting to get dark. Jamie's classes were all in the late afternoon and early evening and he usually didn't have time for much of a social life during the week. But with Scott here, studying seemed a distant concern.

"I just want you. You've taken the exam, right? Could you help me study?"

He asked the last shyly, wondering how Amar would feel about Scott coming over for study sessions and also wondering if those study sessions could be turned into something more. He imagined Scott rewarding him with a kiss for every right answer and knew he would study a lot better with the man in the room, even if he would also be a distraction.

"Yes," Scott said. He sounded victorious, for some reason, and surprisingly serious. "Yes, I'll help you study. You just had to ask. I'll make sure you survive the exam."

Jamie laughed but inwardly he questioned Scott's choice of words. When he said 'survive the exam,' it hadn't sounded like a turn of phrase. Were there people who actually didn't survive, who were killed during the exam? The school had a weird vibe to it, after all, and no one outside the school knew much about it.

First-year students were kept strictly apart from the outside world except for the sister school nearby, which was unusual for a college. Students couldn't leave campus without permission and even then they could only go to the sister campus. The ruling council was extremely picky about who they allowed to enter and it didn't seem to be reliant on grades but rather on the personal interview conducted by the President. Jamie's own interview had been bumpy, with many of the questions concerning his father's untimely demise in the fire six years ago. His father had no relationship to the school, so Jamie didn't understand their interest beyond simple curiosity. He had actually been surprised to find out he had been admitted with a full ride to the pricy university.

Despite Tarragon Academy's oddities, however, it was still one of the most prestigious colleges in the country. All of the graduates – every single one – ended up wealthy or famous or some combination. It was an impressive place, and a weird one, but surely they wouldn't literally kill off the weak when they could just expel them?

"Um, what is the exam?"

"You know I can't talk about that, Jamie," Scott said. "But you should study. Why don't we go back to your dorm and have our first session? I need to meet your roommate, anyway, if I'm going to be making regular visits."

"Yeah, he'll want to make sure you're up to his standards," Jamie joked, thinking of how Amar always brought his serious girlfriends to Jamie for approval.

"More like if he's up to mine," Scott said, but he was laughing and sounded relaxed. "I told you I'm possessive. I want to make sure you're surrounded by good people."

Jamie grinned and a strange pleasure flushed through his body. Scott really cared for him if he wanted him to be surrounded by good people.

"He's great. And maybe after we study, he wouldn't mind leaving us alone for a while. I'd kind of like to try kissing again. I'm not sure I got it the first two times."

"Slow learner, eh?" Scott asked with a pleased smirk.

"Yeah, maybe," Jamie said, trying to sound carefree, as if he did this all the time. He knew he was red as a beet.

Scott lifted Jamie's hand to his mouth and kissed it. "I think we can arrange that. Let's head back now. The dining hall will be closing soon and you'll need food if you want to keep up."

Truly red now, Jamie scooted along behind Scott as they returned to the main campus, dreaming of all the things he could do now that he had a boyfriend. His worries about rejection evaporated into the night as Scott reached out to take his hand and squeezed it gently before they entered the dorms. Jamie smiled up at Scott and knew that nothing bad would ever come between them.

CHAPTER FIVE

First Lesson

"Why are they called the tarragon tribe? Why not the dragon cult or something? And why have Tarragon Academy here when the tribe was in England?"

Jamie thought of the creature in the forest and wondered if it had been a dragon after all. He hadn't been paying attention in class but apparently the tribe they had been focusing on all week believed in dragons, so maybe the knowledge had seeped into his brain and turned into the bizarre forest vision.

"We think tarragon comes from the Greek word drakon. Tarragon is the name of an herb now, but only because the herb has dragon in its name: dragonwort. And you've only studied the British tribe, but there are tribes with similar beliefs scattered across the globe. One used to live right here in Portland. Not the Multnomah or Chinook tribes that you've heard of, but a small group that survives to this day and worships this site as a holy site. Or hadn't you noticed that some of the students are Native American?"

Jamie ducked his head. He came from a rural area on the east side of the state and had assumed everyone on the coast had darker skin, so he honestly hadn't noticed anything. His town was white and of course moving closer to Portland would bring diversity. For the most part, he loved it, but it made him overly self-conscious of his pasty white skin. He felt like a beached beluga much of the time, sickly white and gasping in the sudden sunlight even though there wasn't much sun on the coast.

"I'm from the tribe," Scott said.

Jamie looked up and tried to see the stereotypes from the movies in Scott's face. He couldn't. Scott was just – Scott. Beautiful. His tall, dark, and handsome prince. Jamie smiled at the thought of having his own prince.

"So do you have special powers like the ancient tarragon tribe did?" Jamie teased.

"Yes," Scott said simply.

Jamie's jaw dropped.

"I can see the future," Scott continued. "And I can see that we're done for the night. What do you think?"

He caressed Jamie's cheek and Jamie knew he turned beet red. Damn his pale complexion. Jamie leaned into the caress and took Scott's other hand into his own.

"I think that's pretty accurate. So if you can read the future," he said, feeling playful, "How is tonight going to end?"

Scott grinned. "Well," he leaned forward. A tiny wrinkle appeared in his brow and he seemed surprised by something, but he shook his head as if dismissing the thought. "Let's just worry about how tonight begins."

He leaned into Jamie and the boy shut his eyes, waiting for and enjoying the light brush of lips against his. Scott pulled him closer until they were hip to hip on the couch and kissed him again, and Jamie felt his body go limp against the older man's. Heat flooded his body as Scott's tongue danced with his and he moaned into Scott's mouth and pressed closer. His hands hungrily grabbed the man's hair and then cautiously moved to the powerful muscles of his back.

Scott stroked his neck, his back, then reached his hips and slid underneath his shirt. Jamie skittered backward and broke the kiss, surprised by the touch of flesh against flesh and more than a little frightened at the thought of what might come next.

"What's wrong?"

"It's just, I'm not," his voice trailed off and he pulled his shirt down to cover his hips.

He had just taken a shower that morning in preparation for

his big day coming out, but he still didn't feel clean enough for Scott to touch his body. He was embarrassed by his body, by the hair that sprouted around his belly button even though he wanted Scott to finger it and follow the trail down further to the larger patch of hair above his penis. He ached for Scott to touch him like that. But he would be so embarrassed at the same time and he didn't know which instinct would win out. Right now it was embarrassment and he kept his shirt firmly down so Scott couldn't slip his hands underneath.

"Has anyone ever seen you before?" Scott asked. "Is that the problem? Would it help if the lights were off and we were somewhere more private?"

Jamie hadn't even considered the fact that they were still in the living area adjacent to the front door. If Amar walked in, he'd be bound to see them. Jamie slunk lower in the couch and Scott pushed him down so he was lying on top of the younger man. Jamie knew he should feel uncomfortable being pressed down like this, but he didn't. He rather liked being pinned. He knew that Scott wouldn't go faster than he wanted. Scott's hands were up by his head now, after all, not down by his body that shamed him so.

"I just don't feel clean enough," Jamie said awkwardly, not quite sure if Scott would understand that he didn't just mean physically clean but also pure and worthy of such a beautiful, intelligent man as Scott.

A slow smile crept across Scott's face. "We could take a shower together. I can help you get clean and show you just how good you are."

Jamie flushed, imagining Scott's soapy hands running up and down his body, tracing circles around his nipples before sinking lower and lower –

The door opened and Amar walked in, headphones blaring and completely oblivious. He went straight into the kitchen without noticing them, singing to his music under his breath. Jamie's arousal quieted instantly.

"Why don't you introduce me," Scott suggested quietly as

they sat up.

Amar had his back turned to them and was slathering peanut butter on some bread, still singing. Jamie took a moment to collect himself and then called Amar's name loudly. His roommate turned and did a double take at the sight of Jamie and Scott sitting on the couch together. Pretty close together, Jamie realized. But it was too late to scoot further away now, and Amar already knew his secret.

Taking his headphones off, Amar fumbled with his phone until the music went silent. He grabbed his sandwich and sat across from them in the living area, setting his paper plate down while he reached out to shake Scott's hand.

"I'm Amar. Jamie's roommate."

"Scott. Jamie's boyfriend."

Jamie made a strangled sound. He was thrilled at hearing Scott say it out loud and glad for the confirmation of their relationship, but he was terrified that Amar, despite his earlier reassurances, would suddenly stop being okay with this situation. He valued his friendship with Amar too much to risk losing over Scott's careless words, but he suspected Scott's words were anything but careless. Looking at the older man, he realized Scott was testing Amar to see if he really was okay with Jamie being gay. Feeling a little happier, he hesitantly took Scott's hand. Amar shook his head.

"Damn. I wish I could get a girlfriend that fast."

"You have a girlfriend," Jamie pointed out.

"Well, next time," Amar laughed. "You missed a great fencing meet. We went over a new thrust. I'll show it to you later tonight, maybe. Or tomorrow," he added in an unreadable voice. "If you're busy tonight."

"I won't be here too late," Scott said. "Jamie asked me to help him study for the exam."

"Really? Maybe you can help me, too. No one talks about the exam at all, I have no idea what to study for."

Jamie's heart sank slightly. He had hoped to spend his study time getting close to Scott and building his own confidence, but if Amar were there, Amar would steal the spotlight as always and be the star pupil. Maybe Scott would even like Amar better than him. After all, Amar was nearly as handsome as Scott with his almond skin and hazel eyes. All the girls loved him, why wouldn't the guys?

Perhaps he was Native American, Jamie thought with a start. He had never thought about it before – Amar was Amar. But with his name, he was probably from the Middle East. It didn't really matter, since he was American, but Jamie was a little embarrassed that he had never asked Amar about his family history before. He had just assumed it was as boring as his own.

"We can do some group study," Scott said to Jamie's disappointment. "But tonight I think it'll just be me and Jamie."

"Oh," Amar said, looking between them as if suddenly understanding what their study sessions were really going to be about. Jamie flushed again and wondered if he would ever stop being red. His friend's knowing look was too much and he ducked his head to avoid seeing the congratulations and ribald humor in those hazel orbs.

"Yeah, well, if you get a chance for a group session I'd love some help," he continued. "But you two probably have some stuff to talk about. I'll be in my room. For the night. I'll bring my dinner in my room and stay there. So you can stay out here and study. Or whatever."

He was rambling and Amar never rambled. Maybe he wasn't as comfortable with the idea of two guys together as he liked to pretend, or maybe he just wasn't used to being the one to have to evacuate while the other roommate did the wooing for once. Jamie hoped it was the latter, and hoped he didn't mind too much. He felt more comfortable with Scott at his dorm than he did going to Scott's apartment.

He'd only been to Scott's apartment a couple of times to have pizza and play video games but there was something strange about it, some tension in the air that always put him on edge. Like there was another person in the room Jamie couldn't see. It was bizarre. The dorms were better. Safer. In his comfort zone.

He and Scott said good night to Amar, who took his sandwich and a soda and vanished into his room. Then Jamie looked at Scott, wondering what the man was going to do. He knew he should be the one initiating things, since it was his apartment and he was the host, but he just wanted to sit next to this beautiful man all night and ogle him. He didn't think that was what Scott wanted, however. Scott smiled at him and touched his shoulder. He shivered and leaned closer, hoping for a kiss. Nothing happened. He opened his eyes.

"I don't want to move too fast again. If you want something, I want you to give me a clear signal."

His gorgeous lips were only a few inches away but they weren't moving closer and Jamie made a small sound of disappointment. Scott laughed.

"I'll still kiss you, sweetheart. Nothing would please me more. Just tell me that's what you want. I don't want to rush you. Do you want me to kiss you?"

Jamie tilted his head so his lips were ready to be kissed and closed his eyes. He couldn't say the words, couldn't admit his lust to himself. Yes, he wanted it. Needed it. But to admit it would be giving in to that reckless passion he associated with his father's death.

He had come out to his father and his father had died. He had spoken the truth and told his father his true passion, and now he was alone. If he told Scott his true passion, would the same thing happen? Would Scott laugh at him and abandon him after getting him to bare his heart? Or, even worse, would he fall in love with Scott and then lose him like he lost his father? Could he possibly stand another loss like that?

After his father died, Jamie had teetered on the brink for a long time. He started cutting himself to try to relieve the pain, but it did nothing. Other people said it made them feel good to let the blood run, but he felt absolutely nothing at all. He kept trying, thinking he was doing it wrong, thinking maybe one time he would get it right and he would find release.

Scars criss-crossed his shoulders and thighs where no one

would notice. No one except Scott, he realized. Scott would see them when he undressed. Yet another reason not to get in this relationship.

Jamie opened his eyes and drew away from Scott, who looked disappointed and upset. Jamie scooted away from Scott and folded his hands on his lap, unable to meet Scott's gaze.

"I'm fine," he said. "Um, I didn't realize how late it is. Maybe that's enough studying for tonight. But I do want to see you tomorrow," he added.

Scott was already standing up. He didn't look too surprised as he hugged Jamie goodnight, although he did look disappointed. For a moment Jamie wondered if he really could see the future and he had known this night would end badly back when things were still going so good. He wasn't sure if he was ready to leave Scott forever, but the thought of Scott getting any closer tonight was terrifying. Jamie needed to figure out what to do about the scars first. The scars and the fears they represented.

-

CHAPTER SIX

Mike Ferrin

Mike Ferrin watched his favorite young student closely the next day. It was painfully obvious that Scott had been unable to seal the deal, but Scott did have an entire week to take the young man to bed. The longer he waited, though, the harder it would be for Jamie to adapt.

Jamie performed exceptionally well during class, answering questions easily and readily and seeming to have knowledge of the tarragon tribe beyond what they discussed in class. A little outside research was a good thing, but the teachers had to carefully monitor the students to make sure they didn't find any of the wild rumors circulating on the Internet about the true nature of the college. Those rumors couldn't be learned until after the exam, after the students learned the true nature firsthand.

He called Jamie up after class and the boy seemed a bit nervous. Ever since Mike had attempted to sweet talk the boy, he had been uneasy around the teacher and Mike regretted taking such hasty actions earlier. No, Scott was taking the right approach. This boy needed a slow, steady approach. Or an all-or-nothing assault, Mike thought with a smile, thinking of when he broke Scott in the school hallway two years ago. Jamie was so much the same, with so much sexuality bottled up inside. If someone forced him into a situation and refused to take no for an answer, the boy would say yes just as Scott had done. And it was vitally important that the first time be voluntary. They had just learned that in the past year, after several girls who were raped were unable to complete the exam and suffered agonizing deaths. Mike was just lucky that Scott had consented in the hallway, no matter how half-heartedly or temporarily, to his assault. Otherwise they would have lost one of their most promising students.

Now that Mike was a teacher, he was privy to all sorts of knowledge that students and other graduates couldn't access. He was on the fast track to joining the council, if he maintained his current level. It was just a matter of waiting for a position on the council to open up. That might take one year or a hundred years, but either way, he would be waiting. Scott would also likely get on the council, but not because of his teaching. He would get on because of the strong bond he had formed during the exam.

Every student in the university was a descendent of the tarragon tribe, an ancient tribe of people who worshipped dragons. Although the best-known tribe came from Britain, similar tribes appeared throughout the world around the time of the Crusades. It was believed that the dragons traveled across the globe and created similar societies, because there was no other way to explain the uncanny resemblances between the distant tribes. Physically, people in the tribes experienced adaptations that set them apart from other humans. In order to connect with dragons, the ancient people sacrificed their souls in an eternal bond with the souls of the dragons. As long as the dragons or the descendants survived, so would the other, but neither would be able to survive alone.

Tarragon Academy scoured the world for students who were descendants of the tribe. Some, like Jamie, came from parents who had been identified as tribe members long ago. Others were new finds. If their parents were lucky enough to have lived near Mount Tarragon during early adulthood, then their parents were usually alive. But if, like Jamie, their parents were unaware of their joint fate with dragons, they died young. Many of the students were orphans or adopted for that reason. It was the job of the school to ensure that those students who did make it into their late teens survived the ultimate test for a descendent of the tarragon tribe: bonding with a dragon.

"You did well in class today, Jamie," Mike said.

"Thanks," Jamie said with a sudden bright smile. He must have been worried about getting scolded. "I have a tutor who's helping me."

Mike nodded, but inwardly he was laughing. A tutor? Was that Scott's grand scheme for getting in the boy's pants? Teach him about the tarragon tribe, then teach him about sex?

"That's great," he said. "Remember that the exam is less than two weeks away, so you'll want to meet with your tutor a lot to make sure to learn everything."

Jamie's face fell. "Oh. Have I not been doing well? You should have told me I needed help before. Or is that what you were telling me last time we talked?"

"No," Mike said firmly. "You're doing very well in the class. But the exam tests knowledge from outside of the class as well. Try to get as much help as you can, especially from people who have taken it before. It can only help you."

"Okay," Jamie said, sounding unconvinced.

Mike grabbed his arm and pulled him into a hug, unable to resist the sad puppy-dog eyes on the beautiful boy. The boy resisted for a split second, then dissolved into his arms. Startled, Mike saw that he was on the brink of tears.

"What is it? What's wrong?"

"Oh Mr. Ferrin, I think I really messed up. There's this guy that I like but I was really rude to him and now I don't know if he'll ever talk to me again. He helped me study but he didn't- I mean I told him not to but I thought- I don't know what to do."

Mike resisted the wild impulse to laugh at Jamie's assessment of the situation. He didn't know what had gone on between them but he did know that nothing Jamie said would repel Scott. Even though it sounded like Jamie was giving Scott a run for his money if the boy had specifically told him not to touch him or do anything. Scott was too honorable to touch the boy if he thought it went against his wishes; he was afraid of doing to Jamie what Mike had done to him even though Mike knew it might be necessary.

He stroked Jamie's head gently and held the boy close, wishing the boy weren't crying and they were holding each other for a different reason. But it wasn't bad to establish this sort of relationship with the boy, especially if it helped Jamie. It wasn't the relationship Mike would have liked, but he would make do with what he could get. He sensed that Jamie would become a powerful member of the tribe after the exam, but he had to survive the exam first and to that, he needed to be able to feel comfortable in all relationships, not just the physical ones.

"It's all right," Mike said. "If he really cares about you, he won't give up. But what made you say no? What made you so scared that you risked messing things up?"

"My father," Jamie whispered. "I kept thinking about him, and then about how scared I was that Scott was going to die too. Everyone I care about dies. Or something horrible happens to them. I can't let that happen to him."

"It won't," Mike said.

This was exactly what the council had been worried about. They had reviewed Jamie's case more closely than many of the others because of the violence of his father's death, and Jamie's age at the time of his father's death. Most people in the tarragon tribe who weren't associated with the Academy died young, usually when their children were too young to have many memories. But Jamie's father's death had been a highly traumatic event at a very impressionable age and while the council knew it would impact his capacity to form relationships, they didn't know how much. The council had already given up on Jamie but Mike hadn't; if Jamie gave into his fears now, Mike would be the laughingstock of the council and Jamie would die.

"You've had some bad experiences," Mike said. "But if you don't take a chance, how will you ever form good experiences to counteract the bad ones? Love is always a risk, for everyone, but we take it. It's worth the risk. Just take every moment as it comes and make every memory last, and soon you may find that your joy and happiness far outweigh your fears and you decide that taking a risk was the best decision of your life."

"But what if it's the worst?"

"You won't know unless you try."

"I guess. You really think he doesn't mind? He didn't even kiss me goodnight."

"Did you tell him he could?"

Jamie leaned his head against Mike's shoulder. "Well, no. So he's not mad?"

"I doubt it. But the only way to know for sure is to talk to him. I think he'll be very glad to hear from you," Mike added, unable to keep from meddling. "I've seen him watching you for a while now and I think he really likes you."

Jamie smiled and pulled out of the hug. "Yeah, I think he does. I think I do, too. Thanks, Mr. Ferrin."

"Call me Mike outside of class," Mike offered.

Jamie flushed and looked awkward. "Okay, M-mike."

"Or just stick with Mr. Ferrin," Mike said with a laugh. The boy had obviously never spoken to a teacher on a first-name basis before and even after hugging and practically weeping on his shoulder, Jamie clearly felt uncomfortable. It wasn't a big deal to Mike, so better to keep their relationship going than get stuck on a name. Jamie's embarrassment turned to relief and he left the classroom beaming. Mike would have bet anything that Scott was waiting outside or close by, either watching the scene or, if the man was feeling too honorable to eavesdrop, waiting for Jamie to leave.

Jamie would have no problems getting Scott's forgiveness. If Scott played it right, then Jamie's guilt could lead into intimacy and perhaps even sex. But Scott was rarely the aggressive type, so it was unlikely he could get so far with just a little guilt to work with. It would be interesting to see Jamie's mood tomorrow and see if the boy was still a virgin. And if Scott hadn't succeeded within a week, Mike would be able to build on the sympathy from this little tableau and get Jamie in bed himself. Mike headed towards the teacher's lounge in high spirits.

CHAPTER SEVEN

Seduction

Scott watched Jamie and Mike talking with a strange jealousy in his heart. Mike was a threat, and Jamie was a virgin, like Scott had been. And such an extreme virgin. Scott was willing to bet the boy rarely masturbated and almost never had sexual fantasies, not because he didn't want to but because he wouldn't let himself. Jamie had built up such an extraordinarily thick wall between himself and intimacy of any kind that he didn't even have friends at the school aside from his roommate.

His roommate was a positive influence, Scott thought. Jamie needed a good friend in this place and Amar seemed committed. Actually, a lot of people liked Jamie a great deal, if Jamie ever broke out of his shell enough to notice. Scott had been doing a little research on his soon-to-be lover and was pleased with the results. Jamie would have a comfortable home here once he allowed himself to trust people. People liked him because he was friendly and intelligent, and beautiful, which never hurt. Many people considered him a casual friend when Scott had asked around. But Jamie probably didn't realize how many friends he had, or how well established at the school he really was. He still acted like an outsider, awkward at social events and in class, only hanging out with Amar's friends and a few girls from the sister Academy.

Scott's lips tightened when Jamie and Mike embraced in the classroom and Mike's hand firmly planted itself on the boy's back possessively. He wasn't close enough to eavesdrop and didn't want to be, but he hated watching another man touch Jamie. It looked innocent enough; if it weren't, Mike's hand would be on his ass and not his back. But still. Scott turned away from them and found himself face to face with Amar, who was also watching Jamie and the teacher. Amar gestured at them with a shrug.

"I doubt it's anything, man. Jamie's totally into you. He came out for you, you know. He'd never told anyone he was gay before."

Scott pulled him away from the door into a less crowded hallway.

"And now you're outing him further," he said with a bite of anger in his voice. "Did he give you permission to tell people he's gay?"

Amar seemed puzzled. "Once you're out, aren't you out? And I mean it's not exactly a surprise to anyone who's seen him in clubs. He's had so many girls hitting on him and never given them a glance, but you walk by and he's head over heels. People notice and are talking."

Scott shook his head. "It's a private thing. You tell individuals. I don't know if he's ready to be publicly out yet, even though I want to tell everyone he's my boyfriend."

"Well, people were talking and I figured it was better to give a definitive answer than no answer, because if I didn't answer they'd just ask Jamie and he's not really the confrontation guy."

"Wait, who was asking?"

A confrontation sounded dangerous, and Scott thought of the first-year jocks who gave hell to the gay guys on campus. They never did after the exam, however: the bond with a dragon was just as "unnatural" to them as the bond between two guys and the ones who survived realized how love could strike anyone, regardless of gender. Now that homophobia was less tolerated in society, the council was considering expelling any students who displayed a homophobic streak because they had lower survival rates than more tolerant students. In older times he knew they expelled based on racism, since skin color and ethnicity were other things some students couldn't tolerate. Accepting a dragon into your heart required a level of tolerance that was far beyond accepting different races and genders, and people from disadvantaged groups of all sorts tended to survive better.

"Not the jocks," Amar said as if he knew exactly what Scott had been worried about. He probably did know. He seemed quite protective of his roommate and Scott knew that if the jocks tried to hurt Jamie, Amar would be there to protect him. As would Scott.

"It was this girl, an upperclassman, she's been hitting on him and I've been hitting on her the whole time we've been here. She gave a guest lecture in my bio class this morning and talked to me after."

"Oh, that's probably fine," Scott said.

"I won't tell anyone else. I didn't know how it worked. Um, thanks for telling me, I probably would have told someone."

It sounded like Jamie hadn't talked to Amar about how the night had ended, but then again both boys had eight am classes and not much time to talk. If Amar knew about the upset, this would be a very different conversation and he knew he would deserve every word of the lecture Amar was sure to give. But if Amar didn't know, then maybe it wasn't as upsetting to Jamie as Scott worried and maybe Jamie would come over tonight.

"No problem. Look, can you tell Jamie that if he wants to study, he can come over to my apartment tonight?"

"Moving fast, aren't you?" There was a hint of warning in Amar's dark eyes and inwardly Scott approved. He should be suspicious of Scott, this stranger who was inviting an innocent boy to his apartment on the second date. But it had to happen. He would not let the council send anyone else after Jamie. Especially not Mike. Plus, there was no guarantee that Jamie would come after the hug Mike and Jamie had shared in the classroom. Maybe Mike would get his chance after all.

"We're moving at his pace," Scott said.

"Glacial, huh? I feel you," Amar said with a smile. "I'll let him know. He's been kind of jumpy today. Guess I don't know how guys act when they're in love with other guys but I hope it's a good thing. And don't worry about Mr. Ferrin, that creep tried to feel Jamie up before and Jamie put him in his place."

"He wasn't putting him in his place just now."

"Well, maybe they're friends now," Amar said with a frown. "I won't let him date a teacher even if I get an A out of it. No way. Not Mr. Ferrin. Jamie deserves someone better."

"Someone like me?" Scott asked, genuinely curious.

"Maybe," Amar said. "You're nice enough, I think, but he's a pretty special guy and he deserves a lot."

"I intend to give him a lot, including my love," Scott said. Then he blushed as he realized he said the last part out loud. He hadn't meant to but it slipped out. Amar looked shocked, then he grinned.

"Good luck. I've dated a lot of girls and if Jamie were a girl, I'd say he was almost impossible to reel in."

"But worth every minute," Scott said with a smile.

Amar laughed. "I'll tell him to go to your apartment. See you later."

Scott lingered for a few more minutes, then set off to his apartment to tidy up. By six o'clock, everything was spotless and he had changed clothes twice. He settled on his favorite tight black t-shirt and some jeans. Casual, but the black complimented his dark coloring and the jeans were pressed and dark enough to look a little formal. He would easily wear this on a date. And he would, if Jamie decided to show up.

At seven o'clock, there was a knock at the door. His heart leapt into his throat and began beating a hundred miles per minute. He took a deep breath, ran his hands down his jeans, and opened the door. Jamie was outside.

The boy looked tired from a long day and immensely worried about something. Probably about their night before. Scott gestured for him to come in and he did, rubbing his palms against his jeans nervously just as Scott had done moments before. Scott smiled at the thought and Jamie noticed, turning bright red. Scott loved how easy it was to fluster the boy, and how responsive his skin was. He could only imagine how responsive the rest of his body was and barely managed to stop himself from licking his lips.

"I'm sorry," Jamie said. "I'm sorry I got so weird last night. It's just, we were moving so fast and I'm a little-"

He ducked his head and mumbled, "I'm embarrassed about my body."

Scott's smile grew wider. How could such a lovely specimen be embarrassed? He thought about tying Jamie to the bed and ripping his clothes off, then licking every inch of that beautiful body until Jamie fully appreciated how beautiful he was. His cock stirred at the vivid image and the taste of salty flesh that suddenly filled his mouth and he swallowed hard to regain control.

"It's alright. I was moving too fast. We can do this without taking off your clothes, you know."

"We can?"

The sheer relief in Jamie's eyes was almost sad. Was he that embarrassed about himself? Scott hated to think what had happened to make the boy this ashamed of his body. Had he been abused as a child? After the boy's father had been killed, Scott knew from the council's report that Jamie had essentially been on his own. Had someone hurt him then, humiliated him and done everything except the actual act of sex to him? Scott's fists were clenched at the thought and he relaxed them. This was not the time for anger; this was the time for seduction.

"Yes, we can. Why don't we sit down on the couch? I'll get you a drink. What do you want?"

"What do you have?"

"Um, some soda, apple juice, and water."

"What are the brown bottles?"

Jamie was right behind him, not sitting on the couch. Scott blushed.

"Beer. But you're too young. I'm only just old enough and this is all left over from a party a while ago. I'm not really a beer drinker, I guess. Wine's good, but not beer. Beer just tastes sour."

He grabbed two sodas and handed one to Jamie, then escorted the boy to the couch. They sat down and Jamie set his drink down without even opening it. Scott did the same, guessing that Jamie was ready to move straight into intimacy. Was it really only his fear of being naked that was preventing him from having sex? It had to be more, and Scott would have to be careful not to trigger another fear.

Jamie took his hand and scooted close to him. "Um, could you kiss me?"

Scott's jaw nearly dropped and he thought of all the times he'd fantasized about a beautiful boy like Jamie bashfully asking to be kissed. It was the start of nearly all of his sexual fantasies and already his cock was getting hard. He was going to have trouble taking things slow.

Scott kissed him gently, lips only, and surprisingly it was Jamie who added tongue although Scott was quick to oblige. He caressed the boy's face, his body, careful to keep his hands nowhere near any clothing edges. He wanted to rip the clothes off and stare at this beautiful god in his arms, but knew it would send Jamie away for good to do that. Instead he explored Jamie's body above the clothes, noticing that Jamie tensed when he touched his shoulders and upper arms, and his thighs. The arms were easy to avoid, and he suspected the thighs were a sign of something else. Something growing visibly larger inside the boy's tight jeans even as Jamie shifted and struggled against it.

Scott kissed Jamie's lips, then along his jawbone, nibbling slightly as the boy let out a startled moan. The boy tasted and smelled like warm butter with a dash of sugar; he was delicious to stroke and bite as Scott moved down his neck to his collarbone. But no further, because the shirt was in the way. He remained on the boy's neck, feeling like a vampire and feeling a vampire's urge to suck away at the boy forever. He tasted so good. Jamie was moaning regularly now, and the bulge in his pants was becoming an issue. Scott wondered what his cock would taste like, if it would be as sweet as the rest of him, and he knew that he couldn't let the boy leave until he found out. He just needed to convince the boy to drop his drawers a little, just enough for him to take what was surely a magnificent specimen into his mouth.

Scott caressed his thighs, purposefully stopping before making contact. He needed Jamie to want this. Jamie whined and tried to shift his hips but Scott prevented him.

"Jamie," he whispered. "May I take your jeans off, just a little?"

The boy went still, his eyes wide with fear. Then he shook himself and nodded with a look of dazed desire in his eyes. "Yes, Scott. Please do."

CHAPTER EIGHT

Out of the Shell

Jamie leaned closer. This was right. His cock pulsed with heat and need as Scott unbuttoned his jeans and released him from the increasingly tight confines of his jeans. Jamie moaned with embarrassment as he sprang out, ready and straining against his underpants. Scott chuckled.

"You're ready to go, aren't you? I won't keep you waiting."

His hot breath traveled from Jamie's navel down to the thicket of dark hair around the base of his cock and Jamie's breath hitched. He had never imagined this, never imagined anyone laying next to him with their mouth so close to him like this, about to – about to – Scott's tongue darted out and touched his cock. Jamie cried out, his cock twitching. Scott grinned like a Cheshire cat and stoked his tongue across the sensitive skin of his shaft. As Scott's tongue and mouth worked their way down his length, Jamie moaned and nearly rolled over to stop the incredible pleasure. It was too much: he was going to cum before Scott even did anything.

One of Scott's hands gripped the base of his cock and squeezed just as a feeling of inevitability overcame him. Scott's mouth closed around the head of his penis and Jamie arched his back in pleasure. Amazingly, he didn't cum. The pleasure began to wash over him in waves. Precum dripped from his slit and Scott lapped it up. Jamie shut his eyes, unable to watch anymore, but the image of Scott on top of him, licking him, sucking him, was too strong and burned through his eyelids as he writhed in pleasure.

Then Scott's tongue slid along the head of his penis and he guided it into his mouth slowly, ignoring the panic in Jamie's cries of pleasure. Another firm squeeze at the base of his cock prevented him from cumming and Jamie didn't know whether he was grateful at the other man's skillful control of his body or betrayed by his own primal responses as he tried to bite back the moans and cries that burst forth as Scott's mouth captured new territory. His hands tore into the couch as the waves of pleasure grew closer together and heat flooded his chest and head. Scott's lips brushed against his balls and the walls of his throat closed around him.

Jamie made a pleasured whine and thrust his hips, wanting desperately to feel himself moving in Scott's tight throat, to feel the incredible pleasure of his velvet skin moving back and forth against his cock. Scott began moving on him and all coherent thoughts left his head.

Jamie grabbed Scott's head and helped guide him, aching for him when his mouth moved away, desperate for the feel of his lips against his balls. He fucked Scott's mouth hard and Scott clung to him, giving him control, allowing him to do what he liked.

Scott's mouth left his cock only once, when he leaned down to lick Jamie's balls, tight against his body. Jamie squirmed out of his pants to give Scott more access, not caring that some of his scars were now visible. Scott didn't notice, focused as he was on rolling Jamie's balls over his tongue. He slicked them thoroughly and continued to use his hand to stroke the tightened orbs even as his mouth returned to Jamie's cock. Jamie felt as though he were having heat stroke – his body was on fire, his heart pounded out of control, and though he was harder than he'd ever been in his life, the rest of his body felt uncoordinated and could only thrust desperately towards Scott's welcoming mouth in an ever-quickening rhythm. He was not going to last much longer and no tricks on Scott's part would stop him.

Jamie thrust himself violently as he felt his orgasm coming, bigger than any he had ever experienced. He wanted to be inside Scott when he came. Jamie tugged his head and tried to speak, but words were utterly beyond him. Luckily, Scott seemed to sense what was happening because he firmly planted himself on Jamie's cock and began swirling his tongue in a way that had Jamie squirming for release in seconds. With a final scream, Jamie exploded and came into Scott's waiting mouth, satisfied as he felt his seed swallowed by his lover. He went limp on the couch.

Scott's face appeared before him, lips swollen and cum glistening. They kissed and Jamie thrilled at the taste of his own come on the inside of Scott's mouth. It was salty, like he'd thought it would be, but tangy too, and not at all disgusting as he had worried. He wondered what Scott tasted like and felt his cock twitch despite his exhaustion.

Scott must have felt it too because he laughed, a deep, husky laugh. "Ready for more? I think I might need a moment to re-cover but then I'm all yours."

"Did you-"

Jamie stopped, unsure how Scott would have cum since he was fully dressed and nothing had been done to him. Scott grinned, however, and gestured downward. Jamie gave a start as he realized Scott was unzipped and had apparently jerked himself off while sucking Jamie, because his cock – what a beautiful cock! – was shimmering with moisture. Jamie couldn't take his eyes away from the beauty and he idly wondered what it would be like to have inside him. It was enormous, at least eight inches, and the head was the color and shape of a small plum. Would it hurt much? Jamie flushed as he realized he wasn't thinking of having the cock inside his mouth, but inside his ass as well. He was trying to figure out the logistics of anal sex with such a beautiful monster when Scott kissed his cheek.

"Everything okay?" Scott asked.

"Yeah," Jamie said.

Amazingly, it was true. Everything was okay. All of his wor-ries and fears and concerns just melted away. He and Scott were together. He was with Scott now. He belonged to Scott. Scott could protect him from the nightmares and terrors and fears lurking around every corner.

"Tell me a story," he whispered, cuddling against Scott so that they were fully pressed up against each other and his head was cradled against Scott's strong chest.

"A story?" Scott laughed. "Okay. Once upon a time… Let's see."

He stopped and carded his hand through Jamie's hair. Jamie shut his eyes and luxuriated in the strong man holding him so tightly, loving him so fully.

"Once upon a time there was a dragon," Scott began in a voice full of amusement. "But he was trapped inside an egg. The shell was all the dragon knew, so the dragon thought it perfectly normal to sit around all day not moving, not seeing, not feeling anything. Life to the dragon was empty and meaningless, and sometimes the dragon wondered why he had been born at all. The dragon sensed that there was more to the world, that he was meant to soar in blue skies and breathe crimson fire, but he knew nothing of skies or fire or even colors because none of these existed inside the shell."

Jamie pulled closer to him, caught up in the story. He understood how the dragon felt; he'd felt that way himself for a long time. Trapped inside a cage he couldn't see, unable to truly be himself around anyone for fear of what would happen to them. He hoped the story had a happy ending and suspected it did or else Scott wouldn't be telling it.

"Then one day a man came along and found the egg. Not knowing what the egg was, he kicked it and the dragon fell out. The dragon was shocked. At first he couldn't make sense of everything around him because it was not his shell and he was frightened, and he tried to hurt the man who released him from his shell. But soon he realized that all of his dreams had come true and here was the world he had been waiting for. A world where he could fly and breathe fire and be a real dragon. A world outside the shell."

Jamie felt warm and content. "What happened to the man then? The one who released him?"

"When the dragon realized that the man had been helping him, he vowed his eternal love to the man and they have never been separated since."

Jamie smiled. Eternal love was a bit much, but he was willing to give Scott his heart for opening his eyes to the wonders of pleasure and an intimacy that banished fear. He did feel like the dragon, trapped inside a shell just waiting to get out. He'd been waiting for years, knowing there was something more to life but not knowing what it was. No, he suspected what it was. He was just afraid to go out and get it. But now that he was free, he would never be trapped again.

"Thank you," Jamie said. "For freeing me."

"Freeing you?" Scott sounded confused. "You were the one who did that. I was just the lucky person you chose to help."

"No," Jamie said. "You did it. I was so afraid of everything and everyone, and now I'm not because I have you. There's no one else but you."

Scott was silent and Jamie leaned back to look at him. His dark eyes were somber and he was lost in thought.

"Scott? You okay?"

Shaking his head, Scott smiled weakly. "Yeah, I was just thinking of, well, of something else, if that's even possible with you lying next to me. Do you need more time?"

He leaned to kiss Jamie but Jamie allowed only brief contact. Somehow the thought of more physical contact was far too exhausting, despite the pleasure he knew it would bring. Plus, the mood had turned contemplative and he was rather enjoying it. He didn't feel like riling up his energy and passion again when he could sit back and ponder Scott's story and try to figure out what Scott had been thinking of to make him so serious.

"I think I'm spent," he admitted. "I just want to head home and hit the sack. Is that okay?"

"Yeah, of course that's okay," Scott said. "You can stay here if you want, you know."

Jamie flushed and looked around. There was still something off about the apartment that he couldn't place his finger on. It was fine when he and Scott were talking or doing other things – his mind flashed to Scott's mouth pressing against his cock – but he didn't want to spend the night here and face his usual insomnia in such a strange place.

"That's okay. Maybe next time. Um, can I take a shower here though?"

Scott grinned. "Together?"

Laughing, Jamie shook his head and tried to imagine how red his face must be. He wanted to eventually shower together, but he was exhausted.

"Next time," he promised.

"I'll hold you to it," Scott said, then helped him sit up.

When Scott tried to help him take his shirt off to get ready for the shower, Jamie tugged the shirt down. Scott immediately apologized and Jamie shrugged it off. He didn't mind, really, but he was still embarrassed by the scars criss-crossing his shoulders. Scott hadn't seen them yet. Scott hadn't even seen the ones on his legs, because he'd been mostly dressed while they had sex. He would eventually have to tell Scott about his daily dealings with depression and the times when it got so bad he cut himself, but not now. Not yet. Not when their relationship was just starting out and things looked so bright. Scott didn't protest as Jamie pulled his clothes to cover himself completely before heading into the bathroom to shower and Jamie was grateful for his tact.

He turned the water on hot, needing to burn away the residual lust. He always loved steaming in showers, the water warm enough to turn his pale skin a faint red. Like a sauna or hot tub, only better. He was lucky he enjoyed it: Amar preferred colder showers but since the water was heated locally by the volcano, it was far easier to get a hot shower than a cold one. Of course, the really hot water was in the hot springs that lay between their academy and the girl's academy. Jamie had dipped his toes in once and that was enough, but it was a very popular place for upperclassmen who presumably were used to the heat after years of it.

Steam filled the bathroom and fogged up the mirror and Jamie fingered the scars on his shoulders. He wished he could see the mirror and see how visible his scars were from a distance. Up close they looked like chalky white lines on his already white skin, lines in perfectly symmetrical patterns running down his upper arm. He enjoyed symmetry and it was part of his ritual. Not that the ritual did any good. Perhaps he should have tried sex before, but he knew that sex with anyone else wouldn't have the same effect.

Jamie had tried everything to get rid of his depression. Like the dragon of Scott's story, he felt he was trapped by the world but he was terrified of allowing himself to love or even form a friendship, so he was never able to properly get help. He did everything on his own. He tried cutting himself and just ended up with meaningless scars. He tried masturbating and just ended up with humiliating cum on his hands, no real relief from the pressures he faced. Often he couldn't even reach orgasm because he was so worried he was doing it wrong, or someone would find him, or that his reasons were wrong and he shouldn't masturbate out of fear.

Once, he tried an antidepressant. It made him feel like his head was full of cotton. The very act of thinking hurt and he wanted to scream all day and night because he couldn't even think of stopping the medicine: it hurt too much to be rational. When he finally met with his doctor again after a month, his doctor expected him to feel better but he came in a wreck, unable to sleep or eat or function. He'd been attending school out of habit but the entire month was a blur now and he had no idea what happened during that time except that he survived. The doctor tried to prescribe something else but Jamie refused. He was in too much pain and just wanted to go back to how things were. Sure, they weren't great and he was in a state of deep depression every day, but it was better than not being able to remember anything or think clearly. He had always meant to go back and try again but he never did.

Always, through everything, he was alone. Technically he lived with his aunt, but she barely noticed him. She had her own children to watch out for, young children, and she made it clear on day one that she was only watching him until he turned eighteen and then he was out.

The water hissed and he opened his eyes. There was a shape in the fog and for a wild moment he hoped Scott had ignored him and barged in. But it was too large to be Scott, and it appeared to be on all fours like a giant dog. No dog, however, had a back nearly touching the ceiling. It must be a shadow playing with his senses. Once he thought he saw his father standing in the living room, but when he took a step forward his father became parts of the bookshelf, the jacket thrown on the chair, a stray shadow on the wall. He had stepped back quickly to recreate the illusion but it was gone. This strange beast must be something similar.

He slid open the door just to be sure. The shape was still there and seemed to turn to him. He paused. If he stepped out of the shower, just for a moment, then he should be shifting position enough to see what this strange shape was made of. He wasn't worried about an intruder because Scott was outside, and if it were Scott, well, he wouldn't be upset.

Jamie reached for a towel and wrapped it around his waist as he stepped out, leaving the water running. The shape seemed to dart closer and he raised his hands instinctively as if to ward off a blow. He shut his eyes, then shook himself. It was a shadow, maybe of a dog that had gotten in the bathroom and the mist was enlarging the shadow. Nothing to be afraid of.

He opened his eyes and stared into two black orbs in a green, scaly face. He instantly thought of the forest and knew this was the same creature he had seen. Not a hallucination, or if it was, he was hallucinating again. It didn't feel like he was hallucinating. Jamie held out his hand and placed it on the creature's snout. The creature let out a pleased huff and opened its mouth, exposing hundreds of razor sharp teeth.

Jamie cried out for help and stumbled backwards into the

shower, grabbing the towel from his waist and covering his face with it, as if that would hide him. He heard Scott calling his name and wondered if Scott would believe him. The dragon faded into the mist and Scott barged through the door.

"What is it? What's wrong?" Scott said, looking around for the cause of Jamie's cry.

"There's a dragon in your bathroom and it was going to eat me!"

CHAPTER NINE

Second Shower

Scott breathed a sigh of relief when Jamie left his apartment. He almost had to lie to the boy. Luckily, Narné was gone by the time Scott arrived so he could honestly say that there wasn't a dragon in the bathroom. He could feel Narné hiding somewhere in the apartment, confused that the boy had seen him. Scott was shocked. No one could see the dragons until they went through the exam, or at least that was what he had been told.

He had successfully calmed Jamie down without lying, and the boy left without saying much except asking for a kiss goodnight. It was a sweet kiss, gentle and apologetic, and Scott had to fight the urge to make it something more and drag his lover back into bed. Jamie was so incredibly delicious that just the taste of his lips gave him a hard on, but he knew he needed to keep moving at Jamie's pace and Jamie was finished for the night.

Really it was remarkable they had gotten as far they did. Scott wasn't sure whether or not oral sex was enough to pass the exam, but he suspected it was in this case. Jamie had completely submitted to Scott's caresses and emotionally, he wasn't a virgin anymore even though he hadn't been penetrated. Scott suspected the council wouldn't leave Jamie alone until penetration occurred, however. It was an unfair double standard. Gay men, regardless of their preference, had to submit to another man, but straight men didn't.

When Jamie had left the building, Scott began searching for Narné. It didn't take long; the enormous dragon could only fit in a few rooms even though the apartment complex was designed for dragons. He was in the bedroom curled up on the bed and Scott was grateful that the furniture was designed for dragons as well. Even so, he could see the mattress flattening as Narné shifted at his arrival.

"Off the bed," Scott said. "You're in trouble. How could you be so careless?"

He shouldn't have seen me, Narné said sullenly. He didn't speak aloud; his thoughts just appeared in Scott's head. Scott was the only one who could hear Narné's voice, but the dragons could communicate with each other using this telepathy and Scott sensed that Narné had already reached out to his community to understand how Jamie had seen him.

No one knows why he saw me, Narné continued. *But I believe it is because he will be great. He will find one of the hidden eggs.*

The hidden eggs were the Queen eggs. There hadn't really been a Queen dragon in centuries. Instead, each class from the college relied on eggs laid centuries earlier and the dragons that hatched tended to be violent and bitter when they first broke out of their shells, making the exam deadly for many. But there were rumors of hidden eggs that would allow someone to partner with a Queen, and a Queen's eggs would be fresh: her offspring would be inside eggs for months rather than centuries and therefore much easier to partner with. Unfortunately, not even the dragons knew where the hidden eggs were, and partnering with a Queen had serious downsides.

About fifty years ago, a man had found a hidden egg and partnered with a Queen dragon. He was straight, and when his Queen reached maturity and began mating with male dragons and he was expected to mate with their human counterparts, he refused. The Queen dragon respected his wishes and didn't mate. She also stopped socializing with other dragons because it was too painful for both of them, and eventually she grew too weak to move. The council forced her partner to let her mate and she revived, but he was so humiliated by having sex with multiple men that he killed himself. She died soon after.

It took a certain type of person to successfully partner with a Queen. Only a straight woman or a gay man who enjoyed submitting to others could survive the mating ritual, and they also had to be strong-willed enough to dominate the Queen dragon when she first hatched. Very few people fit that description, but Narné and Scott believed Jamie could do it. He lacked confidence, but he had it within himself to partner with a Queen if he ever found one.

Scott frowned. His mind had drifted to Queens and he sensed Narné's relief at his change of mood. Narné had been feeding him thoughts about hidden eggs to lessen his anger. Occasionally Narné manipulated him like this and it usually worked, but today he wasn't finished being angry.

"We both want him to partner with a Queen," Scott said. "But that doesn't explain why you were in the bathroom watching him in the first place!"

Narné hung his head. *I wanted to see who was making you so happy. He is very beautiful for a human. I just wanted to see him.*

Scott laughed. "You wanted to see him? Can't you see him through my mind?"

Narné snorted in irritation. *It is not the same. And he senses when I'm nearby so I couldn't watch earlier. I meant him no harm.*

"He thought you were going to eat him."

I was thinking he looked delicious, but I did not mean it like that.

"Wait," Scott said, putting a hand up. "You were thinking that? You don't suppose he heard your thoughts, do you?"

Narné raised his head and reared back on his hind feet. The bed squealed in protest. *He did react when I thought that. Perhaps he picked up on the thought unconsciously. I do not think he heard me as clearly as you do.*

"Well, that's a relief. Still, I don't think I'll be bringing him over here again. I'll have to talk to that roommate of his about getting some privacy. Has Jamie-"

He paused, unsure of how to ask whether or not Jamie's chances of survival had gone up after their evening together. Asking would make it seem like he was only with Jamie for academic reasons, because the school ordered them to be together. That was how it began, but from the first time Jamie shyly said hello back to him in the hallway, Scott knew it was something more. And now that they had shared a truly intimate experience, he didn't want to lessen it by thinking of it as a job he was required to do. It wasn't a job: it was love.

I see the same. If Jamie reaches a Queen egg, he will survive.

"But you still don't see where the Queen eggs are, or what will happen if he doesn't reach one?"

No one knows where the Queen eggs are except that they are scattered and well-protected. And he may still survive if he partners with another dragon. I cannot see that path, but it is a path. However, we must focus on finding the location of the hidden eggs. Now that Jamie has been taken care of, you need to begin researching the eggs.

Scott flushed. Taken care of. Sometimes Narné had no concept at all of human emotions. Or perhaps the dragon was being deliberately cruel in order to inspire Scott to stop daydreaming about future dates with Jamie and start working on finding the eggs. Either way, the words stung even as he felt relief. If Narné thought Jamie was taken care of, then so would the council, and Jamie wouldn't have to deal with any more assaults from upperclassmen. Or from Mike Ferrin.

Scott took a quick shower himself before getting to work, and Narné joined him in the shower as always. Narné loved water and could often be found clawing at the nozzles to drink or bathe in the shower. The nozzles were extra large and sturdy just for this reason and Scott was a little surprised that Jamie hadn't noticed, but then against Jamie probably had other things on his mind. Scott smiled and imagined the boy in his shower, soaping his lean, lithe body and thinking of what they had just done. Maybe Jamie had even gotten off in here, before he was disrupted by the dragon.

As the water ran over Scott's body, he imagined it was Jamie's hands running over him, followed by trails of kisses. Someday they would be in this shower together. Scott lathered himself with soap and couldn't help giving his cock a few long strokes as he thought of pressing Jamie's hands against the walls and massaging that sweet ass, working his soap-lubed fingers in and out while Jamie moaned and cried out in pleasure. Scott's hand on his cock worked a little faster as he imagined plunging into Jamie's uncharted territory and feeling his tightness surround him as he whispered for Jamie to relax, relax while he slid inside further and then began to move on him.

He imagined Jamie's hands clenching to fists and his knees growing weak but Scott would wrap his arm around Jamie's belly and take hold of the boy's cock, supporting him and pleasuring him all at once. How long would Jamie last? How long could Scott last? As the image of Jamie's face appeared in his mind, distorted with beautiful pleasure, Scott felt an enormous release and a thick, ropey spray ejected from him and splattered against the shower wall. Soon that would be captured by Jamie, he thought as his body started to relax and go limp. He finished showering, being careful to leave no trace of his activities. He didn't want Jamie to come visit and see cum all over the shower. If that happened, the boy's offer of showering together might vanish.

When he stepped out of the shower, Narné was nowhere to be found. Scott checked for his mind and found the dragon over at the girl's school searching for a female dragon to mate with. Scott felt a little bad that his lust had set off lust in his dragon, but surely there was a girl at the school who wouldn't mind if her dragon had a little fling. It happened all the time. The female dragons were infertile but they still had sexual needs, as did their human partners. Every month the female dragons went into heat and anyone with a male dragon was invited. The dragons chased and fought for rights to the female outside, and inside the dragon's partner was courted and wooed.

Usually she ended up with the partner of the dragon mating with her dragon, but not always. Women in committed relationships made sure that their lover was always present; lesbians made sure that the crowd was filled with women who partnered with male dragons. It was far more common for a woman to partner with a male dragon than a man to partner with a female dragon but it did happen. Men with female dragons went into heat just like their female counterparts, but they often didn't have the mental stamina to survive the experience, leading to a high suicide rate. The man who partnered with the Queen was the most famous example of a man not able to adapt to his female dragon, but it happened at least once every couple of years.

Jamie would survive with a female dragon, but Scott didn't want him to have one unless it was a Queen. The ordinary female dragons were much smaller than the males and could be overpowered. At the parties, too, the human counterpart could be overpowered by strong men made stronger by their ties to their dragons. Many of the women were raped, and Scott would do anything to protect Jamie from that. The council turned a blind eye and said rape was part of tradition, but Scott suspected they ignored it because they were sometimes the ones doing the raping. Frequently a council member would join a mating party and easily dominate both the female dragon and the female human, regardless of her desires. But since they were on the council, no one could do anything.

Scott dried off from the shower in a bad mood. He hated thinking about the corruption in his school, but there was little anyone could do. There were only two sources of authority among the Tarragon clan: the Queen and the council. Since there was no Queen, the council ruled everything. But once there was a Queen, things would change. And Scott would do everything in his power to help Jamie find the Queen egg.

CHAPTER TEN

Dragon Lake

Dragons were real. Jamie knew it. Scott hadn't said so; he had tried to deny it, to reassure Jamie that there was nothing in the bathroom, but his words rang false. He had said everything except the most obvious response: dragons don't exist. And because Scott couldn't bring himself to make that simple, obvious denial, Jamie knew that he had in fact seen a dragon in the forest and in the shower. He couldn't explain it, but he knew it to be true. Scott had said everything except the simple denial that would have put Jamie's mind at ease.

If dragons were real, however, it meant that all sorts of things could be real. All of Jamie's favorite fantasy stories could theoretically be true. Perhaps there were elves hanging around in the woods, and unicorns awaiting innocent virgins. Jamie blushed. He wouldn't count as an innocent virgin anymore. No unicorn would ever appear for him.

He wasn't sure if oral sex counted as real sex in terms of losing his virginity, but the emotional connection that had formed between them during and after was undeniable. He didn't feel like a virgin anymore. He felt like someone who had experienced love in all of its forms. But there was a little tug at the back of his mind that warned him that he wasn't finished yet, that there were still things to try with his boyfriend. Images filled his mind and stirred his cock: Jamie lying on his back, holding his knees to his chest while Scott used lube and his fingers to ease him open before penetrating him. Jamie tossing his head in ecstasy as Scott's length filled him, stretched him, the pain adding to the pleasure as he cried out for more until Scott was completely inside him. The look of concentration and bliss on Scott's face as they moved together in harmony, as Scott took control of Jamie's body and drove him towards an orgasm that made all of his previous orgasms seem like sneezes.

Jamie shook himself out of the vision and realized his cock was tenting in his pants. He glanced around and was relieved to find the park empty. It was a short walk from Scott's apartment to his dorm and it passed by the entrance to the vast national forest that branched between the men's and women's colleges. He paused at the entrance. He had heard that there was a lake inside with icy cold water, a remarkable feat given that they were essentially on a volcano. Jamie needed a cold shower to quiet his lust a little and he knew the dorms wouldn't be any help in that regard, but maybe he could take a dip in the lake.

The sun was beginning to set when he entered the forest and he vowed to leave if he didn't find the lake in ten minutes. A cold dip in the lake wasn't worth getting lost. There were no dangerous animals this close to the campus, at least unless one counted the dragons. Jamie still wasn't sure where the dragons lived, but they definitely existed. He had seen one in the woods over by the football field but that was over half a mile away, way on the other side of campus in the part of the forest that wasn't a national park. And the one in the bathroom seemed at home in the apartment; surely a dragon with access to an apartment wouldn't be out in the woods. He hoped.

Jamie kept a close watch on everything around him but he saw no dragons as he followed the trail heading northeast towards where he remembered hearing about the lake. The woods took on a hazy orange glow as the sun lowered further and he was grateful it was a sunny day. If the clouds had been out as they often were, he wouldn't be able to do this. He walked for several minutes, listening for the sound of water and observing the shadows of the trees growing longer. He ought to turn back. He didn't even need the cold dip anymore: walking through the forest had quieted his lust. But he kept going just a little further, thinking of turning back but never quite doing it.

Finally, after his allotted ten minutes was up, he heard water. He rushed forward along the trail and arrived at the bank of a massive lake spreading farther than he see. An island stood not too far from the bank where he stood and a bright light shone from the island. A house? He couldn't tell, but it looked extremely inviting.

Jamie took off his shoes and rolled up his pants before wading into the water. It wasn't too cold but compared with the nearby hot springs it was heaven. When he was up to his knees and his pants were getting damp even though he was holding them up, he noticed that the floor of the lake dropped off and changed from small pebbles on an ordinary lake bottom to large, round boulders. They looked dangerous and he took care not to go near them. He returned to the shore and picked up his shoes. The forest ground was fairly smooth, without too many needles or pinecones to injure his feet, so he planned to walk barefoot until he dried off a little. But when he looked for the path, all he saw were shadowed trees ringing the lake. He had waited too long.

Jamie's first reaction was to rush to the treeline and try to find the path, but it was no use. The trees were widely spaced and the path could have run between any of them. Without more light, it was impossible to tell what was the compacted soil of the path and what was the ordinary soil of the forest. Panic sprouted in his chest. He was trapped here. He turned towards the lake and the light on the island was brighter. Was someone there? He considered his options. He could stay on the shore and try to get through the night on his own and hope he was right that no dangerous animals lived in this part of the woods, or he could swim to the island and see if he could find shelter.

He had just decided to stay on the shore when a howl erupted into the night. Wolves. He didn't even know there were wolves in Oregon. The sun had dropped below the horizon and everything was in shadows. He backed away from the woods, worrying that wolves would come running at any second. He didn't have much of a choice anymore. He couldn't spend the night on the shore: even if the wolves didn't attack, he would go insane from fear. The island was protected and might even offer shelter if the person or people were friendly.

Jamie set his shoes down far from the water and hesitated. He should strip to his boxers in order to swim better, but he didn't want to end up on the island asking for help in his underwear. His clothes would weigh him down but he wanted to be dressed. He did take off his jacket and leave it with his shoes. Another howl rent the sky, much closer to where he was. So close, in fact, that he wondered if the wolf could see him. He dropped the jacket and ran into the water.

It was hard to see the strange boulders at the bottom of the lake in the darkness but he suspected they were dangerous so he began swimming immediately instead of wading out. He didn't want to risk touching them. As he swam, he was careful to keep his body floating high so he wouldn't accidentally kick them. He swam and swam, and the island didn't seem to be getting any closer. Had he miscalculated the distance? He wanted to stop swimming, reexamine the distance, and determine if he should turn back, but that would require stopping and potentially landing on the boulders. He didn't know how deep the water was and he didn't want to find out. He worried that the boulders were just inches from his feet and he was in constant danger.

He kept swimming until he began to grow exhausted, and then he flipped over and swam on his back for a while. He loved floating on his back and he could do it for hours, not that he wanted to be swimming for hours tonight. But it was peaceful pushing himself along and staring up at the stars. With the sun completely gone now, millions of stars were bursting to life in the growing darkness and he spotted all of his favorite constellations: Orion, the Big and Little Dippers, Cassiopeia. He was enjoying his view of the stars when something hit his head.

He sputtered and flipped over, hands and feet scraping against sand. He was at the shore of the island. He scrambled to his feet and tried to wipe some of the sand away. He wondered how this beach could have sand while the other beach had rocks, but he wasn't complaining. If he had run headfirst into a rocky beach he would probably be bleeding right now instead of just feeling a bit banged up. He looked around for the light but it was nowhere to be seen. The beach was only a few feet wide before forest started, and he figured the house, or whatever it was, must be somewhere else on the island.

He began walking along the beach in search of the house or wherever the light had come from when he noticed more of the boulders from underwater scattered among the trees. The boulders seemed almost deliberately placed, as if someone had scooped them from the bottom of the lake and used them as decorations on the land. He approached one of the boulders and stared. How had the boulders in the lake gotten there, anyway? The lake water should have worn them down. There was no real explanation for why the lake bottom should be covered with boulders unless someone or some force of nature had put them there.

The boulder in front of him looked like marble in the darkness. He could see veins of color shooting through the rough grey surface and he wondered if the boulders were the result of an old mine. He reached out to touch the boulder but at that moment a light flashed from nearby. Snatching his hand back, he turned towards the light. Perhaps he wasn't supposed to touch the boulders and the person with the light was warning him. The light was small and seemed to be at a great distance from him, so Jamie set off again.

He marveled at how his fortunes had changed and let a little smile slip onto his face. In just a few days, he had come out to his friends, gained a boyfriend, lost his virginity, and now he was on a quest that seemed entirely unreal. He knew he ought to be afraid and he had felt real fear when the wolves howled, but he sensed that he was safe now, that nothing could hurt him now that he had reached the island. And what a story he would have to tell tomorrow when the sun rose and he swam back to shore.

As he walked, the light grew weaker but he knew he was drawing closer. Finally, he reached the place where he knew the light came from. Only there was no house, no person, no lantern or flashlight or anything. The light seemed to be coming from one of the boulders, only that made no sense. Then again, nothing on this night seemed to make sense. Jamie approached the boulder and yes, the rock was emitting light. It was veined like the other rock, like fine marble with a rough texture. He held his hand out to touch the boulder and this time no flashes of light stopped him. His hand came to rest on the boulder and he cried out in fear and pulled his hand away.

The boulder was warm, and he could feel something inside moving in response to his touch. He put his hand back, horrified yet fascinated, and felt the rock stir again. Then the boulder began to splinter into glowing shards. But only the outside of the boulder. Inside the boulder was something else, something living and breathing. At first he couldn't make out what it was because of a layer of liquid almost like placenta covering the creature, but then a snout tore through the fleshy lining of the boulder and a creature fell out.

It was a dragon. A very small dragon, nothing like the one Jamie had seen in the forest and in the shower, but he recognized it instantly. The hands and feet were enormous, as was the creature's head, but the body was miniature and looked half-starved. It lay in a heap on the ground where it had fallen out of the boulder and Jamie's eyes widened as he realized the boulder was an egg. Did all of the boulders hold dragons? But this line of questioning vanished when the creature lifted its enormous head on a wobbly neck and snarled at him with pure hatred.

The dragon lunged at him and its claws ripped through his t-shirt and into his side. He gasped at the sudden pain and backed away from the furious dragon. Unbidden, Scott's story sprang into his mind and he wondered if the little creature was angry about being born. There had to be some way to communicate that the creature was better off.

"I'm trying to help you," he said. "You were trapped before, now you're free."

The creature spread its tiny wings. They were too small to support its weight and it screamed in protest before lunging at Jamie again. He backed away and stumbled on a tree root, falling ass-first on the ground. The dragon pounced and closed its jaws around Jamie's shoulder. Needle-fine teeth pierced his flesh and Jamie shouted and tried to dislodge the beast, but everything he did seemed to make the situation worse.

"Stop," he begged. "Stop and think for a moment. I'm not hurting you. I want to help you."

The creature kept its teeth buried in his shoulder and with its hind claws began tearing away at Jamie's belly, leaving deep scores in his flesh. Jamie sobbed and tried again to get the beast off of him. The beast's movements were spasmodic and un-controlled and Jamie wasn't sure if it could even hear his pleas, let alone understand them. The sense of surrealism that had surrounded this night was gone; the pain was all too real and he realized that if the beast kept digging into his belly, eventually it would strike a vital organ or disembowel him. Tears ran from his cheeks and he went limp. He couldn't fight off this little beast. All he could do was play dead and hope the thing left him alive so he could get back to Scott.

The newborn dragon must have sensed his surrender be-cause it finally let go of his shoulder. Those dagger teeth turned to his face and Jamie flinched, but didn't try to fight. He shut his eyes and silently begged the creature not to hurt him anymore. The creature's teeth were right in front of his face; he could feel its breath and smell sulfur and ash. If only there were some way to communicate, to make the dragon realize that he meant it no harm, that he hadn't known what he was doing when he touched the boulder, perhaps the dragon would forgive him. But the dragon didn't seem to understand anything except rage at being released from its shell and Jamie squeezed his eyes tighter so he wouldn't have to see the dragon as it dealt the final blow.

Scott, he thought. *Scott, please save me.*

But Scott was nowhere to be found.

CHAPTER ELEVEN

First Year Exam

Scott's phone woke him up in the middle of the night and he answered without checking to see who it was. He had it set so the ringer would go off for only a few important people so he already knew it was an important call. He hoped it would be Jamie, mostly because he had just been dreaming about Jamie. When it was Mike's voice on the other end, all of the pleasure of sleep left him.

"What do you want, Mike?"

"Is Jamie with you?"

Scott snorted softly. "No, but you don't have to worry about him. Things are great."

More than great, he thought with a pleased smile. Jamie hadn't just allowed physical contact, he had been an active participant. Scott could still feel Jamie's hands wrapped in his hair as he begged him to keep going, not to stop. Jamie had been able to lose himself in pleasure and Scott was willing to bet that was the first time Jamie had ever allowed himself to be out of control. Jamie tried so hard to be self-sufficient, and no one had ever taken the time to take care of him. It was an honor to be Jamie's first and Scott hoped he would also be Jamie's only.

But none of that explained why Mike was calling in the middle of the night. If Jamie had been here, a call from Mike might have ruined everything.

"Let's hope they're great," Mike said. "The first-year exam is starting. I'm gathering the students but I can't find Jamie."

"Wait, what do you mean it's starting?"

All sleep vanished from Scott's mind. Jamie wasn't ready for the exam. There was still so much to do. Scott still had two weeks until the exam began.

"I mean one of the students found the nesting grounds and the first egg has been shattered. We have to get the rest of the students ready immediately. Do you know where Jamie is?"

"He left my place hours ago. He was heading to his dorm. You don't think he's the one-"

There was silence on the other end. Scott shut his eyes and tipped his head back. If Jamie had found the eggs on his own, then he was totally unprepared for what he would find. The other students would receive advice on how to deal with newly hatched dragons but Jamie would be on his own. Scott still remembered the terror he felt when Narné emerged from his shell and attacked.

"There are three freshmen who can't be located," Mike said. "It could be one of the others."

"Or those two could have snuck over to the women's college for the night."

"We're checking. They're gathering their freshman for the exam as well so we'll know soon enough. It could have been one of them."

"It's not, though. It's Jamie," Scott whispered. He could feel the truth of it reflected in Narné's mind. But was the boy ready? Could he form an attachment with a dragon and would the dragon even let him?

"This could be good," Mike said. "When the students go to the exam together there's almost no chance of him finding a hidden egg. But if he went on his own, then perhaps he found a Queen."

"He might have found one, but can he keep one? Queens have a tendency to kill their partners rather than bond with them."

Mike was silent again. Inwardly, Scott was trembling with fear. He had wanted Jamie to find a Queen egg, true, but as part of the exam. At the exam, students were given swords and advice for fending off their dragon's initial attack. Jamie was alone and unarmed somewhere, and Queen dragons were notorious killers. It was one of the many reasons they were so rare. Of course, it was hard to prove at times that Queens and not regular dragons had killed students. The bodies of first-year students would be found slashed and hacked to death with no dragon in sight. Only a Queen dragon was strong enough to survive for a time without a human, so those deaths were attributed to them. If Jamie did find a Queen, he would be utterly unprepared mentally and physically and he would stand little chance of surviving.

Mike sighed and Scott was willing to bet that for once the two of them were worrying about the same thing.

"Look, Scott, I need your help with these freshman. Can you give me a hand preparing them? I was expecting more time as well and they aren't ready, but I won't let this year turn into a massacre."

"Of course. I'll meet you at the trailhead."

They set up a time to meet and Scott got up and tossed on some clothes before checking in on Narné. The dragon was in the guest room built specifically for a dragon, with a massive dragon bed in the middle. Although the dragon appeared to be asleep, Scott knew he was awake and worrying about Jamie.

"Any news? And how did a student wander onto the nesting grounds without any of you noticing?"

Narné rolled his head from side to side in embarrassment. *We do not protect all of the nesting grounds, only the newer ones the school uses. There are others. He went to a nesting ground that has not been used in nearly a thousand years. It is a very dangerous place.*

Scott climbed up into the dragon bed and curled into Narné's giant arm. It was well known that the longer a dragon stayed in its shell, the angrier it became when released and the more it would fight the person who released it. A nesting ground as old as Narné described would be lethal even if Jamie didn't find a Queen.

The school used newer grounds whose eggs were from the last Queen, well, the last Queen not counting the one whose human killed himself. Those eggs were only a century old and were considered relatively safe, but frequently individual students would be drawn to eggs in different nesting grounds. Scott had been drawn to a large clearing in the woods with a hollowed out nest in the middle filled with eggs. Narné had been in his shell for just under four centuries, much longer than the other dragons from Scott's class. The longer they were in the shell, the harder they fought but also the more powerful they tended to be. Most of the council had dragons that had been in the shell for at least two centuries. Mike's dragon had spent over three centuries trapped inside its shell; he was another student who ended up in a different nesting ground.

Narné's warmth soothed Scott, as did the dragon's assurances that everything would work out. Scott couldn't tell if the dragon was lying or using his ability to see glimpses of the future, and he wasn't going to ask. It was enough that Narné had faith in Jamie's abilities.

"Can you tell if Jamie found an egg?"

An egg was opened. That is what triggered the exam. You know that there is only a small window of time for hatchings each year. Twelve hours from when the first egg is hatched. You humans try to have this hatching at set times, but nature has taken her own course this time.

"Yeah, I guess so. Is there any way to tell if Jamie is-"

He stopped, not ready to ask if Jamie was alive or if the worst had happened.

Not until he leaves the nesting ground. We do not go to the nesting grounds during the hatching. The little dragons would attack us instead and you humans would be unable to bond with us.

"I still don't understand why attacking is such an integral part of the process."

We are dragons. We fight. You must learn to accept this about us, Narné chided. *Now go and help the little humans. Time is running out.*

69

Scott sighed and left the comfort of his dragon. His fight with Narné at the hatching had been fierce and he still had scars across his chest from where the dragon had clawed him. He wondered how many scars Jamie would end up with. Assuming he survived. Even the weakest dragon in a nesting ground that old would be a formidable challenge, especially without a weapon to ward the creature off.

When he reached the trailhead, Mike was already there giving instructions and handing out weapons and flashlights. Most of the students looked highly skeptical, as if they thought this were some sort of initiation prank. For people who didn't believe in dragons, it did sound like a prank: go out into the national park in the middle of the night with a sword, find a dragon egg, and fight the dragon. It wasn't something a reasonable, rational person would do. But Tarragon Academy was anything but rational and most of the students were taking this in stride. The ones who didn't believe, who wanted proof first, those were the most likely to be killed.

The students were sent up the northeastern path one by one. Scott didn't understand how the forest worked, but he knew that this specific path changed destinations depending on the person. For those without dragons, it led to nesting grounds. For those with dragons, it led to a canyon where most of the dragons lived. Only Narné and a couple dozen other dragons lived in apartments with the humans. The rest lived in the canyon and kept an eye on things.

When Scott arrived, the students were already being sent off down the path but the remaining students swarmed him, demanding answers and reassurance that this wasn't some trick on Mike's part. Scott assured them that everything Mike said was true and emphasized the importance of holding off the dragon's initial attack without hurting the dragon. A few of the skeptics looked disgusted, as though disappointed that Scott too was telling a lie. They would learn soon enough that it was no lie, and hopefully they would get a dragon who gave them time to get over their shock before attacking. The students continued heading down the path one at a time, laughing nervously. Only a few students were left when the girls arrived with the other two missing boys. If there was any doubt about who started the exam before, there was none now. Jamie was the only person unaccounted for.

As the women were sent off down the path, one of the female instructors pulled Scott to one side.

"I hear Jamie was the first. Has he returned yet?"

"No," Scott said. "No one has returned yet."

"Well, your boys just went out. It's too early to expect them. But if the dragons are correct, and they always are, then your Jamie hatched his egg almost four hours ago. That's more than enough time to return. Was he... properly prepared?"

Scott wanted to punch her. What an arrogant prick. She had to know how worried he felt and how very aware of the timing he was. And it wasn't her business if Scott and Jamie had slept together. Or at least it shouldn't be, except that she was favored to be on the council in the future and he couldn't be rude to her.

"He's as prepared as possible without knowing anything about the exam," Scott said coldly.

"I see. You know the council had concerns about him."

"Those concerns," Mike interrupted, joining their conversation to Scott's great relief, "will have nothing to do with any failure on his part. If something happens to Jamie, it is because he is unarmed and hasn't been told about dragons."

"But Jamie will be fine," Scott added, not sure if he was making a statement or asking a question.

The woman sniffed and walked back to the girls. Scott thanked Mike and the two sat down on a fallen tree trunk to wait for the freshmen to return, dragons in tow. Scott could hear Narné's voice in his head narrating some of the events. The dragons couldn't go into the nesting grounds but they could see who went in and out and they shared that knowledge freely between them. Not all dragons were able to communicate with their humans as easily as Narné and Scott did, however, so Scott always had an advantage. Even Mike, who could communicate with his dragon, frequently chose not to because he said having the dragon's thoughts in his head felt like an invasion of his privacy. Mike and his dragon spoke aloud, and rarely used telepathy.

From Narné, Scott knew that most of the freshmen ended up in the usual nesting ground. Only two ended up in alternate nesting grounds and both were fairly recent ones. When the first freshman left the nesting ground with his dragon, Scott shared the news with Mike, who smiled and relaxed against the tree.

"I'm so glad," he said. "This is my first year in charge of the exam, you know, and I want it to go smoothly. I was afraid none of them would make it out."

A few minutes later the boy emerged from the bushes with a proud glow in his eyes and a baby dragon in tow. Scott smiled indulgently at the little creature, remembering Narné at that age. In his mind he felt Narné grow indignant.

I did not look like that ridiculous little thing, Narné insisted. Scott just laughed, and the boy and his dragon joined in even though they didn't know why he was laughing. The boy was so happy the laughter seemed to stream straight out of him and the dragon kept head-butting his knees and nearly knocking him over. They were assigned a spot by the fire the women had built while everyone waited for the rest to return.

The other freshmen returned in a steady stream with dragons in tow. None of the dragons were especially powerful and none seemed to have special gifts, but all were a blessing. Two students returned with deep injuries and Mike stitched them up carefully. They would be sent to a real doctor and perhaps even a plastic surgeon later, but for now everyone waited together. Finally, after three hours, all but three of the boys and most of the girls had returned. But still no sign of Jamie.

Mike seemed deep in thought, no doubt talking to his dragon Eraxes about the chances of the three missing boys being alive. They had all been at the normal nesting ground and it was unlikely that there were any extenuating circumstances that would prevent them from returning. Aside from death, that is.

No one could enter the nesting grounds until sunrise, so there was no way of knowing for sure until then but traditionally the group left after four hours, and they had waited here nearly six. Dawn would be in another three hours, but the students with medical injuries needed attention soon. They couldn't all wait on the off chance that Jamie or the other boys were just taking their time leaving, but Scott refused to leave until Jamie was at his side.

"What do we do, Mike?" Scott asked. "We can't leave without him. We know he's out here."

Mike's face took on a hard set. "We have to consider the fact that he might be dead, or unable to leave the nesting ground. I have to take my students back. Some of them need medical care and all of them need rest. But I can't stop you from staying here tonight."

"You'll just abandon him?"

"No," Mike said. "I'm leaving him with you. I know you'll find him if he doesn't show up."

Scott sighed. Mike was right; the other man had responsibilities to the other students and needed to leave, but he wasn't abandoning Jamie. There was no one in the world who cared about Jamie more than Scott. Scott would find a way to locate Jamie.

Mike and the students left, and after another hour the women left as well. Four of their students were still missing and they asked Scott to keep an eye out for them. They left the campfire burning in hopes that the remaining students would see it and find their way back to the trailhead, but Scott knew it was mostly wishful thinking, especially for Jamie. It was pitch-black inside the woods and unlike the other students, Jamie didn't have a flashlight. If he tried going anywhere he would end up lost.

Scott sat up straight as the realization of what he had just thought sank in. Jamie didn't have a flashlight. He couldn't leave the nesting ground even if he survived. He would have to wait until sunrise no matter what happened with his egg. Scott took a deep breath to calm himself. The fact that Jamie hadn't returned yet meant nothing, and he shouldn't have doubted Jamie for even a minute. Jamie was a fighter and would get through this. There was nothing to worry about until sunrise. But if sunrise came and Jamie still hadn't left the nesting ground... Better not to think about that. Better to focus on the positives, Scott told himself. Jamie could handle anything.

CHAPTER TWELVE

Marisol

Jamie lay motionless and the little dragon seemed to lose interest. She hopped away from him to explore the area and he curled into a ball around his wounded belly. The injuries were deep; he was losing too much blood. There was no way he could swim back to safety. He was going to die out here alone.

Hours passed as the little dragon vanished from his sight and he focused on staunching the blood from his wounds, but he knew it was a lost cause. If they were on his limbs he could have put a tourniquet on them, but there was nothing he knew how to do for his abdomen aside from applying pressure and not giving up. The bleeding slowed, but never really stopped as the sky finally began to lighten. It was a miracle he was still alive and he knew it. But as the stars grew dim and the horizon turned a fiery salmon from the soon-to-rise sun, the dragon returned and he worried that she was here to finish the job.

She sniffed around him while he remained tightly curled around his injuries. She didn't try to attack or bite this time, but then again there was no need. He was dying and all she had to do wait. Mentally he pleaded with her to help him, but he knew it did no good. She probably still thought of him as an enemy and would kill him if he tried anything.

The dragon's head swung towards him and a buzzing sound filled his head. He moaned and grabbed his temples. It hurt worse than his belly. It felt as though someone were trying to force his way into his head with a jackhammer. His mind and body were filled with foreign emotions and thoughts that terrified him in their intensity. Pain and pleasure made him scream as he huddled around his torn belly. Everything became saturated with color and a different emotion swept over him with each new color – anger at the red of the dragon's wings, sorrow at the water lapping against the jealous shores. He shoved the bizarre thoughts and feelings out of his head as forcefully as he could and it was like a door slamming in his face when everything stopped.

The dragon made a strange humming sound and turned back to her inspection of the area. He didn't know how she had caused his experience, but everything about her was sharp and painful and he was willing to bet she had caused the horrifying sensations, too.

The dragon sniffed the other eggs but didn't touch them and Jamie was grateful. The last thing he needed was another monster running loose to hasten his death. At least this one seemed to recognize that he meant her no harm. She turned to look at him and the buzzing filled his head again. After a second, the emotions swept over him again like the inexorable tide rising over the head of someone tied to a rock. He was that someone, and there was nothing he could do this time as the moonlight glittered playfully and the shadows traumatized his senses. All of his senses were saturated with emotion this time; the earthy scent of the soil under his face radiated comfort but the boulders exuded sheer panic and it was hard not to react to that ozone scent. The dragon with her angry scales and excited clove aroma reared back and let out a call that deafened him inside and out and he shut his eyes, but he could still see the colors and feel the pain.

Please stop, he thought desperately. It's bad enough that I'm going to die out here, can't you at least let me die in peace?

She made a snuffling noise and returned to his side. He curled up tighter in the fetal position, protecting his vital organs in case she started clawing at him again. It didn't matter; one kick and he was flat on his back with the wind knocked out of him, seeing stars. At least his physical pain was better than the emotional pain being inflicted on him by the harsh world around him. If this was how she perceived the world, no wonder she was fighting. Fresh tears ran down his cheek as she leaned over him and licked the blood from his belly wounds. He braced himself to be eaten and tried one final time to convince her that he meant no harm.

"Please," he whispered. "You're better off outside that egg. I know. I used to be trapped as well, and life is so much better here. I know it's scary, but you'll get used to it. The colors and scents will fade. Please don't kill me."

She cocked her head and the buzzing filled his head again, only this time he could almost make out words.

"Are you talking to me?" he asked, hope lighting up his voice. If she was talking, then maybe she wouldn't kill him. Maybe she could turn off whatever switch she had opened in his head and make the world go back to normal.

Her head wobbled in what he took for a nod. She really was beautiful when she wasn't trying to kill him. Her scent had changed to one of excited reassurance, lavender and cloves. Then her head lowered and she licked up more blood, and thoughts of her beauty vanished. She was still going to eat him. Oddly, he couldn't smell himself or his own blood and he wondered if he smelled as good to her as a well-cooked steak did to him.

I will not eat you, he heard a voice say in his head.

It was a female voice, young and annoyed, and there was no buzzing to accompany it. He looked around to make sure that no human had wandered up, but there was only the dragon. She had spoken to him in a voice that again carried reassurance.

You woke me from a deep slumber and I thought you were here to kill me, she said.

No sounds were being emitted, the words were entirely in his head and he could feel her emotions as she said them, as if her entire soul were adjacent to his and they were sharing everything. He panicked, wondering how much of him she could feel.

"Everything," she said. "You are not hiding from me. That is how I know you will not hurt me."

"But you hurt me," he said. He curled back into a ball to try to stem the blood loss. He was so dizzy and his skin tingled where she had licked him. "My world is broken! Why should I trust you?"

She cocked her head and stared at him with large, black eyes. She really was beautiful. Her scales were crimson except for a single creamy stripe running from the top of her head to the tip of her tail. The stripe formed a triangle on her forehead and he was reminded of a viper or other poisonous snake whose heads were always larger than their bodies. She was definitely deadly, but he could feel her mind and soul now and he sensed that her aggression was simply rage at being locked up for so long. He tried to figure out how long she had been locked in the egg but it felt like an eternity and he could get no definite answer from her mind.

And she could be trusted, he sensed. She was allowing him to read her soul freely and he suspected she would not allow such an invasion of privacy often, but she wanted him to know that she meant him no harm. Then why had she licked him? He dug into her mind for the reason and was surprised to see that forming a blood bond between them was the only way to establish the kind of mental communication they had. They were now bound together for all eternity and the little dragon seemed quite happy that he was the person to wake her. She had searched through his mind thoroughly, he saw, and deemed him worthy of a relationship with her.

He suspected she approved of him partially because he had freed her, and also because when she attacked he had been willing to submit to her and know when to stop fighting. He thought of Scott and how he had fought against his attraction to the upperclassman, and how he had eventually submitted to Scott as well. Submission had its perks, he decided. He saw in her mind stories her mother had sung to the eggs about heroes who woke the dragon eggs to kill the dragons and realized that she had assumed him to be one of those heroes. Her mother had never mentioned that there were kind humans who didn't enjoy violence.

Finally he realized that the world outside had grown calmer. Colors were a bit more normal and looked less like a badly tuned TV, and his sense of smell, while still heightened, was no longer overwhelming him with information. She snorted and suddenly the connection between them was gently but firmly shut and he was back in the real world, suffering from the real pain of blood loss. There was no time to realize that he could see everything as clear as day even though the sun had yet to rise in the sky, or that he could smell every living thing within a mile and tell what it was and what it wanted. He was too busy maintaining consciousness.

He nearly blacked out but she licked his shoulder where she had bitten him before and he noticed the blood flowing slower. Did her saliva have clotting abilities? The bleeding on his belly where she had licked him had come to a stop, he realized. Was it just the passage of time or had she done something? Either way it was too late; he had lost too much blood already and there was no way he could survive the trip home. The least he could do was learn her name.

Marisol, she said as she nuzzled his uninjured shoulder. *And you will survive. I will make sure of it.*

"Marisol," he repeated in a weak voice. "It was nice meeting you. Tell Scott I love him."

She cocked her head and her eyes gleamed. *You will tell him. His dragon is nearly here to carry you back, but they must wait until daybreak.*

He frowned and inhaled deeply. Just at the edge of his senses was a large creature and as it drew closer he recognized the scent of cloves that Marisol exuded. That must be the scent of dragons, he thought. There were two of them hovering about a mile away and both emitted a hopeful cinnamon in addition to the cloves. They smelled like pumpkin pies on the way to rescue him, he thought with a delirious smile. Then he glanced at Marisol and his brow creased.

"What about you? You can't fly yet."

Marisol flapped her wings in protest, but they were far too tiny for her bulk, even though she was mostly feet and head. She looked so unbalanced trying to fly with her enormous head and feet on her scrawny little body that he couldn't help but laugh, a proud yet painful laugh. She was his, and he would take care of her until she was properly proportioned and as big as the other dragons.

After trying to fly for a few minutes, Marisol gave up with a disappointed squawk. Sharp onion filled the air and Jamie blinked back tears at the scent and her sorrow.

Another dragon is coming to carry me, she said in a dejected tone.

"Don't worry," Jamie said. "You'll be flying in no time, and you'll race circles around those other dragons."

Her head rose regally and she nodded once. Then she curled up next to him. Her scales were soft and cool, like a snake's, and she smelled of smoke and cloves, content to wait with him. He leaned his head against her tiny back and shut his eyes. He could feel his pulse dragging against his veins and it was starting to become hard to breathe. Each breath grew shallower but when he tried to take anything deeper, a stabbing pain crippled him as though barbed wire were constricting around his lungs.

He tried shifting position but when he laid flat on his back, the barbed wire tightened uncontrollably and he couldn't even gasp. He couldn't breathe at all; no air entered his lungs and his body was paralyzed. He desperately reached for the dragon in his thoughts as the world started to fade to gray.

Marisol awoke instantly and nudged him onto his side and air started flowing again. She nuzzled his back and licked his wounds again, but it was growing harder and harder to breathe. Soon even shallow breaths were too much and he had to space his breathing to avoid the crippling, paralyzing pain. Just when he thought he couldn't take it anymore, the sun appeared over the horizon and Marisol bellowed.

A shadow covered them and an enormous green dragon landed beside them. It was the same dragon from the bathroom but Jamie wasn't worried about getting eaten now. He could feel death lurking nearby and he just wanted to get to Scott before it happened. Another shadow and another dragon appeared. This one was blue and Jamie had never seen it before. Both dragons studied him lying there, barely able to breathe and dying before their eyes.

He is too weak, the blue one said. They were speaking silently but he felt their voices clearly in his mind. He couldn't feel anything of their souls, but he could smell Marisol and she was angry.

Save him, she demanded. *Carry us back to your doctors and make him better.*

I will carry him, the green dragon offered.

He will not survive the trip, the blue dragon said. *We should give him peace.*

Jamie knew without a doubt that giving him peace meant killing him painlessly and for a moment he considered. The dragon was right; it was unlikely he could be picked up by a dragon and survive when he couldn't even lie flat on his back.

"No," he whispered. He would not accept an easy death; he would go out fighting if there was even the slightest chance of seeing Scott again.

Marisol hopped up and down and stretched a wing towards him. *You see? He wants to live.*

He heard me?

The blue dragon seemed disturbed by this for some reason. Its large head swung over Jamie and the sight was frightening, but not as frightening as death.

"Yes," Jamie whispered.

The dragon turned away from him and snarled. *I carry the baby. You carry the boy. Protect him.*

The green dragon seemed to roll his eyes and wink at Jamie, as if amused by the other dragon's sudden change of heart. He carefully wrapped his claws around Jamie and lifted him. Jamie could still breathe, but barely. Speaking was beyond him, so he tried to use his mind to explain to the dragon that he couldn't be flat on his back or he would stop breathing. The dragon nodded once before unfurling its massive wings and leaping into the air on its one free leg. Jamie looked back to make sure Marisol was all right and saw the large dragon carefully holding her the same way he was being held and leaping into the air. Then the pain consumed him and he began his struggle to breathe again.

CHAPTER THIRTEEN

Exam Results

Scott paced at the campfire, waiting to hear from Narné. While the dragon was in the nesting grounds, he couldn't sense the dragon at all and he was desperate to know if Jamie was alive. The night had passed in slow, agonizing minutes ever since Narné had received a plea for help from the nesting ground where Jamie had gone. That meant that Jamie had successfully bonded with a dragon, but was unable to return on his own and his dragon had needed to call for reinforcements. Eraxes, Mike's dragon, had gone as well to make sure Jamie and his dragon were all right, but neither dragon could enter the nesting grounds until sunrise or they would risk waking the multitudes of eggs surrounding Jamie.

Just the presence of a grown dragon so close to the hatching was enough to cause eggs to hatch even without a human present, as the academy had discovered centuries ago. But any dragon who hatched without a suitable human partner died within hours, so the adult dragons were extremely careful to avoid the eggs. Normally they avoided the nesting grounds altogether, but Narné and Eraxes were willing to risk it in order to save Jamie.

Jamie. He had bonded with a dragon, which was a relief, and his dragon was intelligent enough to know how to speak to other dragons without being taught. That boded well. His dragon was also requesting help for Jamie, so perhaps there hadn't been much of a fight. Scott knew that hope was misguided; the strongest relationships were formed after the fiercest fights. He fingered the scars along his abdomen and remembered Narné kicking against him with those powerful hind legs. Baby dragons were almost entirely claws and teeth and they were born knowing how to use them. Scott imagined Jamie's body ripped open and bleeding, the porcelain skin stained red in places and whiter than a ghost in other places as the blood slowly left his body. He shuddered and tried to banish the thoughts from his mind.

Jamie is alive, a voice in his head said suddenly, and Scott was seeing through Narné's eyes and feeling his emotions. He felt Jamie's tense body in his claws as the boy struggled to breathe and Scott's own chest clenched in horror. Jamie was very, very close to death. Narné was bringing him straight to the doctors and Scott needed to be there, because there was a chance Jamie wouldn't survive.

Scott started running. He felt Narné try to tell him something about Jamie's dragon but he ignored it, ignored everything except the earth under his feet and the brambles and tree branches that sprang in front of him as if the planet itself were trying to prevent him from reaching the gymnasium where the doctors were stationed for the exam. He ran and tried to empty his mind of everything except the rhythm of his feet against the path. He would not think about the agony Jamie was in, or the likelihood that Jamie would not be able to pull through. He ran and reminded himself that the academy called in the best doctors for the first year exam in case something like this happened, and Jamie would be in excellent hands. He ran and felt his pulse against his ears and his breath within his chest and wished he could give some of his blood and breath to the boy gasping in Narné's claws. He ran and ran, and still it was ages before the campus came into sight and he arrived at the makeshift hospital in the gymnasium.

He didn't even glance at the other injured students. He went straight to the back where Narné was just landing with Jamie. Mike was already there, directing Narné and Eraxes to put their passengers down gently and then fly back outside. Scott couldn't see Jamie; he was behind his dragon's bulk, so he came closer despite the doctors telling him to stay back. Finally he was close enough to see his boyfriend and he let out a horrified moan and nearly sank to the floor.

Jamie's face was utterly white and his entire body was crimson and black with dried blood. His shoulder had been bitten open and his entire abdomen was a mass of deep lacerations, some so deep that Scott could see the bone of his ribs and possibly even organs inside. He wasn't moving, not even to take a breath, except for his eyes, which scanned the room until they landed on Scott. As soon as he saw Scott, his chest rose slightly as he took a breath, and a small smile appeared on his lips. Then his eyes closed and he went completely limp.

The doctors were already busy with him when he went limp and had already hooked him up to several machines, and when he went limp they started shouting and brought out paddles. Mike appeared from out of nowhere and blocked Scott's view as the doctors began yelling, "Clear!"

"Come on, Scott," he said. "The doctors need space to work."

"No," Scott said, pushing past Mike in time to see Jamie's body jolted with electricity in an attempt to start his heart. "I have to be here!"

Mike sighed and took his hand. Oddly, the gesture didn't bother him and Scott clung to Mike's hand as if it were the only thing holding him together. Narné was just as frantic about Jamie's condition, especially since he was now stuck outside the gym and couldn't witness the action firsthand, and he was hardly a reassuring figure as Jamie's body was jolted a second time. The monitor still showed a flat line. The paddles were placed on his chest a third time, and Scott closed his eyes. He reached out to Jamie as if he were reaching out to a dragon using telepathy.

Please, Jamie, he thought. *Don't leave yet.*

Jamie's body went rigid a third time, and then the monitor began beeping. The flat line became a series of peaks and valleys and Scott almost shouted in joy. The doctors immediately began preparing to move Jamie into a more sterile environment and one of the doctors informed Scott and Mike that they couldn't follow, but Scott didn't mind now. It seemed to him that Jamie had passed the worst of it and now he had a chance of survival. As long as Jamie had the will to survive, he would. Tears welled in his eyes and he turned to Mike and surprised the other man with a hug. Mike held him a little too tightly and he wondered why the other man had been so concerned with Jamie's health.

"You did it," Mike said. "He bonded with the dragon. Thank you."

"Jamie did it," Scott said. "He's the one who survived."

One of the doctors who had remained behind cleared her throat. "He's not out of the woods yet. And Mike, I need to talk to you about retrieving the other boys."

Mike's expression darkened and Scott felt a wave of sympathy and sorrow wash over him. Jamie had survived, but the other three boys who hadn't returned last night had died. Since Mike was in charge of the exam this year, it was his duty to retrieve the bodies of the boys and their dragons. If any of the dragons were still alive, it was also his job to kill them to spare them the agonizing death that dragons faced when their human died. Mike followed the doctor in the direction of the woods and Scott was grateful that he didn't have that kind of responsibility. He wondered which boys hadn't made it, and if Amar was one of them.

Amar survived, Narné chimed in. *He has a beautiful blue dragon.*

Scott smiled. Blue dragons were often at odds with the green dragons, but Narné had a fondness for his aqua brethren. They were most at home in water, whereas the green dragons preferred the forest. He wondered which kind Jamie had ended up with and realized he hadn't even thought about Jamie's dragon. He sent a question to Narné and learned that Narné and Jamie's dragon were just outside the building. She wanted to meet him.

He was delighted by the "she". He had hoped that Jamie

would bond with a female dragon, because it would make their relationship smoother. When dragons mated, their owners felt the emotions strongly and almost always were driven to have sex at the same time. If the two humans having sex were bonded to the two dragons mating, sex was supposedly a mind-blowing experience. Scott had never tried it; Narné had chased females in heat before, but Scott handled his pleasure privately. If Jamie had bonded to a male dragon, they would never be able to experience the pleasure of dragon-human sex, but since he was paired with a female, the possibilities were endless, as long as Narné and Jamie's dragon got along.

Scott went out to the back and for a moment, he only saw Narné. Then he remembered how tiny dragon babies were and he scanned the ground. She was curled up at Narné's feet, and she was red. He blinked and shook his head, then looked again. Red. A slow excitement built in his chest as his heart rate began to pick up. A red dragon. A Queen. Jamie had bonded with a Queen.

No wonder Jamie had been so close to death, he thought. Not only was she a Queen, she was from an ancient nesting ground and likely had incredible strengths. She looked innocent now, curled up like a kitten, but Scott knew how deceptive appearances could be.

As he watched her, breathless and speechless at her beauty and the wonder of her existence, she slowly opened one eye. Seeing him, she opened the other and lifted her oversized head above her frail body. Their small size at hatching was so deceptive, he knew, because in just a day or two she would have doubled in size at least once, more as long as she was kept properly fed and her dead scales were scraped off. The freshmen would spend their entire summer in an endless routine of feeding and scraping to make sure that their dragons matured properly. Jamie might not be able to care for his dragon, however, at least not for a while with his injuries, so the duty would fall to someone else and Scott knew that he wasn't about to let anyone besides him touch that beautiful Queen.

"I am Marisol," she said.

His jaw dropped. She was newly born and already knew how to talk.

"You are Scott. You are very important to Jamie."

"Yes," he said, not sure which of her comments he was agreeing to and still stunned that she could speak. "He's in good hands now. I think he might make it."

"Of course he will," she said with a snort. "He has me and you to live for."

"He almost gave up," Scott said, a little annoyed at her certainty.

He still remembered how Jamie had seen him and gone limp, as if the boy had wanted to live long enough to see him one last time and then gave up his will to live. Scott still felt that his attempt to communicate with Jamie telepathically was the reason Jamie's heart had restarted, even though he knew humans couldn't communicate that way.

"I felt that," she said, sounding puzzled. "But you were there. Why did he give up if you were there?"

"It's complicated," Scott said.

A great weariness was beginning to settle on him and he was overcome by the desire to curl up next to her against the safety of Narné's bulk. He wanted to check on Jamie and make sure he was doing all right, but he suspected that the doctors wouldn't let him in. They had tolerated him before because Jamie had been in such a large, open area, but now that Jamie had been whisked away to a real doctor's office there was little chance of seeing him until he was stable.

"I'm sorry I hurt him," Marisol said. "He frightened me when he woke me up. I didn't mean to hurt him so badly."

Narné nuzzled her. "It isn't your fault, little one. That is how we bond with our humans."

She was silent and Scott hesitantly reached out to touch her. Sometimes dragons attacked everyone besides their bonded human for weeks after the hatching, but Marisol seemed to already possess an adult mind and abilities, even if her body was that of a child. She leaned into his caress and several scales fell off into his hand. Scott smiled wryly. She was already growing and she hadn't even eaten yet. It seemed that child's body of hers was anxious to become an adult.

"Come with me, Marisol. We'll get you something to eat, and I'll scrape your scales for you. How does that sound?"

She let out a chirp and fluttered her little wings as she leapt to her feet, nearly knocking him over in the process. He laughed and led the way to the academy's farm, where they had been breeding animals for months in preparation for the babies. Every dragon required red meat to grow, but luckily, green dragons also ate leafy matter and blue dragons also ate fish or else they would never be able to produce enough food for all of the babies. Red dragons, however, were rumored to only eat red meat and Scott hoped that they wouldn't have to start importing cattle when Marisol grew older. A full grown dragon ate one cow every month and grazed or fished to supplement that diet, but Marisol would need a steady supply her entire life and the campus farm, while large, might not be big enough. Scott would hate to have to import factory animals who lived their lives in cages. The animals on the campus might be bred to be eaten, but they were well taken care of and lived full, happy lives.

It was a worry for another time, Scott thought as they passed the campus doctor's office where Jamie must be lying, surrounded by machines and fighting for his life. Marisol seemed confident that Jamie would pull through but as the doctor had said, Jamie wasn't out of the woods yet. Marisol was a good distraction to Scott's anxiety, but he knew that Jamie would be lurking in his thoughts and fears the entire time he fed and scraped the little Queen. And once she was taken care of, he would be at Jamie's side no matter what the doctors said.

CHAPTER FOURTEEN

The Council

Mike pressed an ice cube against Jamie's swollen lips. The boy opened his mouth obediently and tried to pull the ice cube into his mouth, but Mike held it firm. Jamie was unconscious but still capable of some ordinary movements, and the boy began sucking on the ice, working his lips over the melting surface as Mike held it still. He could see Jamie's tongue flickering against the ice cube inside his mouth and he wondered what it would feel like if it was his cock and not an ice cube. Melted water dripped down the boy's chin and Mike shivered with desire.

It would be so easy to take Jamie. He was on so many drugs he wouldn't even remember. Mike would prop his legs up gently so as not to disturb the bandages, and he would prepare Jamie's opening with his fingers before plunging in. As much as he ached to feel Jamie's tightness around his cock, he longer to finger the boy even more, to watch his eyes widen and those moist pink lips form an 'o' of surprised pleasure as he rode Mike's hand and Mike taught him the pleasures of sex. Scott hadn't touched him – Mike was sure of it – and Mike wanted to be the first to feel that silky interior and stroke the boy's prostrate until he begged for release.

The ice cube was practically gone and Mike released it, watching Jamie suck the remnants into that sweet mouth with his eyes closed in drugged bliss. He must be beautiful when he came, Mike thought, when he allowed himself to lose control. Mike was determined to help Jamie reach that point and now that Jamie was bonded to a Queen, it was a strong possibility.

It was unlikely that the council would allow Scott and Narné to mate with Jamie, since they were so young and rebellious. No, Marisol's first mating would be limited to the council, because the Queen's mate held a great deal of power. Mike might be allowed to participate, however, since he was favored by the council, but Jamie would have to specifically request him. Surely Scott and Jamie would rather have Mike in bed with the boy than one of the much older council members. Mike thought of the head of the council, Peter Ashton, in bed with Jamie and shuddered.

Once Marisol went into heat, all bets were off. She would fly away from the males and the fastest, strongest male would claim her. Jamie had a close enough bond with Marisol that he would likely lose all sense of himself during the flight and become Marisol, which would allow the victorious dragon's partner to take the boy at the same time his dragon was taking Marisol. If it was someone Jamie didn't want, he would be unable to resist and it would be like getting raped twice.

Mike had no qualms about forceful seduction, as he had done with Scott years ago and many students since, but even then he always was careful not to proceed until they stopped fighting. He knew Scott thought that what had happened between them was rape, but Mike had waited until Scott said yes. The council members would take Jamie even if he was screaming no, and Mike was determined to stop that from happened.

"You're quite taken with the boy," a voice said, coming from the doorway. Mike looked up and his heart stopped for a moment. It was Peter Ashton, head of the council and the man in charge of the entire academy and all of its graduates. For a moment, all Mike could see was the man's smile the night they had first met, when Mike had gotten on his knees and Ashton had parted his robes. Then he was back in the present and he realized that he was in an equally dangerous situation.

Although Mike was the new rising star of the council, he still had to tread carefully to keep their respect. Overstepping his bounds would earn him punishment, if not death. To Mike's relief, a doctor came in behind Ashton, preventing the man from saying anything more. Ashton could have ordered the woman out, but he didn't. Instead, he just watched Mike with a look of amusement on his face as the rest of the council filed in. To Mike's surprise, Scott came in the room as well.

Mike moved away from Jamie's side quickly when Scott entered, but apparently not quickly enough because the other man scowled at him. Mike said nothing and glanced at Ashton to see whether he would be allowed to stay or not. Ashton nodded and gestured for him to take a place at his side. Cautiously, Mike sidled up against him. Ashton grabbed his ass, but because they were so close, no one could see what the man was doing. Mike felt himself blushing and looked down, commanding his body to stop reacting to the man's skillful touch while the doctor gave her update on Jamie's condition.

Because Jamie was partnered with a Queen, his condition was important to the entire council. Even so, Mike was surprised they were all here. Perhaps they were checking him out to see who they would potentially be having sex with. Mike was especially surprised that they allowed Scott in the room, since he would almost certainly not be allowed in the mating flight.

"He's lost a lot of blood," the doctor said. "Even though he's gained faster healing abilities, it might be weeks before he fully recovers."

Mike's mind wandered as the doctor gave her report. She had already told him everything earlier in the day. Mike watched Scott stroking Jamie's hand and wondered if he had any idea how lucky he was that the council had let him in the room at all. Even though Scott would probably become a council member eventually, he was considered too unruly and disobedient right now and the council hoped to mold him into shape before allowing him onto their board.

They hadn't succeeded in breaking him yet, but Jamie was excellent leverage and Mike could already see Scott bending under their pressure. Already, Scott had agreed to participate in the yearly seductions just so he was assigned to Jamie, and soon the council would force other concessions out of him for the privilege of sitting beside Jamie's hospital bed like this. Mike was sure of it. But for now, the council seemed content to allow Scott to remain at Jamie's side and take care of Marisol.

Their decision about letting Scott care for Marisol was not just for selfish reasons, however; the young dragon refused to let anyone else come near her and the only dragons she tolerated were Narné and Eraxes. Since she allowed his dragon, she would probably also allow Mike to come near her but he hadn't tried. He had stayed near Jamie's side ever since the boy had been brought to the hospital three days ago.

The council thought he was there for all of the injured students, not just Jamie, and commended his commitment to his students. Really, though, he just wanted to make sure the council didn't try anything on Jamie while he was unconscious and unable to fight. He didn't think they would kill Jamie, but if they suspected that Jamie wouldn't be a pliable, obedient child, then they would break his spirit to make sure that he didn't rebel against them. Above all else, the council hated disobedience, especially the head council member Peter Ashton. His word was law, and anything he wanted, he got, as Mike had learned when he began being considered for the council, and as he was constantly reminded by Ashton's gropes in hidden places or when no one was looking, like now.

There was a group within the community, a secret group, that wanted to overthrow Ashton and change many of the unjust and corrupt laws that governed Tarragon society. The council, after all, ruled not just the Academy but all of its graduates scattered across the globe. Before leaving the Academy, each graduate had to swear on the life of his or her dragon to obey the council. Most never had their obedience questioned, but there were enough dragonless graduates to serve as warnings to anyone who dared challenge the council.

Anyone who fought against the council lost their most precious friend and a part of their soul, as the older rebellion members had learned the hard way. The new strategy consisted of getting new council members sympathetic to the cause. Mike was their primary focus right now and he was on the shortlist to be added to the council. His voice alone wouldn't change much, but he would then have the privilege of voting for other new members and in time, they could establish a strong minority and perhaps even a majority within the council. Eventually they hoped to have enough strength to be able to get rid of Ashton, who was continuing to stroke Mike's lower back as the doctor spoke.

The rebellion's plan would change, of course, if a Queen dragon appeared. Everyone dreamed of it happening, and now it finally had. The Queen outranked the council, but since she was young it would be her mate who made the decisions. Marisol was growing quickly and would be ready for her first mating in weeks, if not earlier. Jamie's state of mind would affect her readiness, since the two were so closely linked. It was said that the bond between Queen and her partner was the strongest of any dragon, and the human partner could even experience the world the same way that a dragon did.

The first mating would be the most important day of Jamie's life, and Marisol's. And despite what both of them would want, Scott would not be allowed to participate. It would only be council members, to ensure that control of the Academy remained within the council. It wouldn't do for a disobedient child like Scott to suddenly have more authority than the council, after all. Ashton no doubt expected to be Marisol's partner, but Mike had a plan and he hoped Jamie and Marisol would go along with it.

Mike figured that since he was so close to becoming a council member and had proven himself an obedient member of the society, and because his dragon was one of two that Marisol tolerated, he should be allowed to participate in Marisol's first mating. The council would probably agree, because in the mating it was a race to see which dragon caught the Queen dragon first and they would falsely assume that Eraxes, as the youngest dragon, wouldn't know the tricks of the mating game as well as their older, experienced dragons. Ashton's dragon Arion in particular was known for his skills in the mating chase, and he practiced those tricks on a regular basis despite Ashton being far older than most of the dragons and partners he chased. Nearly everyone partnered to a female dragon had slept with Ashton at one time or another, willingly or not, and Arion's skills were legendary.

Eraxes and Mike, on the other hand, didn't know as many tricks and it would be a challenge to ensure that they were the ones who caught Marisol, but he had been in enough matings to know that the dragon's preference made a difference. If Marisol wanted him, she would only submit to him no matter what tricks the other dragons used.

Scott wouldn't approve, of course, to allowing Jamie have sex with Mike. He wouldn't have much choice in the matter, though. It was either Mike or one of the council members and Mike knew enough about the council to know that most of them had a strong streak of sadism. It was one of the reasons Mike hated the council so much, and a reason why Mike's underground group was trying to change the balance of the council.

Mike knew firsthand how cruel the council could be. When he was selected to be in charge of the exam this year, he hadn't earned the position solely through his teaching or leadership abilities. He had been called in to the council's dark chambers in the basement of the Academy, a stone chamber where Mike could imagine beheadings and torture taking place. Even the stone tile seemed smeared with dried blood, although surely it was from a leftover dragon's meal and not from a human. It was a place designed to inspire fear and it worked.

Mike had gotten down on his knees before them and explained why he was best suited to take over the exam. The head of the council, the powerfully built Peter Ashton whose grave face was framed with wings of gray in his ebony hair, had stepped forward. They were all dressed in black robes with red dragons embroidered on the breast and back. The other council members watched as Ashton walked up to Mike and carded his hand through Mike's hair. Mike had gulped, almost knowing what was coming.

He had heard rumors, been warned by the underground group what kinds of things the council did behind closed doors, but this was his first experience with the council's secret rituals. He could feel Eraxes's discomfort in his mind and realized that his dragon was being surrounded by the council's dragons and whatever was about to happen to him was going to happen to Eraxes as well. He thought about fighting to protect his dragon – he had never imagined that his dragon would be harmed – but it was too late. He knew he would be killed if he tried to leave now, and nothing had even happened yet.

Ashton stroked his hair and must have been waiting for the tension to leave Mike's body because as soon as Mike realized the inevitability and hopelessness of his situation and accepted what had to happen, Ashton tousled his hair as one would a pet.

"Good boy," he murmured. "Now let's see what you can do."

Ashton had opened his robe. With Mike kneeling, the man's cock was directly in front of his face and it was already getting hard. It was enormous: a voluminous shaft with a purplish head. Mike would be able to fit some of it in his mouth but there was no way anything else was happening.

At Ashton's command, he hesitantly put the monster on his tongue, then began licking and stroking with his hands and mouth. He could barely fit the head into his mouth, it was so large, but he kept trying because he knew his plan depended on this. He had given head to men before, but never like this, kneeling on the floor while a crowd of people silently watched. It gave him chills and he shivered. Normally he would get off sucking something so substantial, but this was different. He didn't want to be here or do this, but there was nothing he could do about it.

Ashton pulled away from him without warning and gestured for him to stand up. He led Mike to the wall and pushed him against it.

"Wait," Mike said, realizing what was about to happen.

Again, a sense of inevitability came over him. He reached out to Eraxes, horrified to think that his dragon might also be getting raped, but there was silence. Eraxes had closed off communication between them, probably so that Mike wouldn't know what was happening.

Ashton laughed and pressed him against the wall, forcing his hands over his head. Then he grabbed Mike's cock and Mike groaned in surprise. Although he wasn't aroused, he was extremely sensitive and Ashton had him hard in a few skillful strokes.

"I want you to enjoy this," Ashton had whispered.

Then Ashton plunged into him and Mike couldn't control his scream. He felt himself being ripped open but Ashton didn't stop until he was fully inside him. Ashton kept stroking his cock, keeping him hard against his will, and Mike lowered his head in shame and defeat as his body responded to the arousal and the incredible sensations of Ashton thrusting into him, pain and pleasure alternating as Mike couldn't help but spread his legs to give the man better access in the hopes that it would hurt less and feel better.

When Ashton came, it was like an explosion and the sudden pressure of liquid against his insides tipped Mike over the edge and he came as well. It was several minutes before he could breathe normally and look around at the other council members. Some of the men had their cocks out, and several women were rubbing themselves as they watched.

Mike had collapsed to the floor in humiliation, but they had given him the first year exam. He had never gotten the courage to ask Eraxes what had happened and his dragon never spoke of it. Since then there had been a gulf between them and they rarely used telepathy anymore, relying instead on spoken language. He missed his friend dearly, but he knew that other dragons were relying on him to get on the council and it was for the greater good.

He had succeeded, after all. Ashton had kissed him and told him he showed great promise, and since then Mike had been like a favored pet, given perks such as being in Jamie's room when only council members were allowed in. All he had to do was put up with occasional gropes, which was a small price to pay. It would be a larger price if he wanted to join Marisol's mating, but if he was willing to sleep with Ashton again, he was almost certain that he would be allowed to do it. After getting Ashton's permission, it would just be a matter of dealing with Scott and convincing the council that he wasn't a threat until Marisol was old enough to defend herself. He didn't think they'd try to kill a Queen, but he wouldn't put anything past the council. If Marisol ended up choosing someone besides Mike or a councilmember, her life and Jamie's life would be in grave danger.

CHAPTER FIFTEEN

First Light

Stray flickerings of light crossed Jamie's vision, followed by a quiet roar in the distance. Something was missing; something that should have been beside him was not. The scent of antiseptic spray overwhelmed his senses and he wrinkled his nose in an attempt to smell past it to other, more important smells. There was another person in the room, a person with a scent that he vaguely recognized but not the one scent he was looking for. Scott wasn't there, but even though he ached for Scott it wasn't Scott that he was missing. He was looking for cloves, but who went with that smell? Who could possibly be more important than Scott?

Jamie squinted and the light almost blinded him. He kept his eyes open, though, not wanting to prolong the business of waking up. He remembered being attacked, the world turning strange, and the weakness. He remembered hearing Scott's voice in his head telling him to hold on, and that voice had given him the strength to keep fighting. And another voice, an annoyingly persistent voice that didn't let him give up the whole time he was being carried back to campus. The dragon.

He couldn't move except for his eyes, and he still couldn't see because of the light. He remembered the dragon and how she had become kind towards the end, how their minds had seemed to mesh together into a single entity. Marisol, that was her name. Where was she? Had she and Scott abandoned him?

I am here, a voice whispered in his mind. It was the dragon, speaking very quietly as if afraid her voice would upset him. *Are you awake now?*

Yes, he thought. *Where are you? Where is Scott?*

We are waiting for you outside. Scott will see you before I can.

There was a hint of melancholy in her voice and he was surprised that she would be upset about not seeing him first, but he could sense that she valued him deeply, despite attacking him earlier, and he couldn't deny that he felt an inexplicable bond between them. But he wasn't sure if he fully trusted her yet; the pain in his body was still present and now he had even more scars to worry about hiding. Although perhaps now his scars from cutting himself would be less noticeable. He could blame them on the dragon and never have to acknowledge the desperation that had led him to draw the blade across his skin again and again, desperate for some kind of release. Marisol made a reassuring sound in his mind and he saw an image of her trapped in the egg, biting her tail over and over in order to feel something other than the dreary monotony of life. They both had scars.

Jamie opened his eyes a little wider as the lights became manageable and he saw a man sitting on his bed, not touching him but watching him closely as if waiting for him to awaken. He was familiar and Jamie squinted to make sure he saw it right. Yes, it was Mr. Ferrin. Jamie couldn't figure out why Mr. Ferrin would be at his bedstand, but the teacher had seemed to care for him before the attack. In fact, Mr. Ferrin was known for taking good care of his students and had visited one of the other boys when he was hospitalized for a broken leg earlier in the semester. It wasn't unusual for Mr. Ferrin to be here, Jamie told himself. But it still felt strange waking up from a deep sleep after a severe attack and seeing his history teacher instead of the man he loved or the dragon who completed him.

"It's all right, Jamie," Mr. Ferrin said reassuringly. He placed his hand on Jamie's and Jamie was too weak to pull it away. "You've been through a lot, but you're going to be fine."

"Scott?" he managed to ask. He wanted to ask about Marisol,

but there was a chance Mr. Ferrin didn't know about dragons and he didn't want to sound crazy. At least he had an excuse with all the pain killers that were probably in his system.

"Scott is outside with Marisol."

Well, that put that idea to rest. Mr. Ferrin knew about Marisol and didn't think he was crazy. Jamie's heart fell as he heard that Scott and Marisol were together, however. They were probably having fun while he lay here immobile and upset. Why weren't they at his bedside?

I am too big, Marisol said apologetically, and Jamie realized he had been thinking too loudly.

Not all of my thoughts are meant for you to hear, he said with a little anger. She wasn't too big; she could easily fit in the room. And she had no right invading his thoughts. Bitter anger swept over him and he felt Marisol retreat. Jamie glared at Mr. Ferrin, the only one close enough to be a target of his rage. But Mr. Ferrin seemed prepared for anger and he gestured to a bouquet of wild flowers next to the bed.

"Scott has been bringing you new flowers every day when he visits, and he spends much of the day with you but Marisol needs to be fed and groomed. Once you're better, you can take up those responsibilities. I'm sure now that Scott knows you're awake, he'll be here shortly."

Jamie stared at the flowers. He didn't know what kinds they were, but they were beautifully arranged and he could imagine Scott clipping the stems so that the cornflower blue bells were just lower than the brilliant mini-sunflowers and surrounded by the little white flowers that seemed to grow everywhere in the spring. Only it wasn't spring, it was fall. Where did he find the flowers? It was a lovely arrangement, especially if the person they were intended for might not even see them.

"How long?" he asked. He meant to ask how long he was asleep, but the words were still too difficult. It must have been a long time because his body felt numb and strange, but perhaps that was the drugs.

"One week. The doctors put you in a coma so you wouldn't

feel the pain. You almost died," Mr. Ferrin said.

Jamie looked down at himself. He was covered in a blanket and he tried to lift his arms to remove the blanket and look at his injuries, but his arms wouldn't move properly. They felt locked into place and he could only move them side to side, not up and down.

"You're covered in bandages," Mr. Ferrin said, no doubt guessing what he was trying to do. He lifted the blanket for Jamie to see and Jamie gasped. His entire upper body was a large bandage, from his neck to his hips. He was naked below that and he blushed and gestured Mr. Ferrin to lower the blanket, hoping the man hadn't seen anything. He still wasn't sure if Mr. Ferrin had been hitting on him that one day after class, although the chat they'd had about Scott had reassured him a little that Mr. Ferrin was someone to be trusted.

A doctor ran into the room glaring at Mr. Ferrin and shooing him out. Mr. Ferrin promised to be back before allowing the doctor to push him outside. More doctors came in, swarming the room, and the first one sat where Mr. Ferrin had been sitting and began a barrage of questions about how he felt. Then she began a series of simple questions relating to math and logic and he realized that whatever had happened could have been bad enough to cause brain damage. That was the only reason he could think of to test his simple addition skills. His memory was tested, too, but he remembered everything, even the doctors yelling clear and the shocking pain of the jolt that had restarted his heart. The doctor seemed disturbed that he remembered this, but made a note of it in her notebook and made no comment.

Finally she gave him a chance to breathe and he asked when he could get up and see Marisol. She hesitated and he realized she probably had no idea who Marisol was. But she had to know about dragons; they were what had carried him to the gymnasium and saved his life and she hadn't batted an eye when he told her that. She didn't seem to think he was crazy, so she must know about dragons. Did everyone know about dragons? Was it some adult secret he had never been let in on, or something his life had just never exposed him to? It was like the opposite of Christmas: instead of finding out that the magical creature you've believed in all your life is a lie, you find out that the magical creature you thought was a lie was actually true.

"You can start moving as soon as you feel comfortable," the doctor said. "We'll have to get the bandages off and see how well you're doing first. Do you want us to start now?"

"Yes," he said without hesitation. He knew that he wouldn't be able to see Marisol bound up like this, and he needed to see her. He felt bad for yelling at her, even though he could sense that she understood his anger. Finding a balance between them would take time.

The doctors worked quickly and soon Jamie was able to move. He tried not to look at his body and kept his eyes closed, but eventually the curiosity was too much. He had to see what the dragon had done.

Three long gashes ran across his abdomen from the center of his chest to just below his left ribs. They were stitched up and weren't bleeding or anything, but he knew without being told that he would have those scars the rest of his life. The rest of his body was healing well. He was covered in minor bruises and contusions, and a scattering of smaller stitched wounds, but nothing that he thought would be serious or last more than another week. He seemed to have healed fast and he remembered Marisol licking him to stop the blood loss. Perhaps she had done even more and started the healing process while he was still out there.

The doctors helped him sit up gingerly. There was no pain, undoubtedly due to the drugs he was on. His body felt limp, but he pushed himself to try to stand, with them holding his arms and prepared to catch him at the slightest sign of weakness. He put one foot on the ground, then the other, and gathered all of his strength to hoist himself up. He nearly fell forward and would have, if the doctors weren't there to stabilize him. One of the doctors helped him slip a robe over his body and he was grateful – he didn't mind being naked in front of doctors but if anyone else came in he wanted to be covered.

He had a great deal of respect for doctors; he still remembered sitting by his mother's bedside at the hospital before she passed. The doctors had done everything for her and if the injuries had been less severe, he had no doubt the amazing doctors could have saved her. But she had been caught in a fire that killed two others as well, and her burns were too severe for her body to recover. The doctors kept her alive, trying to find ways to revive the dying flesh on her body, but it was too late. Jamie had been a child at the time but he still remembered the doctors trying to save her and one doctor in particular who had refused to give up. In the end it didn't matter, but doctors were firmly planted in his mind as heroes and they were some of the few people that Jamie trusted without question.

Jamie took a few steps towards the window with his escort, thinking that perhaps he could see Marisol outside. He carefully sent a thought to her asking if she could go outside the building so that he could see her. She responded with a gleeful cheer and he could feel her moving. For a moment, the sensation of her moving overcame him and he felt as though he were moving too. He reached for the doctors to stabilize himself and forced his mind back into his body, which, he was glad to discover, was standing absolutely still.

He came closer to the window but it was difficult because part of his mind was flying and it was hard to distinguish between the two.

It will be easier in time, Marisol said. *I can feel you, too. It is very strange.*

At least he wasn't the only one. Perhaps there was a way to work it to his advantage, Jamie thought. He tried to draw on Marisol's healthy energy to take more confident steps and it worked. The doctors exclaimed in surprise as he strode towards the window without hesitation and waited for her to show herself. He could feel her spinning in circles with delight. There was another dragon outside his window spinning in circles and while it looked vaguely like Marisol, there was no way that giant beast could be his delicate Marisol.

Marisol laughed with delight and the dragon outside turned to face him. When he saw its eyes, he gasped. It was Marisol. But this dragon was nearly as big as the other dragons he had seen. How could she possibly grow so quickly?

Scott is feeding me well, she answered. He didn't scold her for reading his thoughts because it was a question he actually wanted answered. *And I am a Queen dragon! They all say so.*

A Queen? What does that mean? You get to be in charge?

Inwardly he laughed at the thought of the little dragon fresh from her egg bossing around all of the larger dragons. They weren't much larger anymore, though.

Yes, she said and her voice turned solemn. *Is that okay with you? You will have to be in charge too someday. Not until you are much older, but someday.*

I don't have much choice, Jamie said dryly.

He thought of being in charge of the academy but the idea seemed preposterous. That was the council's job. Surely they wouldn't let some freshman push them out of power. And there had to be other Queen dragons, right? Others who were in charge? Maybe he and Marisol would eventually get on the council, but he doubted her status meant anything more than that.

He smiled as his dragon did a somersault midair in an attempt to cheer him up. It worked; worries about leadership vanished and he was caught up in admiring his beautiful girl. Scott had been taking good care of her, and perhaps he could even forgive Scott for not being at his side when he woke if he was taking care of Marisol. But where was Scott now?

CHAPTER SIXTEEN

The Silent Arrangement

Scott ran into trouble outside Jamie's door. For the first time, the door was shut and the windows drawn and two forbidding men stood guard in suits that looked more like club bouncers than medical personnel. Mike was being escorted from the room and the doors were closed firmly behind him. Scott rushed up and tried to open the doors, but the bouncers blocked him.

"Jamie's awake," Scott said. "I need to see him."

"Not without permission."

Mike took his arm. "Scott, I know who can get you permission but we should talk first."

Scott snatched him arm away. "I don't need permission. Jamie wants me. Let me in."

The bouncers just looked at him impassively. Scott wondered if they were even capable of thought, or if they could only follow orders. As strong as Scott was, there was no way he was getting past these two. He allowed Mike to drag him into the empty hospital room next to Jamie's. For a moment he thought there would be a secret door or entrance, but it was just an ordinary room. Mike pushed him on the bed and Scott immediately tensed, thinking for a moment that Mike was planning on seducing him, but Mike began pacing and seemed to have other matters on his mind.

"Scott, I don't know how to explain this so I'll just say it. You aren't going to be allowed in Marisol's mating flight and I think it would be in Jamie's best interests if he were taken by someone he knows, someone who cares about him."

Scott laughed. "I suppose you mean you. Well, no thanks. I'm going to be his partner in every mating flight he has, no matter who else is chasing."

"Sooner or later I'm going to be on the council and you would be wise to have an ally there."

"How do you know I won't get on the council first?"

Scott knew it was a ridiculous question but he was angry at Mike and his presumption. Just because Mike seemed to be on the fast track for being appointed to the council didn't give him the right to propose having sex with Jamie. What kind of man even brought up such a possibility, especially when Jamie was awake for the first time just next door?

"You won't. Besides, you know better than anyone how kind I'll be to him."

"What's that supposed to mean?"

"I didn't hurt you, did I?"

Scott's jaw dropped and his hands curled into fists. Mike dared to pretend that he hadn't hurt him? Sure, physically Mike had been gentle and there hadn't been any real pain, but emotionally he had been shattered. If he hadn't found Narné, he didn't think he would have lasted much longer. Narné had helped him piece together his life and his soul and even so, he had never allowed himself to be interested in anyone until Jamie. He would not allow Mike to inflict the same agony on Jamie, even if it meant alienating the council.

There wasn't much they could do, anyway. Once the mating flight began, any nearby dragons would follow, and the Queen would be caught by the one she decided was the most worthy. When the dragons' partners were in a relationship, the female dragon almost always chose the dragon of the partner's lover, so it was a safe assumption that Marisol would choose Narné. Perhaps a Queen's mating flight would be different – there hadn't been one in ages – but it couldn't be that much different than a normal mating flight.

"Look, Scott, if she weren't a Queen, no one would be interested," Mike said. "But the Queen has to mate with a council member in order for the balance of power in the academy to be maintained. Don't you see? I'm not on the council, but if you and Jamie request me, then I should be allowed to participate and at least you'll know he's safe."

"Safe?" a strange voice boomed from just outside the door. "Safe from what?"

A large, powerfully built man emerged into the room. He wore all black with a red dragon sigil on his breast marking him as a council member. He looked familiar. He had been in the room the other day and he was one of the men who had forced him to agree to sleep with other students in exchange for being assigned to Jamie. Scott instantly disliked him. The man strode into the room and placed his hand on Mike's shoulder as if in greeting, but the younger man shied away from the touch as if embarrassed or afraid.

Mike was pale and looked guilty, as though he'd done something wrong, and the man was smirking at him. For a moment, neither Scott nor Jamie existed and the man cupped Mike's face with his hand in a strangely sexual manner. Scott wondered if the two of them had been lovers – it would certainly explain why Mike seemed to be getting so many favors from the council. Scott wouldn't put it past Mike.

"Whatever do you think you're doing?" the man asked Mike softly.

Mike took a deep breath and seemed to compose himself, though he didn't pull away from the man's touch. In fact, he leaned into it as if he enjoyed it.

"Marisol is only allowing two dragons near her. One of them is mine. I thought perhaps Eraxes could participate in her mating flight, to ensure that she picks a dragon."

The man was still smirking, but he seemed pleased by Mike's actions, not angry.

"Oh, I know your reasoning, child. I've been listening outside the door to your attempts to persuade Scott."

Mike's cheeks flushed bright red against his still-pale face and he cast his eyes down at the ground. Scott slammed his fist into his palm. He was tired of being ignored, especially when it didn't matter. Nothing they said mattered. He just wanted this conversation to be over so he could be with Jamie.

"Narné is flying with Marisol," he said. "I don't see why you're even questioning it."

The man released Mike and turned to him.

"Do you know who I am?"

"No," Scott answered honestly. The man looked familiar, but Scott couldn't place his face.

The man's smirk faded and he became serious.

"I am Peter Ashton, head of the council. My word is law at this academy, and it is my decision – the council's decision – that you will not be allowed to fly with Marisol during her first mating flight."

Scott narrowed his eyes. "I don't see how you can stop me. When a dragon flies, everyone is free to give chase."

"Not for a Queen. Only approved council members will be allowed to participate, as Mike here has already told you. This decree will be enforced and your dragon will be the one to pay the price."

Scott stared at him. He couldn't be saying what Scott thought he was saying, but it sounded as though the council would harm Narné if they attempted to join the mating flight. That had to be impossible, though. The council's whole purpose was to protect all of the dragons. Scott didn't always like the ways they chose to do that, but he had never before questioned the fact that the dragons came first for everyone in the academy. That was the only reason Scott had any respect for the council in the first place: they protected the dragons. How could a group devoted to protecting dragons suddenly threaten his dragon if he disobeyed?

"Mike's offer is a generous one," the man said, turning back to Mike. "If you agree to let him be in the flight, then he will be allowed. He has already proven his loyalty to me. It will be interesting to see how he thinks he can outrace my Arion. Arion is from the same hatching ground as Narné, you know," he added to Scott. "Perhaps someday brother can race against brother for the privilege of the Queen, but not on her first mating flight. Have I made myself clear?"

"If that's true, then I'm not sleeping with anyone else," Scott said angrily, thinking of the promise he had made in exchange for the honor of being the person assigned to Jamie.

Mike winced and the man laughed. "You will. You already swore to it, Scott. The council can compel you to obey even if it is against your will. I think you'll find that promises made to the council are always kept. So why don't you give me your word right now that you and Narné will not participate in Marisol's first mating flight?"

Scot glared. "Even if your dragon is the one to catch Marisol, I'm not letting anyone touch Jamie."

"You won't have a choice," Mike said. "Scott, be reasonable. Let me be in the chase and I'll take care of Jamie."

"If you catch him and I don't," the other man said. Scott couldn't bring himself to think of the man as Peter Ashton, head of the council and most powerful man in his world. It was easier to think of him as just a man; it was easier to disobey him when he didn't have to worry that Ashton would order some attack against Narné.

Narné was oddly quiet, Scott realized with a start. What was he up to?

"Where's Narné?"

Mike paled yet again and looked at Ashton. The man was smirking and a chill ran down Scott's spine.

"Each of us here have special dragons with special gifts," he said, fixing his eyes on Scott. "Arion's gift is the ability to prevent a dragon from speaking with its partner. Normally it's temporary, but if you disobey and try to fly with Marisol, you will never hear Narné's voice again. Am I making myself clear now, boy?"

Scott shut his eyes. He didn't doubt that this man would harm Narné. He thought of Mike and Eraxes and the strange silence between them. He had always wondered why they didn't speak telepathically even though they could. Had Ashton done something to make it impossible for Eraxes and Mike to speak? He would not let that happen to Narné. It was too difficult a decision: protecting Jamie or protecting Narné, but he had to trust that Jamie had Marisol looking out for him now, while Narné had no one besides Scott. He had to err on the side of protecting Narné.

"I understand," Scott said. "But I don't want anyone besides me laying a finger on Jamie until then."

"You're just making it harder on him," Mike said. "Break up with him now and let someone else step in. It'll be better in the long run."

"No way," Scott nearly shouted. "You just want him to yourself because you're jealous. He is mine, and I won't let you or anyone else have him."

Ashton chuckled. "And what do you think he'll say when he finds out you were assigned to seduce him? You think he'll still be in love with you then?"

"You won't tell him," Scott said in a half-plea, half-command.

"He'll find out," the man said. "You can't hide the truth forever."

The three of them looked towards Jamie's room and Scott deeply regretted not being already in the room when Jamie woke up. If he had already been inside, no one could have dragged him out, even the two thugs now guarding the door. But Scott didn't like to see Jamie in the hospital, helpless and in pain, so Scott had been spending a lot of time with Marisol. He knew he shouldn't be leaving Jamie's side but Marisol needed a lot of attention and caring for her was like caring for Jamie. Plus, Jamie had no idea what was going on. His coma had been supposed to last until tomorrow, when the doctors planned to wake him up.

Scott hadn't realized, however, just how many visitors Jamie was receiving and how potentially dangerous they were. He had known that Mike spent most of the day with Jamie when Scott was elsewhere, but what was Mike doing? Was he whispering secrets to Jamie, or seducing him while the boy was helpless?

And how often did Ashton visit? The man looked comfortable enough at the hospital. It was said that the better two humans knew each other, the more likely their dragons were to mate together, so was Ashton trying to increase his odds?

Scott shuddered at the thought of the older man raping Jamie while Marisol was attacked by the much larger dragon. It was a good thing her first mating flight was still weeks off. Or at least he thought it would be. She was growing so much faster than he expected that it was hard to predict. Already she was the size of a sedan and she ate a whole calf every day. She would eat less once her size stabilized and her body switched to maintenance rather than growth, but she was still eating far more of the academy's supplies than they had anticipated and the farm workers were starting to complain every time she showed up.

It didn't help that she was so aggressive, even if it made sense. She was in a strange place with strange customs, surrounded by other living creatures instead of her shell, and her partner wasn't awake to help her navigate. Any dragon would be confused.

Scott searched for Narné again in his mind, wondering if he was with Marisol somewhere, but again the dragon was silent. Did Arion have to be close to Narné to prevent them from speaking? Was Arion attacking Narné right now, giving him the dragon's version of a stern lecture with tooth and claw?

Scott tapped his fingers nervously. He needed to find Narné but he couldn't leave Jamie like this. He knew it was exactly what Ashton wanted, and probably the reason Arion was interfering in the first place. For whatever reason, Ashton wanted him out of the hospital and no matter how much Scott wanted to be with Jamie, he was compelled to make sure Narné was all right first.

"I'm going to find Narné," Scott said reluctantly. "And when I return I'm going to see Jamie no matter how many guards you have."

The man, Ashton, smiled. "You have my permission to see the boy anytime until his mating flight. You might want to warn him about what will happen during his flight, just so he doesn't panic. We all want the flight to go without a hitch."

Scott's brow lowered. If Jamie knew that Scott had agreed to let another man sleep with him, would Jamie still love him? He shook his head sharply in an attempt to rid himself of his doubts. The dilemma with Jamie might be weeks away, and he had a far more pressing matter at hand – his still silent dragon.

CHAPTER SEVENTEEN

Separation

Only an hour after waking up, Jamie was outside with Marisol at his side. It was all thanks to the man sitting with them, the head of the council and President of the Academy. Jamie remembered him from his interview to get into the school. Mr. Ashton – or just Ashton, as he had asked to be called – had asked a lot of questions about Jamie's father that had seemed irrelevant at the time, but now Jamie could see how they fit into Tarragon Academy. If Jamie were still in mourning for his father, then perhaps he wouldn't have been able to form such a close attachment to Marisol. There had to be more to it than that, but at least Ashton's questions made sense now.

Marisol butted his cheek playfully with a snout as large as Jamie's entire torso. She was gentle, however, because Ashton had warned her how delicate Jamie was. Jamie knew she also smelled the fresh blood on him from his injuries and he knew she would have been gentle even if Ashton hadn't warned her. Still, he appreciated Ashton's concern. Ashton was sitting outside with him, to keep an eye on him and to teach him the first, most important lesson of having a dragon: separating his mind from Marisol's. Jamie was eager to learn, as he had already experienced problems with her slipping into his mind and vice versa.

"Marisol," Ashton said. "Why don't you fly around?"

She perked her head up in astonishment. Jamie knew that she hadn't been allowed to fly yet. She had only been able to fly outside his window earlier because no other dragons were around to stop her; Narné, Scott's dragon, had vanished somewhere and couldn't guard her as usual. He could feel her excitement coursing through his veins and he jumped to his feet, eager to fly. She stretched her wings and he held his breath, remembering when she was just a hatchling and she had tried flying with no luck. This time, however, her wings were properly proportioned and she took off with no problem.

Jamie saw through her eyes as the ground dwindled below her and he saw himself and Ashton standing under the tree watching her. He was fully in her mind, completely unaware of his body as Marisol soared through the sky. She flew circles until Jamie grew dizzy and asked her to stop, and he vaguely became aware of his own body collapsing into Ashton's arms. Ashton was whispering something but he didn't want to hear it: he was flying!

Another loop and he grew dizzy again. Perhaps he should listen to Ashton. Marisol delighted in circles and didn't want to stop, but he couldn't handle much more. The strange feeling of twirling in the sky while not moving would make him throw up if he didn't stop soon. He tried to focus on his human body instead of letting his mind soar with Marisol. Instantly, Ashton's words made sense and he felt both his body and Marisol's body clearly in his mind. Marisol shrieked as he doubled over in confusion. She didn't want to hurt him, she told him, but the feeling of two bodies was too foreign and he crouched in fear.

"Focus on yourself, your body," Ashton was saying. "Let Marisol be Marisol. You are here. You are in my arms. You are safe. Just focus on yourself and let Marisol slip away. She will always be there, but you have to let her go now."

Jamie tried. He focused on his body, but he couldn't let go of Marisol. She was too real, too loud; the sensations of flying were too strong to fight. She turned another loop in the sky and before his stomach started churning Jamie forcefully shut her out of his mind as he had once before. To his astonishment, it worked. He was alone in his body, but he could still feel her presence. He had returned to himself without cutting her off.

The process was unusually exhausting and Jamie collapsed to the ground with Ashton still holding him. Jamie leaned against a nearby tree and studied Ashton. He asked Marisol what she thought about Ashton. Images of a large blue dragon filled his mind along with a name, Arion. Ashton's dragon. She didn't trust Arion and when he asked her why, she turned a slow loop in the sky and let out a puff of air.

He does not respect me, she finally said.

You're a kid, Jamie said in amusement. *Do any of the dragons respect you?*

I am a Queen, she said haughtily. *Narné and Eraxes respect me. That is why I do not allow anyone else near.*

Jamie laughed, then realized how odd he must look to Ashton. He apologized, but Ashton just smiled and shook his head. Jamie related the conversation to Ashton, who laughed as well.

"I will try to convince Arion to be more respectful of the little Queen," Ashton said. His eyes glinted strangely. "Does she require anything else?"

"Oh, no," Jamie said. "She's just being fussy. You've been so kind to her, and to me. I don't know how to repay you."

"You're one of us now, Jamie," Ashton said. "There is no repayment."

Jamie flushed and ducked his head. All his life he had needed to watch his spending, most often using his meager earnings from his part time work on food because his worthless aunt refused to take care of another mouth, especially a hungry teenage boy's mouth like his. He had taken care of himself ever since his father died, working various jobs when he could, but never able to hold anything for long because his aunt also expected him to be a babysitter whenever she needed it, and if he didn't do what she wanted, he would get tossed to the curb without a roof over his head.

Tarragon Academy was the first place since his father died where he didn't worry about money, or work. The council, and

Ashton, had made it very clear when he enrolled that he was to focus on schoolwork and let them take care of all the finances. It was more than a full ride; it was peace of mind for the first time ever.

Jamie couldn't even imagine how much the hospital bills were, especially since they hadn't really told him what all had been done to fix him. But it was probably more money than his aunt made in a year, if he knew anything about how hospitals worked. And Ashton just brushed it aside like it was nothing, like it was part of the package. The last time he felt so secure and taken care of was when both his mother and father were still alive, before he had to learn to fend for himself.

Ashton reminded Jamie of his father a lot. They would be about the same age, he thought, although Jamie's father had died when he was much younger. But if Jamie had to imagine an older version of his father, it would look a lot like Ashton, only with copper hair like Jamie's instead of black. The only time Jamie hadn't felt safe with his father was when he came out. He honestly hadn't known how his father would react to hearing that his son liked other guys.

His father had been surprised, and possibly a little hurt, but he said the hurt was only because Jamie had waited so long to tell him. He loved Jamie for who he was. His father didn't have much time to accept the news, however. He had died only a week later in a fire that was eerily similar to how Jamie's mother had died, except that his father had died instantly and his mother had survived the initial fire. Jamie tried not to think about the coincidence; the circumstances were entirely different.

Jamie's mother had been spending the night at a friend's when a still-lit cigarette butt engulfed the house in flames. She had been drinking, Jamie knew from reading the reports when he was much older, and didn't act fast enough to escape without fatal burns. Jamie's father died under more mysterious circumstances. His car had crashed and caught fire, killing him almost instantly. But no one could find the cause of the crash or the fire.

For a long time it was classified as a homicide, but after a year had passed with no leads or possible motives, the police had come to talk to Jamie and explain that it was probably just a freak accident and they would never know the truth. It became a cold case, although there was nothing cold about Jamie's grief. Jamie tried not to be afraid of fire, but he avoided bonfires and passionately hated people who smoked. Luckily, Tarragon Academy was a smoke-free campus and he had never seen anyone violating the rules.

Deep in his mind he worried that dragons meant fire, but since Marisol had shown no signs of spouting flames, he pushed that concern aside for now. Instead, he focused on the present, and in the present he wondered what Ashton thought about Jamie being out of the closet. He had been out for such a short period of time, but by now everyone must know that he was dating Scott and he was terrified that people would hate him or even want to hurt him because of his orientation.

He also wondered about the way Ashton and Mr. Ferrin – Mike, he reminded himself – had touched each other when leaving the room. Jamie had almost missed it. Ashton had grabbed Mike's hand just before the other man left the room and squeezed it. Mike seemed surprised, but he had looked at Ashton with a small smile on his face. It was almost like they were planning some clandestine meeting and the handshake was a signal. He already suspected that Mike was gay, given the way he had acted earlier in the semester, but Ashton was a powerful man with a lot of influence. Surely he wouldn't be gay.

Jamie didn't have any gay role models and if Ashton was gay, perhaps Jamie would feel a little more comfortable being openly out the way that he was now. He wanted to know, but didn't really know how to ask. He had never associated with gay people before out of fear that he would be labeled one, and now he felt awkward and trapped by his inexperience.

He asked Marisol what she thought and she replied that all humans seemed alike to her, but she sensed attraction between Mike and Ashton. She could only tell gender in dragons, she said solemnly. Jamie shook his head. He hadn't seen many dragons but he read books, and he had never heard of a way to tell a dragon's gender and there was nothing in Marisol's body that indicated that she was female. Marisol must have picked up on his thoughts because she grew indignant and flew further away from him, purposefully spinning in a way that made him sick. This time, though, he was prepared and knew how to pull himself away from her mind.

Jamie took a deep breath and decided to dive right into the gay conversation.

"Are you and Mike… together?"

"We have been, and will be again," Ashton said with a smile that was half-smirk and half-sincere. "Why do you ask?"

"Just something I noticed. I was surprised. I didn't know he had a boyfriend."

"He doesn't. People with dragons are a little more flexible with relationships than people without."

"Not me," Jamie said, thinking of Scott. "There will only be one person for me."

Ashton shrugged. "You say that now, as do many. But once you realize the reality of your situation, you may change your mind."

"What reality?"

"Well," Ashton said slowly, as if choosing his words carefully. "Did you ever wonder why Scott was hanging around your classroom the first time you met him? Or why he chose you to talk to instead of any of the other students?"

"He said he'd been crushing on me the whole semester and finally got up the nerve to talk to me."

"Did you ever wonder why he pressured you to have sex?"

Jamie grew hot and knew he was beet-red. It was true that Scott had pushed the relationship a little, but Jamie had pushed it more. And they hadn't actually had sex, not real sex at least. And no matter what, it certainly wasn't Ashton's concern!

"That's none of your damn business," Jamie said, peppering in one of his few swear words in an attempt to indicate how serious he was. He reached to Marisol for comfort but she was busy enjoying her flight. She was also a little angry that he didn't recognize her feminine charm. He posed a stronger question to Marisol, purposefully breaking through her enjoyment because he needed reassurance.

What do you think of Scott?

She was annoyed, but she settled down on a branch nearby while she formulated an answer. He could feel all sorts of emotions swarming through her mind at the name Scott, mostly positive but some negative as well. Finally, he felt her snort and toss her head.

He took very good care of me. But maybe he should have been taking good care of you instead.

She flew off and he felt her erect a barrier, almost a Do Not Disturb sign in her mind. She wanted to enjoy flying and didn't want to be interrupted by his human doubts.

Ashton placed a hand on his back and Jamie jolted back to reality. He must have been sitting in complete silence for several minutes. No wonder the man was concerned. But he seemed to understand, because instead of asking if Jamie was okay, he asked what Marisol said. When Jamie told him Marisol's response, Ashton nodded.

"Scott was a godsend for us because Marisol would only allow Scott and Mike near her, and she needed constant care. But of the two of them, Mike was the one at your bedside. Scott visited, but didn't stay long."

Jamie flushed again. Mike had been at Jamie's side, not Scott. But Scott had brought him flowers every day, Jamie remembered. That meant Scott visited. However, Scott hadn't visited since Jamie had woken up several hours ago. Was Scott abandoning him? Or was Scott only interested in the dragon, and his interest in Jamie had been faked in order to get close to Marisol?

No, Jamie told himself firmly. The feelings between him and Scott must be real. Scott had been so kind and respectful, even when Jamie rejected him. Scott would never have ulterior motives; it just wasn't in his nature. And he would have a good explanation for his absence. Once he showed up.

CHAPTER EIGHTEEN

Reunited

Narné was not in Scott's apartment, or in the forest, or in any of the usual places Scott expected to find him. Normally it was easy to find the dragon: he simply listened for the dragon's thoughts and knew exactly where the great beast was and what he was doing. This time, however, there was only that chilling silence. He could feel a faint vibration and knew that Narné was alive, but the connection wasn't strong enough for him to tell anything else.

In his mind he heard his parents laughing at him for losing his dragon over such a small thing as a crush. They were both graduates of Tarragon Academy and looking back, he realized that they had done everything in their power to make him an ideal candidate for the school, teaching him how to fight from a young age and encouraging him to have various and multiple partners when he started dating.

He had even been a minor celebrity when he was a child, appearing in dozens of commercials and even starring in a television series before the age of five. At five, he finally figured out that the men with the cameras weren't his friends even though they gave him cookies and candy, and he stopped being obedient. While the show had been cancelled, his commercials lived on and some were still played today, much to Scott's chagrin. He had grown up and no one ever recognized him from those early ads for pillows where he danced around and fought the Nightmare King, but it was still humiliating every time one came on.

He prayed to god that Jamie didn't see one and recognize who the little child star really was. Jamie might have fears about his body, but Scott had fears about his past. The past would inevitably come out, just as Jamie would inevitably have to accept his body, but maybe it would wait a while.

Scott also didn't want Jamie to know he was an actor because he didn't want Jamie to think his actions and emotions were fake or forced. Jamie would already have questions about why he wasn't there when Jamie woke up, and if Ashton was right and Jamie started thinking about how they met and figured out that Scott had been assigned to him, Jamie would be alienated completely and their relationship would likely be over. There had to be some way to explain to Jamie that yes, Scott was assigned to seduce him but the reason he was assigned was because he cared for Jamie so much. Narné would know how to explain it; perhaps Narné could even explain it to Marisol and Marisol could relay the information the Jamie. But Narné's voice was still quiet.

Scott took a deep breath and shut his eyes. He was about a block from his apartment complex. He let his mind go blank and focused on the hum from Narné. Narné was alive, he could sense it, but when he tried to do anything more, like locate him or talk to him, the fuzzy hum scattered in his mind and he had to start over. There had to be an easier way to find the dragon.

"Scott? Is that you?"

Scott opened his eyes to see Amar with a small blue dragon beside him. Well, small compared to Marisol and the adults. The dragon's back was as high as Amar's shoulders and was undoubtedly several times bigger than on hatching night. Scott hadn't even paid attention to the survivors on hatching night; all of his attention was on Jamie. Now he held out his hand to the dragon cautiously, aware that some dragons took more than a week to learn manners around people.

The dragon didn't bite him, though; he just sniffed Scott's proffered hand and sneezed. Amar and Scott laughed. Babies had delicate senses and new experiences tended to send them into sneezing fits. Marisol had never sneezed, but when Narné was a baby he had sneezed at nearly everything.

"What a beautiful creature," Scott said appreciatively. Even Narné had commented on the beauty of Amar's dragon, he remembered. "What's his name?"

Amar beamed. "Tephis."

Scott could just make out a scar running from Amar's ear to his cheek. He started to ask Narné whether Amar had been at an older hatching site, but there was silence and it struck like a fist to the gut. He had never been unable to communicate before.

"What's wrong? Are you sick? Is it Jamie?"

Scott took a deep breath and tried to compose himself before the young student. "No, it's not Jamie. He's doing fine. He just woke up and should join the rest of the students once he's healed a little more."

"Good," Amar said, and Scott was surprised to notice that the other man was on the brink of tears. "I've been so worried. I heard he was almost killed and no one has heard anything from him since we got back. Tephis keeps telling me that Marisol thinks he's getting better, but not even Marisol knows anything because she's stuck outside."

"He just woke up," Scott said. "Just a few minutes ago."

"Shouldn't you be there?"

Amar's body language shifted dramatically from one of sorrow and confusion to one of scolding disapproval. Scott approved of his disapproval, but there was nothing Scott could do. Nothing bad would happen to Jamie as long as he had Marisol protecting him, but Narné had already been threatened twice. His priorities were clear and unfortunately, as much as his heart ached to be with Jamie, he had to find his dragon first.

"I'm looking for Narné. You haven't seen him, have you?"

"No, but maybe Tephis has."

Amar stared at his dragon in silence and swayed slightly. Scott knew he was communicating with the tiny creature. Scott wanted to hit himself in the head for not thinking of asking a dragon first. Of course the dragons would know where Narné was. They all kept tabs on each other and there were no secrets between dragons. All he needed was one dragon to talk to – or rather a dragon's partner – and he could gain access to all of the dragons' group knowledge and find Narné in no time.

After nearly a minute watching Amar stare blankly at his dragon, the boy shook himself and seemed to come back to reality with a small frown on his face.

"He's near the hot springs with Heron. She was in heat. What does that mean? Is Tephis going to go into heat?"

"No, males don't go into heat," Scott said, but his mind was racing. Narné had left to chase a female? That didn't sound like Narné at all, but Amar had no reason to lie and neither did the dragons he was getting his information from. Scott started heading towards the hot springs. He hadn't looked there because it was a site notorious for dragon couplings and not much else, and he hadn't expected Narné to be having sex at a time like this.

"Wait!" Amar cried. "Aren't you going to explain what's going on?"

"Ask your teacher," Scott said, glad once again that he wasn't a teacher at Tarragon Academy. He had never appreciated how difficult Mike's job was before – dealing with the bodies of the students who didn't survive the first year exam, and then dealing with the students who did survive. No wonder Mike was keeping himself sequestered in the hospital and letting the other teachers take over.

Scott jogged to the hot springs and only had to perform a cursory search to find the two. They weren't bothering with camouflage and were lying on top of each other, exhausted, in one of the hottest springs. Briefly Scott imagined Marisol lying underneath Narné like that, while Scott and Jamie panted for breath in the comfort of their bedroom. Sweat would slick off of all four of them, the two dragons entwined in some of the hottest waters on earth and the two humans joined together in the fieriest passion ever seen. Scott knew that once Marisol became involved, Jamie would be forced to drop his protective shield and his entire sensual nature would be on display.

For Jamie was a sensual creature, Scott knew. The way he caved so quickly as soon as he felt safe, the way his hands fisted in Scott's hair while Scott pleasured him, the moans that he didn't even try to stifle, all told of a passion burning deep within Jamie just waiting to burst forth. The thought of another man seeing that passion cut into Scott like a dagger to his heart and he ached, but the thought of losing Narné hurt worse.

Not that the ungrateful creature seemed to care. Here Scott had abandoned Jamie to find Narné, and the beast just rolled his head to stare at Scott with swirling, satiated eyes.

"Narné," Scott said, frustrated that he had to speak aloud and worried that he still couldn't feel his dragon in his mind, "We need to talk."

Narné shook his great head like a dog shaking off water and the female growled low in her throat. Narné nipped her lightly and she tossed her head and slithered out from underneath him, scattering scalding hot water as she went. She took off and soared back in the direction of the dragon canyon. That meant her partner was a more traditional woman, as opposed to Scott and the younger crowd who lived in the apartments. He wondered who she was and if she minded having the dragon but not the partner – some women preferred it, but some women refused to take a dragon unless the partner was a willing participant. He hoped she was one of the former but couldn't ask Narné.

Narné slithered out of the hot spring as well and must have sensed Scott's anger because he kept his head down. But once he was out, his head reared back and there was stifled rage in his eyes. Scott took a step back. The last time Narné had looked like that had been the hatching and Scott had been severely injured. Now that Narné was full grown, there was no way Scott would escape with his life. But why would his dragon turn against him?

Scott took a breath and tried to recapture his anger. Narné was keeping him from Jamie. Narné had abandoned his duty protecting Marisol to go chase some random female and he didn't appear to show any feelings of remorse. Scott had every right to be angry. But he wasn't angry. He was just terrified because he still couldn't sense anything from Narné, even though the creature was standing just a few feet away and they were practically touching. Scott had never felt so alone than he did at that moment and he just wanted to rush into Narné's warmth and hear the creature's comforting voice inside his head.

"Why can't I hear you?" Scott said, setting aside everything except the pain of their separation. There would be a time for anger, but it wasn't now.

Narné looked truly confused. He was silent for a moment, then he reluctantly spoke. "You cannot hear me still? Arion said you would be able to hear me after the mating."

"Arion?" A shot of fear ran through him. "Why were you talking to Arion?"

"A female was mating," Narné said. "I wanted to join, but I knew you were busy. Arion appeared and offered to dull our connection for a while. I accepted. I did not want my mating to interrupt your talk or your time with Jamie. Why aren't you with Jamie?"

Scott glared. "Because I thought you were hurt! Ashton said I'd never hear you again if I disobeyed him! I thought I'd lost you! How could I stay with Jamie when I thought something happened to you?"

Narné lowered his head. "No, it was my choice. I have used Arion before. Most dragons do. There are many times when we want to be silent to our partners. I am very sorry that it came at a bad time but I wanted to be in the chase."

"It wasn't a bad time, it was Ashton's plan! Arion is his dragon, doing what he wanted to make me think you were hurt. And since when do you abandon Marisol to go chase some female?"

Narné snarled at him, the rage back in those giant eyes. "You do not have a right to judge me. You have been blind to me for days; Arion barely had to do anything."

"How have I been blind? We've spent almost every minute together!"

"No," Narné said and he reared up on his hind legs. "You have spent every minute with Marisol, and you expect me to be there to babysit. You did not ask if I wanted to be there. I did not object, because I hope to mate with her someday and I want to please you, but I have my own needs. It never occurred to you that spending so much time around a female would make me ache for a chase, and Marisol is too young and even when she grows older, she is a Queen and we are not ranking dragons. I needed release and you were not giving it to me, so when you left and Arion showed up, I asked him to help me and he obliged."

Scott stood in stunned amazement. It was true: it had never occurred to him that being around Marisol would trigger lust in the much older dragon. Scott's own reaction to Marisol had probably made things worse, too, because when Scott was around Marisol he thought of Jamie, and his thoughts were rarely chaste. Male dragons didn't go into heat, but they preferred to join mating flights every two or three months.

The last few weeks must have been especially hard on Narné, with Scott busy seducing Jamie. He remembered how Narné had shown up in the forest and in the shower to watch Jamie. That was the closest Narné had gotten to sex for months, and then Narné was expected to babysit the creature who would someday be his mate? No wonder Narné had left for a mating flight. And no wonder he had succeeded – all of that suppressed rage had probably frightened off any other contenders in the flight. Scott just hoped the woman didn't mind having an angry dragon as a mate.

But none of it explained why he still couldn't hear Narné. He wondered if the problem lay in himself. He had been ignoring Narné lately, but it was because his priority had been Marisol and Jamie. Today, by going after Narné, he was clearly placing Narné back as his number one priority, where Narné would remain. He would have to be much more vigilant about his dragon's feelings. It was easy to forget that the dragon was a separate person with thoughts and feelings of his own, and not just a reflection of Scott.

Scott approached Narné, who settled back down on all fours and accepted Scott's hug by curling his head around him. Scott was entirely surrounded by green scales and he inhaled deeply, ignoring the spicy scent of dragon sex and instead focusing on the leathery smell from the scales. He loved Narné with all of his heart, more than he loved Jamie, even. He and Narné were halves to a whole and nothing would ever separate them.

I know, Narné said in his mind.

Scott didn't move but a smile broke across his face. Narné was back in his mind and for the first time in weeks, Scott actually examined his dragon. Narné was worn out, tired, and emotionally drained. Just like his owner, but for different reasons.

I'll never take you for granted again, Scott said.

Yes, you will, Narné said in an amused tone. *But I will forgive you. Now you must return to Jamie, and I am ready to return to Marisol.*

Scott nodded and released his beloved dragon. Then his brow creased.

"Narné," he said aloud. "You mentioned that we wouldn't be allowed to mate with Marisol. How did you know that?"

I am not a ranking dragon. I have known that we could not be together since she hatched, but you have ignored that knowledge.

"What is a ranking dragon? I thought all dragons were equal."

Narné sniffed and tilted his head to one side. *Our society is complicated. We do not explain it to humans. I should not have spoken of it to you.*

"The council members all have ranking dragons, don't they?"

No, Narné said to Scott's surprise.

"What about Mike? Is Eraxes a ranking dragon?"

Narné nodded his head.

"How do you become a ranking dragon?"

Narné rubbed his snout against the ground. *I should not be telling you, but it is determined by age and power. I will be a ranking dragon when I am fully mature – many months more. Not in time for Marisol's first flight.*

"But then you'll be able to mate with Marisol."

Narné's eyes gleamed. *Yes.*

Scott thought for a minute. "Does Ashton know all of this? I mean, about ranking dragons and all that?"

Arion may have told him, just as I am telling you. You must not share your knowledge, though, even with Ashton. The other dragons would not be pleased with me. I might be banned from mating flights.

Scott's eyes widened. That was a significant punishment. Still, he wondered how secret the knowledge really was. Narné hadn't been too discrete with his information, and Ashton had to know something because he was willing to let Mike join Marisol's mating flight but he had also said that only select council members would be participating. Perhaps knowledge of dragon society was something that all partners knew, but none ever talked about for fear of harming their dragons. Well, Scott had already proved that he would do anything to prevent Narné from harm, so he could easily keep this secret.

Together, Scott and Narné began heading back to campus, Narné in the sky and Scott on foot but their minds connected. Now that he had Narné back, his only task was finding Jamie and making sure that the boy was still safe.

CHAPTER NINETEEN

Childhood Scars

Marisol's thoughts grew stronger in Jamie's mind and for a moment, he was flying with her again only now there was another dragon in the sky, a friendly green dragon that Jamie recognized from the forest and the shower.

Narné, Marisol told him. *Scott's dragon.*

Marisol twirled in a loop to show off her flying abilities to the green dragon and Jamie clutched wildly for something to hold onto as his sense of direction vanished and it felt as though he too went in a slow, lazy loop in the sky. Marisol had no problems with gravity but Jamie did.

When Marisol righted herself, Jamie realized he was clutching Ashton and Ashton was repeating the instructions to distance his mind from the dragon's mind. It was the third time in the hour they had been talking that he had needed those instructions due to Marisol's antics. He gratefully listened and soon he was back in his own body and mind, away from the frolicking dragon. Ashton was embracing him in a protective, paternal way and for a moment Jamie was reminded of his father holding him after a terrible nightmare. Even their scent was similar, although Jamie hadn't possessed superior scent when his father was alive. But they wore the same cologne and Jamie imagined his father would smell of the same oaky musk underneath.

When Jamie was a child he had been haunted by nightmares on a regular basis. Turning the lights on didn't help – Jamie was more terrified of seeing the monsters that lurked at night than he was of the monsters themselves, so he preferred the dark when he wouldn't see their slobbering, distorted faces. He had seen a monster once, a twisted thing that scrabbled into his room on four stick-thin legs and came just to the height of his bed, like a large dog only this dog was covered in broken scales and horns and had a face that seemed sideways, with the jaw offset so that its pointed teeth overhung each other in a threatening way.

Jamie had never been able to shake the image of that creature and how easily it had gotten into his room. Thinking back, he now realized that it might have been a dragon, although it was nothing like the sleek, handsome dragons he had seen so far and it didn't have wings. If it was a dragon, it was a mutant and it acted like one, too. The monster had opened its mouth and a bit of flame had appeared by its crooked mouth, but Jamie had screamed and the scream seemed to startle the monster. It leapt up on its straw legs and scuttled back out of the room like a cockroach.

His father had rushed into the room and listened to Jamie's sobbed story with great understanding. He had checked under the bed, in the closets, out in the hall, and assured Jamie that the monster wouldn't be coming back. He had even pulled out the sleeping bag and slept in Jamie's room that night when Jamie couldn't be consoled. With his father sleeping across the threshold of his room, Jamie had been able to fall asleep. His father had needed to sleep in his room an entire week before the fear subsided and turned into nightmares instead. Even when Jamie was older, he would sometimes pretend to see the monster just so that his father would come in and hold his hand until he fell asleep.

He embraced Ashton longer than he needed to and the man let him, stroking his back and reassuring him that in time he would gain control and not lose himself in Marisol's mind as readily. In truth Jamie didn't care; he just wanted to hold this man who reminded him so strongly of his father. Even though they were close, he was always "father" to Jamie and never "dad". Jamie had stopped calling him "dad" when his mother died.

Then another scent entered his awareness, another familiar smell but this was one that stirred his loins and not his memory. Scott.

Jamie leapt up and searched for his boyfriend, who was still out of sight. Ashton chuckled.

"I imagine Scott is nearby? I'll leave you two in peace, then."

He stood up and cupped Jamie's face in his hand. "If you need any help with Marisol, please come to me."

Jamie leaned into the touch, so similar to his father's. "I will, Mr. Ashton."

Scott appeared at that moment and froze, as if he were shocked to see the two of them together. He approached slowly as Ashton lowered his hand from Jamie's face and they held hands. Jamie remembered Ashton's questions about Scott and wondered if there was anything to them. He squeezed Ashton's hand in thanks and then stepped forward to embrace Scott.

Scott held him gingerly, as if afraid he would break, and for the first time Jamie remembered his injuries. They had completely slipped his mind with Ashton. Irrational anger filled Jamie: why had Scott reminded him of something he wanted to forget? And if Scott was so concerned with his injuries, why hadn't he been at Jamie's side the way Mr. Ferrin was?

Scott must have sensed his anger because he released Jamie abruptly and awkwardly. Jamie returned to Ashton's side. The man had a strange smile on his face, as if he had won some sort of victory. As comforting as his presence was, though, Jamie knew he and Scott needed to talk in private. Ashton nodded at the two of them and turned as if he could sense that his presence was no longer necessary. Jamie would be sad to see him go, but there were things he and Scott needed to deal with by themselves.

"If you'll excuse me," Ashton said. "I have other matters to attend to and I'm sure Jamie is in good hands."

"He is," Scott said, moving up and wrapping an arm around

Jamie.

Jamie gave a start at the anger in Scott's voice and wondered why Scott would be so mad at Ashton. A little voice in his head wondered if it were perhaps because Scott suspected that Ashton had told him something, whatever the thing was that Ashton had hinted at earlier. If Scott were hiding a secret and Ashton knew, then that would be reason for Scott to be acting so strangely. Jamie's heart sank a little at the thought that Scott might have been lying to him, but there was no other reason for the anger, was there? He tried to take comfort in the arm around his shoulders but it was hard when Scott was so upset and Jamie didn't know why.

Jamie said goodbye to Ashton and turned to face his boy-friend. Scott's dark complexion was flushed red and he looked truly upset, but as soon as his eyes returned to Jamie, the anger vanished and sheer happiness raced across his face. The change was startling and Jamie's heart skipped a beat. Maybe Scott had been upset about something else. Because Scott wasn't faking the relief and love that Jamie saw now, and it warmed Jamie from his easily blushing cheeks to the tips of his toes as Scott's embrace became gentler and pulled him in closer.

"You're awake," he said. "And you're safe. I was so worried, Jamie. I know I should have been with you when you woke up and I'm sorry. There were guards outside your door and I couldn't get in, and then Narné..."

Jamie stopped him. "It doesn't matter," he said. "You're here now."

Looking at Scott, he realized that Ashton had no idea what he was talking about when it came to Scott's feelings. Scott's relief, his concern, his grief, were all too real to be faked. Scott would never keep a secret from him. Whatever had been the cause of his anger, it wasn't related to Jamie. There was nothing but love in those eyes.

"There are things I have to explain," Scott said. "Things about your future. You won't like them."

"Let the future be the future," Jamie said, stepping further

133

into Scott's arms and luxuriating in his embrace. His scent was sweeter than honey and as fresh as a dandelion, and it was intoxicating. Jamie barely even heard what he was saying and he refused to worry about the future yet. For this moment, he was with Scott and everything was right.

Scott sighed and stroked Jamie's hair.

"I don't want you to hear it from anyone else, sweetheart."

Jamie mumbled something against Scott's chest, some sort of soothing reply that didn't quite make sense. He could feel Marisol at peace beside Narné and her relaxation was seeping into him and taking away his words. It was a pleasant feeling, unlike his previous times linking to her mind. He didn't mind feeling her relaxed and asleep. Scott's arms held him tightly and he imagined how wonderful it would be to let himself fall into a deep sleep right here and now, with Scott holding him and keeping him safe just as Narné was doing for his dragon. He heard amused laughter from Narné and the green dragon prodded his mind away from Marisol.

Speak with Scott, Narné said. Then his voice was silent again and he was only a warm presence in Jamie's mind.

"Narné wants me to talk to you," Jamie murmured.

"Is that what Marisol says?"

"No, Narné said it."

Scott went still around him and the hand that had been gently stroking his back stopped. "You can hear Narné?"

"Only when he wants me to. It isn't like with Marisol. I hear her all the time. Does she talk to you?"

"No."

Jamie leaned back to look at Scott. Something in his tone was strange, as if he were in shock or deeply surprised and disturbed.

"What's wrong?"

"It's just, well," Scott began, then he pulled Jamie close again. "Maybe it's because you're partnered to a Queen. I knew you would be different but I didn't expect this. Most dragons have to communicate verbally, through human speech. Only special dragons can communicate through telepathy, and only with their partners. I've never heard of a human who can hear more than one dragon."

He paused and Jamie saw a smile brighten his face. "Is it just Narné? Perhaps we have a special bond between us."

Jamie hated having to wipe that smile away, but he didn't want to lie. "No," he said. "I heard Eraxes as well, and a couple other dragons said hello to me when I first came outside. They seemed surprised that I could hear them but I didn't know why at the time."

As Jamie had worried, the smile vanished from Scott's handsome face and the man shook his head. "I guess that was too much to hope for. Jamie, we have to talk about Marisol and what happens when she gets older."

"Ashton was telling me some of my duties, the things you've been doing for her. Thank you," he added shyly. "I hear she's been growing a lot and that means she's happy and well taken care of."

"I'll still help you take care of her," Scott said. "But I meant after she's an adult. Jamie, we have to talk about her first mating flight."

A rock sank into Jamie's belly. Ashton had mentioned something about this but Jamie had been too nervous so he changed the subject. A mating flight, where a bunch of strangers tried to get into bed with him. It sounded like a nightmare, worse than the nightmares he had as a child. But Scott would be there; Scott would always be there. Scott would fight off the other men and protect Jamie, because that's what boyfriends did. Jamie held Scott closer and longed to devour his clean, fresh scent and make it a part of him, to gain protection from him even when Scott wasn't there.

Scott tipped Jamie's head until they were centimeters apart and looked like he was about to say something, but Jamie pushed forward and kissed him. Lightning sparked from where their lips touched and he could feel Marisol's interest peak in the back of his mind. Scott tried to pull away but Jamie was determined never to let Scott leave his side again, so he wrapped his arms around the man and opened his mouth, tracing the outlines of Scott's lips with his tongue. Scott moaned and allowed Jamie access, then took over and invaded Jamie's mouth. One of his hands ran through Jamie's hair while the other hand cupped his ass and Jamie gasped in surprise.

It felt incredibly good to have Scott feeling him up, massaging his cheeks while his mouth was being plundered. He felt helpless in a perfectly pleasant way and his knees began to quiver with the effort of standing up. Scott must have felt it, because he wrapped Jamie in his strong arms and lowered them both to the ground. Jamie gasped for breath in the momentary pause in the action, and he nuzzled Scott's neck before taking the daring move of stroking his back. He longed to feel those powerful muscles under his hands but he hadn't ever been bold enough before.

He knew they were exposed here in the woods just outside the hospital – hell, the nurses could come for him at any moment! – but he didn't care. He just knew that he wanted Scott, and they were finally together. It felt like a lifetime had passed since the last time they were together, not just a week.

But Scott didn't resume the kissing, although he didn't stop Jamie from touching him and he kept running his hands along Jamie's body. Only on one side of his body, though. Jamie looked down to see why and the bandages stood out like a white sail against his scant hospital clothing. In the heat of the moment, he had completely forgotten. He was dressed in sweat pants, not a gown, but his top was mostly exposed except for the bandages. It hadn't bothered him before because he didn't care what Ashton thought about his body, but now he realized that he had been parading around half-naked in front of Scott this whole time. And worst of all, his scars were on full display and Scott was stroking them with a special interest!

Jamie pushed away from Scott but from his position lying under the man, there was little he could do. Scott pursed his lips and examined Jamie with sorrow in his eyes. *This isn't happen-*

ing, Jamie thought. *He can't know about the scars yet, because I haven't figured out how to explain them!*

He will understand, Marisol said, popping into his head unexpectedly in the way that normally bothered him. Right now, though, he didn't mind. *He has scars of his own.*

No he doesn't, Jamie said. *He's flawless except for the dragon scars!*

Not all scars are physical, she said in a sad voice.

Jamie looked at Scott more closely. The sorrow in his eyes was clear, but there was also understanding. Without a word, Scott leaned to his shoulder, to the scars, and kissed them. Jamie blinked in surprise, and found tears in his eyes. Scott kissed the scars on his other shoulder as well, then kissed him on the lips but it wasn't a passionate kiss like before. There was no lightning. It was a kiss of possession, a promise that nothing would hurt Jamie as long as Scott was around. More tears streamed from his eyes and he was embarrassed as his nose began to stuff up. Scott kissed him again and again as Jamie wept, and when he was finished kissing he just held Jamie close. There were tears in his eyes as well, and some anger, but the two of them found solace in each other's arms. Scott's lips brushed against Jamie's ear in another kiss.

"I love you, Jamie," he whispered.

CHAPTER TWENTY

Sweet Punishment

"Come in, Michael."

Mike shivered as he entered Ashton's private chambers. Ashton, like many of the council members, had a suite of rooms carved into the mountain where the dragons lived. Everyone else lived below, in the small canyon along the mountainside nearest the academy. Mike's quarters were near the top of the canyon in one of the more desirable quarters with a view of the nearby lake, as befit his dragon's status, but he had never been inside one of the upper chambers before.

Three of the boys in his class would never see this view, he thought sadly. Three had died during the exam, and a fourth was still in the hospital barely clinging to life. As much as Mike tried to distract himself with thoughts of Marisol and the mating flight, he could never quite escape the memories of his students lying cold in the forest, their dragons screaming in pain. He wondered if they would have enjoyed the view and tried, once again, to push the memories out of his head. He was alive, and the view was spectacular.

He didn't even have to strain to see out the window – one entire wall opened directly to the air and the view was incredible: the canyon with dragons flittering about and tiny, nearly indistinguishable humans trodding the well-worn paths, the lake that seemed to stretch forever but in reality contained several of the oldest nesting grounds known to exist, and the academy buildings breaking through the forest with their elegant architecture. The academy was modern, but the design blended with the forest rather than stayed apart from it.

When Mike had finished gawking at the view, he turned to Ashton and his heart sank. He knew he was going to be punished for his arrogance at suggesting that he join the mating flight, even though Ashton had agreed and even seemed amused at the request. The way Ashton had caught his hand when Mike was leaving let him know that it wasn't over, and then Eraxes had politely informed him that Ashton requested his presence. At least he could still hear Eraxes.

He hadn't realized that blocking dragons' voices was Arion's skill and now he was rethinking the evening when Eraxes had gone silent. Mike had assumed it was because something horrible was happening to Eraxes and the dragon didn't want him to know, but what if nothing had happened except for a few threats from Arion? Mike had never asked Eraxes, so he didn't know. If nothing had happened, then he had been walking on eggshells with his dragon for months now for no good reason, and he had almost lost his dearest friend. He was determined to have a conversation with Eraxes, but not now. Not when Ashton had requested his presence and was looking at him with a strange glint in his eyes.

Ashton gestured for him to come into a different room and Mike stumbled when he saw that it was the bedroom. It was neatly furnished and fairly simple, with a large bed dominating the space. There was a window looking out on the same spectacular view, but small enough that someone flying by on a dragon wouldn't be able to see in as they would the enormous window in the other room. Whatever Ashton wanted, he wanted it to be private.

"Do you really think you have a chance in the mating flight?"

Ashton's voice was polite and curious, without any hostility or resentment. Mike glanced at the bed and wondered how long it would be until they were both naked with Mike squirming underneath him. Why waste time on the niceties when it would inevitably end there? He tried to ignore a little part of him that was looking forward to that inevitable end; Ashton was not a lover but a rapist, he reminded himself.

"Yes," Mike said, his attention wandering between Ashton and the bed. "Eraxes is the one who carried Marisol out of the nesting grounds, and I have a close connection to Jamie."

"But not a sexual connection," Ashton said. "And dragons, no matter what you think, do not have as much control during their flight as you seem to give them credit. When Marisol flies, she won't see Eraxes as Eraxes, she'll just see a male dragon, same as the other male dragons chasing her."

Mike shrugged. He didn't want to disagree, but in his experience the female could choose her mate if she concentrated and didn't get caught up in the emotions. Just like male dragons could trick the female dragons if they didn't get caught up in their emotions. In both cases, all it required was a bit of restraint on the part of the human partner, a small brake to the hormones that rushed through the bond between human and dragon and made everyone look the same. Ashton, however, probably had never had a female refuse to mate with him, so he didn't realize the females did have a choice. After all, what woman wouldn't want to have sex with a council member? Ashton's experience was probably vastly different than Mike's, but he didn't know which was more accurate when it came to Jamie.

"You'll see," Ashton said. "I just spent some time with the boy and he is extremely close to his dragon. He gets dragged into her mind at the littlest things. It's quite remarkable, actually, to have someone so close to a dragon yet able to keep their own identity. But in the mating flight, Jamie will have no control whatsoever."

"Then what's the harm in letting me join?" Mike asked, still wondering when the other foot would drop and the punishment would arrive.

"No harm, and if, by some fluke, you do become Jamie's partner, I think you understand your place well enough. Don't you?"

"Yes," Mike said, lowering his eyes.

A cruel smile lit Ashton's face. "I've been watching you eye the bed. You really think sleeping with me is punishment? Most

140

people would consider it a reward."

"I don't-"

Mike stopped. He didn't know what to say. He could imagine making love to Ashton and it being pleasurable, but only in fantasy. Never in the real world, where Ashton had so much power over him. Unless Mike was in control, he had never enjoyed sex.

"You will sleep with me, but only when you want it. Until then," he rubbed his hands together and his eyes sparkled. "Take off your pants and come over here."

He sat down on the edge of the bed and patted his lap. Mike flushed, but he toed his shoes off. He was about to reach down to take off his socks when Ashton stopped him.

"Leave them on. I don't want you to feel too naked."

Mike gulped and undid the button on his slacks. Ashton watched him eagerly and Mike hid a smile, his fears subsiding. He had gained a kind of power in this situation: Ashton was the helpless viewer while Mike was the one in control of undressing. He had stripped for men before, but rarely for anyone who watched with such rapt attention. He unzipped his pants and slowly pulled them off. He let his hands trail along his body as he stood back up.

He was a little hard when his hands slid under the waistband of his boxers and he watched Ashton's face as he stroked himself under the boxers once before slipping the waistband down. Ashton smiled in approval as Mike finally exposed himself and tossed the boxers to the ground. He felt strange with his shirt still on, the coarse material teasing his tender nipples, but Ashton had been specific. Pants only. He hoped boxers were included in that and with a blush he realized that he had done far more than was required.

"Come here," Ashton said, patting his lap again.

For a moment, Mike remembered his first sexual experience. It was similar to this: an older, handsome man asking him to sit on his lap. Mike and his parents had been moving from Dripping Springs, Texas to Portland, Oregon and on the first night while his parents enjoyed the hotel's bar, Mike had gone for a swim and encountered a man so beautiful it was love at first sight. The man had taken him upstairs and patted his lap just like this, and what followed was the most perfect, earth-shattering sex that Mike could imagine. Nothing had ever compared to it in the years since.

But of course the man had just been taking advantage of a young boy, as Mike knew now, and it wasn't love. With Ashton it wasn't love either, but Mike could feel an excitement building in his chest that he hadn't felt since that night long ago.

Mike cautious sat on Ashton's lap and Ashton immediately flipped him over so he was bent over Ashton's knees, his ass in the air. He squirmed and tried to right himself but Ashton just laughed and kept him in place with a hand to the back of his neck.

"You deserve to be punished," Ashton said. "But I believe in mixing punishment with a little pleasure, don't you?"

"What-"

Ashton's hand smacked his ass and Mike gasped. Ashton was going to spank him! Another slap, this one hard enough that Mike's knuckles went white.

"Stop," he said. "It hurts!"

Ashton slapped him harder and he couldn't stifle a cry. The older man laughed.

"I think that's about your tolerance. Now let's see how long you can last."

Ashton began spanking him again and again, each blow hard enough to make him cry out in pain. But despite the pain, something about the placement of his hand or the rub of Ashton's knee against his crotch was getting him hard. He wasn't a masochist, but he was really getting turned on with each spank. His cries became moans as Ashton continued, as the sting from each blow sensitized his ass and spread warm circles throughout the region into his groin.

He rubbed against Ashton, trying to get some friction as he got harder, hoping the pleasure would wipe out some of the pain. He could feel Ashton's erection pressed against his side and knew the older man was really turned on, but still the spanks continued. Just when he thought he couldn't take the pain any more, Ashton started massaging his ass instead of spanking it.

"How does that feel, pet?"

Mike gasped and tears sprang to his eyes as Ashton firmly worked his fingers into the tenderized flesh of his ass. It was incredibly painful and arousing at the same time. Ashton's fingers worked their way closer and closer to his opening and Mike moaned and tried to shift his body to get Ashton inside. He felt something cold slither down his crack and the fingers returned, sliding along his skin easily. It must have been lube, he thought. Then Ashton touched his opening and he nearly howled in pleasure. He wanted Ashton inside him, now, no more playing games of punishment. He knew it would be painful to take Ashton's size into his sore ass, but he needed it more than anything else. He felt ashamed of his desire, but there was no way to hide it with his hard cock pressed against Ashton's legs. Ashton knew what he wanted, and he was going to oblige.

Ashton worked one finger inside of him and Mike moaned in pleasure and tried to spread his legs to give the man better access. Two fingers had Mike panting and rubbing against Ashton, but the angle he was being held wasn't ideal for getting friction. He was pressed against Ashton's knee and part of his thigh, but Ashton wasn't letting him move. It was torture having his cock trapped the way it was as Ashton slid three fingers inside and focused on gently stretching him.

"Let me- Let me-"

Mike couldn't think clearly enough to get the words out but Ashton knew what he wanted. Ashton leaned over and kissed his back, then finally allowed him to sit up. The loss of the fingers was only temporary, however, because Ashton laid back on the bed and ordered Mike to straddle him. Mike longed to slam down on the man's erect penis, but he knew he would be sore for days if he tried to take him that suddenly. No, he would have to be slow and work his way to what he wanted. His cock twitched at the thought of slowly lowering himself on Ashton's cock and Mike reached down to stroke himself, but Ashton slapped his hands away.

"No hands, only me, pet," the man purred, pulling Mike into position.

Mike nodded his agreement and positioned himself so that he could feel the bulge against his opening. Slowly, carefully, he lowered himself. He gasped. Ashton was bigger than he remembered and he had to remind himself to breathe and relax. If he wasn't relaxed, then there was no way he could take it all. He lowered himself more and his body screamed in pleasure. He wanted to be filled – needed it – and the only way he would ever feel complete was with Ashton inside him. Slowly he kept going, each inch another inch closer to feeling complete, until finally he was resting again Ashton's body and he was completely enveloping his cock. It hurt a little, since his ass was still sore and stinging from the spanking, but Ashton's rough pubic hair scratched against his balls in the most delightful way and he leaned forward to feel more of the texture. As he moved, the change in position caused him to gasp in surprised pleasure.

In all of his sexual exploits, Mike had only been penetrated a couple of times and always from behind. Even his first encounter had been from behind after the foreplay. He had never imagined that so much pleasure could be achieved when he was straddling a man like this. He shifted again, gently rocking back and forth. Ashton groaned and clutched Mike's thighs. Mike began lifting himself up and lowering himself again as he rocked, and soon he had a rhythm going that he knew would bring both of them to an orgasm quickly. He slowed his pace. He wanted to enjoy this.

Ashton was murmuring the entire time, words and phrases that Mike could only sometimes make out. "Yeah, baby," and "That's it, pet," were the only recognizable phrases he heard and he was thrilled that he was able to send the powerful Ashton into a nearly incoherent state. He was on top and in control, even if he was the one getting pierced. It was exhilarating.

Ashton's hands on his thigh gave the man a little control and soon, the hands grew stronger. Ashton didn't allow the slow rocking anymore; he demanded a faster pace and Mike obliged. Sweat was pouring off his body and as hard as he was, he knew it would only be minutes before he came, less for Ashton.

When Ashton came, the man arched his back and somehow penetrated Mike deeper than he had before, and the feeling of being complete washed over Mike stronger than any orgasm. This was where he belonged. He luxuriated in the warmth and physical completeness for a long moment before he felt a tightening in his balls. His own orgasm hit and squirted across Ashton's muscled chest exposed under his opened robe.

Exhausted, Mike collapsed forward onto Ashton's chest and knew he would be covered in cum the same as Ashton, but he didn't care. Ashton helped him disentangle and soon they were lying side by side in the large bed. Mike was surprised that Ashton was letting him stay; he had assumed that once the sex was finished, Ashton would kick Mike out. But the man seemed in no hurry, and Mike was too fatigued to figure out his motives. Ashton stroked his back gently as they lay together and Mike felt at peace for the first time in a long time. He belonged at Ashton's side and he would do anything to stay here. Ashton made his first sexual encounter seem like the stumbling adolescent adventure that it was – this was adult love and he already longed to experience it again. Spanking would never have the same connotation, he thought with a smile.

Mike was drowsing into sleep when Ashton turned to him and kissed his forehead.

"Did you enjoy that, my pet?"

"Mmm."

Mike snuggled closer to him. He had never been called someone's pet before but he found it highly erotic. The submission it implied went against his normal preference for domination, but he was willing to submit to Ashton. After the explosive sex they had just shared, he would do anything to please Ashton even if it meant becoming his pet. Ashton carded his hand through Mike's hair and he leaned into the caress.

"That is the sort of fucking that young Jamie needs," Ashton said in a musing voice.

Mike's eyes snapped open and he went stiff. "What?"

"When I spoke to him today, he was so tense and quiet. He needs to find a good release and once the mating flight is over, I plan to provide him with that release frequently."

"No, you can't do that to him," Mike said. He sat up and stared at Ashton. The man looked utterly serious.

Mike's stomach dropped. During the sex, he had felt special. Unique. Loved. And at the end, the sense of completion he felt was unmistakable. He had never felt it for anyone else, and he had assumed that Ashton had felt something similar. Was that just an ordinary fuck for Ashton? Did he always convince his lovers to do those things, and participate so fully and willingly? Did he not realize that Mike was special, that he was different? Tears welled up in his eyes. He and Ashton had just shared what he thought was incredibly passionate love, and immediately Ashton began talking about fucking someone else. What kind of man did that?

Mike stood up and winced. His entire body ached, especially his ass. He wouldn't be able to sit for days without the pain, but it was from the spanking and not the sex. Ashton watched him without a word as he pulled on his pants. Then he looked down at his shirt and realized that it was covered in his cum from when he had leaned against Ashton. He looked around, not sure what to do. He could go without a shirt, but now that he was a teacher there was a chance that a student might be nearby and he needed to be dressed. Dressed, but not in soiled clothes. His eyes fell on Ashton's wardrobe.

"Um," he began, kicking the ground nervously and feeling like a schoolgirl. "Can I borrow a shirt?"

Ashton smiled, a completely unreadable smile. "Of course, pet. Take your pick."

Mike opened the wardrobe and grabbed the first thing that wasn't a council uniform – Ashton had a lot of those. Then he turned to face Ashton, his lover.

"I have to go," he said.

"I know. But I'll see you again. Whenever you get the urge, feel free to find me."

Mike nodded, but in his heart he vowed not to return. Ashton was using him for his body and while Mike had feelings for him, Ashton felt nothing in return. It was just like all of the men Mike had seduced, he realized sadly. At the council's request and sometimes by his own choice, Mike had seduced dozens of men in the eight years he had been working for the council. He wooed them, made them feel special, made love to them, and then dropped them. He had never imagined how it must feel from their end.

He wondered if Scott had felt this betrayed when they broke up. Perhaps, Mike thought, it wasn't the rape that bothered Scott so much as the fact that Mike had almost completely ignored Scott afterwards. He should have been gentler and more respectful of the boy's feelings, because it was clear that Scott had developed feelings for Mike. Still had feelings, just of a different sort. And it wouldn't have been a lie. Mike had been watching Scott jealously ever since the rape, unwilling to admit that Scott was more than a man to seduce. Scott had actually touched Mike and Mike had genuine feelings for Scott, even though he couldn't express them.

Because he knew the council wouldn't approve of a continued relationship between him and Scott, Mike had been cruel: parading his latest conquests in front of Scott, always making sure Scott knew that Mike had completely forgotten him. But in reality Mike never forgot him and the big show was an attempt to hide the fact that Scott was still one of the most important people in Mike's life.

Maybe it was the same with Ashton, Mike thought with a flash of hope. Maybe Ashton did have feelings for him, but he couldn't express them because of the council so he was trying to push Mike away by talking about Jamie like that. It would make sense, after all. Mike was trying to get on the council, Ashton was head of the council, surely the council would cause a ruckus if the two of them started seeing each other.

There was a reason, Mike knew. He might not know it, but he knew that he was special to Ashton even if the man couldn't admit it. The trick was in finding out why he couldn't admit it, and then finding a way to work around it. But first, he had to make himself so desirable that Ashton wouldn't want anyone else. He had to become Jamie's mate no matter the cost.

CHAPTER TWENTY-ONE

Trigger

Scott waited in tense anticipation as he watched Jamie's reaction to his confession of love. Jamie's face was oddly unreadable, even though he was normally quite expressive. Or else Scott was so nervous he was unable to read anything into it. Jamie was smiling widely but did that mean he was pleased or was he just humoring Scott? Tears still glittered in his eyes: were they new or from his tears before?

The words had just slipped out. He had been planning on telling Jamie about the mating flight, about his betrayal, but the simple truth had gotten the better of him. He loved Jamie. The scars on Jamie's shoulders and what they represented had struck him powerfully. He didn't know whether someone else had scarred the boy or if Jamie had done it himself, but either way spoke of a childhood far darker than any he had imagined. They made him realize the full extent of the painful life Jamie had lived, and he knew that he would never let Jamie go through another day of pain.

The realization of how deeply he cared for the boy was like a trigger for him: the words slipped out and now he realized with a kind of abstract terror that he didn't even know if Jamie loved him. The boy's eyes were welling with tears and Scott still couldn't read the situation. Was Jamie overwhelmed with joy? Sorrow? Regret? He sent a message to Narné asking for Marisol's reaction, but Marisol had tired of flying and had fallen asleep. Of course, Scott thought.

"Say something," he said, unable to take the waiting any longer.

"Oh, Scott," Jamie murmured. "I- I don't know what to say."

Scott's heart fell and he looked away. Then Jamie grabbed him and kissed him fiercely and passionately, letting his tongue do the talking. Scott was overwhelmed and found himself barely able to keep up as Jamie began kissing his cheeks, his nose, his eyelids, his forehead, kissing and claiming him in a way that had tears springing to Scott's eyes. That had to be a sign that Jamie loved him.

Scott ran his hand through Jamie's hair and kissed him back, lavishing that pale skin with kisses and sucking on him until hickeys appeared along his neck. Jamie laughed and pushed him away playfully, but Scott held him tightly and resumed his sucking until Jamie was red all the way from his neck to his shoulder. With Jamie's healing abilities hastened by the dragon bond, the marks would disappear in hours but Jamie didn't know that and Scott was delighted that the boy was letting him mark him so.

Jamie flinched when he got near his shoulders and Scott deliberately kissed his scars again and ran his tongue along the neat, horizontal lines. He couldn't ask what they were from. Inwardly he raged that his Jamie had ever been hurt like this, even if the hurt was self-inflicted. If it wasn't self-inflicted, Scott knew he would never rest until he found the bastard who did it and made some cuts of his own. He couldn't ask, though, not now. Not yet, perhaps not ever. Jamie needed to be handled delicately and lovingly at all times. Jamie deserved better, and Scott vowed that he would protect Jamie so that the boy would never be hurt again. No matter what the council wanted.

He understood the pain that Jamie seemed to associate with the cuts, though. Sometimes as a child he had looked at the world around him and wondered if it would be better if he weren't around. But those thoughts were fleeting, and his parents were good about keeping him happy. Jamie hadn't been so lucky, with both of his parents dying in fires.

It was a strange coincidence, the fires, and one that had

bothered Scott for a while now. Both of Jamie's parents had tarragon blood but weren't in the society, so they didn't have dragons. People with blood but no dragons died young, but Jamie's parents hadn't died naturally, the way most did. They died in fires, which occasionally happened on campus when students began learning how to control their dragons' fire. Marisol wouldn't be mature enough to produce fire for months; Narné was just mastering the skill now and it was likely the reason everyone categorized him as too young for the mating flight.

It was a dangerous time, nearly as dangerous as the exam. One of the reasons the academy was in Portland was because of the constant drizzle that made fires easier to contain. Still, there were deaths. According to the university, Jamie's parents did not have dragons, but perhaps they had been in contact with a student. He didn't want to think of the darker scenario where a dragon had deliberately killed Jamie's parents. No, surely the council wouldn't go as far as to kill people outside the academy. Jamie's parents must have had a friend who had a dragon and that friend must have been present for both deaths.

The guilt must be overwhelming, Scott thought. Being responsible for the deaths of friends. He was careful to keep Narné in the field when they practiced, away from any trees or people. Narné didn't like the fire, but it was a natural instinct and if he didn't learn to control it, people would die.

Scott knew that he would say none of this to Jamie. Jamie had suffered enough without having to start worrying about the real cause of his parents' deaths as well. When Jamie was older, he would figure it out on his own. Until then, Scott would shower Jamie with the love and affection he should have gotten all of his life.

Scott was in the middle of licking Jamie's shoulder while the boy moaned in pleasure when a doctor approached them. Jamie noticed first, stiffening and shoving Scott away. At first Scott refused, thinking it was a game, but then he heard the footsteps and removed himself quickly but reluctantly from the salty tang of Jamie's skin.

The doctor frowned when he saw the light bruising along Jamie's neck and shoulder and glared at Scott in accusation. Scott shrunk a little. He had forgotten that Jamie was injured. Leaving the marks wasn't such a good idea after all, even though they would heal quickly. Jamie needed his healing abilities focused on his real wounds, not the kisses that Scott had inflicted.

"Scott," the doctor said. "Your class is about to start. I need to take Jamie back and see if he's ready to move back to the dorm. If you're ready," the doctor continued, turning to Jamie, "then you'll go back to classes tomorrow. We'd like to get you back on a regular schedule as soon as possible. It isn't good for your body or mind to sit around in a hospital ward all day."

Scott glanced at his watch. As a senior, he was taking very few classes and he was being excused from most of them right now while he cared for Marisol. The one class he couldn't skip, however, was his dragon training course. Jamie would be taking it too, although his would be very different. Scott trained one-on-one with a council member to learn about fire, flying, and other advanced skills. Jamie would still be learning basic precautions with his entire class.

He thought of Ashton and was relieved that he hadn't been assigned to that man for his trainer. His trainer was a much younger man, the youngest man on the council, in fact, and Scott had a lot of respect for him. Ashton might be okay with harming dragons, but Scott was willing to bet that his trainer knew nothing about it and would have no problems allowing Scott into the mating flight.

Perhaps if he gained support from enough council members, Ashton would change his mind. Scott brightened as he gently kissed Jamie goodbye and promised to check in on him again first thing in the morning before the boy's classes. He was not prepared to let anyone else touch his precious Jamie and if there were any way to persuade the council, he would take it.

When he arrived at the field, Narné and Eric, the trainer, had already started. Narné was belching fire into the air and attempting to control how wide the spout of flames went.

Breathing fire was a natural process for mature dragons. Their digestive tracks shifted once they reached maturity and many of the natural gases that resulted from eating began to be exhaled, and because of some mechanism like a rock and flint in the upper portion of a dragon's throat, it occasionally caught on fire. The mechanism, known as the trigger, was unconscious at first but dragons could learn to control it. Had to control it, actually, because if they didn't then they would spout flame at unexpected times and people could get killed.

The dragons undergoing this training were housed together and forbidden from human contact until they mastered the process. They were immune to each other's fire so no harm was done when they accidentally spouted fire on each other. Narné had mastered the trigger almost immediately, as did most dragons who came from older nesting grounds. Scott wondered if perhaps they were the ranking dragons. Now Narne had to learn to control the flow of his fire stream.

It was an advanced skill and not one taught to all dragons. If a dragon could control his trigger, after all, then he didn't necessarily need to control the fire: he could just choose to prevent the fire in the first place. It didn't hurt the dragons if they never emitted fire, but many of the dragons delighted in the process and there was an entire chamber in the dragon canyon designed just for firing, as it was called.

Scott's presence at this training wasn't really necessary, but he wanted to stay updated on what his dragon knew and often his trainer had assignments for him as well. Today, though, he wanted to talk. Narné's fire wavered and ceased, and the dragon met his gaze.

Be careful, Narné warned.

"Ah, Scott," Eric said. "I was starting to think you wouldn't show up today. I was just teaching Narné some new controls."

He briefly explained how the control worked and how Narné could fine-tune his trigger to get the precise flames that he wanted. Normally Scott appreciated knowing the details of his dragon's training, but as soon as Eric started talking about firing, Scott's mind leapt to Jamie's parents again.

"Excuse me," Scott interrupted just as Eric was explaining how Narné squeezed the mechanism in his throat to the left to get a wide-angle fire and to the right to get a narrow stream.

Eric seemed surprised at the interruption but gestured for Scott to continue.

"Has anyone outside the academy ever been killed by a dragon's fire?"

The trainer's face darkened. "It has happened, yes. That's why we train so much, and why we keep the dragons isolated until they can control their trigger. Why do you ask?"

"What happens to the dragons?"

"What do you mean?"

"If they kill someone outside the academy. What happens to them?"

"Nothing happens to them," Eric said, a bewildered tone in his voice. "They can hardly be punished for something they can't control. The partners always take it hard. No one likes to have a death on their hands. But it's part of being a dragon's partner."

"How often does it happen?"

"It's rare," Eric said. "Are you worried about Narné? He has exceptional control, you really don't need to worry. Unless there's something you haven't told me?"

He looked at Scott, then at Narné, who was watching them with dismay. The dragon shook his head. Narné hated verbalizing, but he did when necessary and he did now.

"No," Narné said. "Scott is just curious. Can we continue?"

"It's because of Jamie, isn't it?" Eric asked. "You're thinking of his parents. Well, I can assure you that no student was involved. In either death. Does that help?"

Scott wanted to say that no, it didn't help, it just raised more questions. Why specify that no student had been involved? That implied that someone other than a student had been involved, maybe even a council member. Maybe even Ashton, although it seemed a little extreme even for him. But he felt a powerful nudge by Narné to drop the subject, coupled with a warning that pursuing the issue would end very, very badly for both of them.

"Yeah," Scott said. "So I've seen some of the older dragons shoot balls of fire instead of streams. Is Narné going to learn that?"

"Next week," Eric said, sounding exasperated. "Have you even been listening to me? This week is width, next week is duration. Now then, I was explaining how Narné controlled his trigger."

Eric went back to his lecture while Scott pondered the implications of everything he was learning. He had never before stopped to think about why dragons learned things like fireballs, but with the death of Jamie's parents in his mind, the lessons were taking on a dark overtone. What if the dragons were being trained to kill? Because there really was no real need to teach dragons how to control their fire. That was well-established.

Sure, dragons enjoyed showing off their firing tricks in front of each other, but was that really a reason to teach it to every dragon capable of learning it? The Academy was creating an army of dragons capable of camouflaging themselves, capable of communicating without speaking, and capable of delivering targeted, precise destruction wherever they wished. Any government in the world would kill for that kind of army.

He felt another nudge from Narné, another warning of dire consequences if he followed this train of thought. That meant it was true, he realized with a shudder. And Narné was trying to protect him. How much did the dragons know that they were keeping from their humans? If Scott and Narné were allowed to join the mating flight and became equal to the council, what kind of power would they wield?

More than you imagine, Narné said. *But don't think of it now. Eric is suspicious and he is on the council. Be happy today. Jamie is awake.*

But the council has forbidden me to be with him. I have the right to sulk.

Do not sulk so publicly, not after bringing up Jamie's parents,

Narné said sharply.

Scott inwardly nodded and outwardly he pulled himself together. He had hoped to talk to Eric about the mating flight, but given Narné's warning, it wouldn't go far. Eric was on the council and as far as Narné was concerned, the council was a single unit, not individual people who could be persuaded. It would probably be best if Scott thought of them the same way. The rest of the lesson went without incident but when they were leaving, Eric grabbed his arm.

"I just want to make sure you don't have any more questions," Eric said. "I understand this is a trying time for you."

Scott sighed. So Eric knew about the council's decision on the mating flight. "I don't suppose the council will change its mind, will they?"

That seemed an innocent enough question, asked in such a way that it didn't seem like he was trying to figure out how to overturn the council's decision. Eric smiled and patted his back and Scott knew his deception had worked.

"I'm afraid not, Scott. We have our reasons. But after the first flight, I'm sure you'll be welcome to join."

Scott smiled hesitantly and moved away from the man's touch. Did he actually expect Scott to quietly accept the council's decision? Did they really expect him not to fight?

Yes, they expect that, Narné said quickly. *They have had unquestioning obedience for so long they can no longer recognize deception unless it makes itself known, so keep your thoughts to yourself and make them believe you will obey.*

"As long as I fly with him eventually," Scott said, and turned away from the trainer. He went to Narné and stroked the beast tenderly while Eric made his way across the field towards the dragon canyon where he lived. Scott was his only class for the day.

As he watched Eric leave, he could feel some of his innocence leave as well. Tarragon Academy was steeped in more corruption than he could have imagined. Someone needed to clean it up. Since obviously the council wouldn't do it, it would fall to Marisol and her mate. That mate would be Narné, and Scott would wipe this place clean as soon as he was in control. He just needed a plan.

CHAPTER TWENTY-TWO

Back to School

Once again, Jamie was sitting in class waiting for the class to end. It was the last week before winter break started but the school insisted on holding classes even though the final exam – the hatching – had already taken place. The night before had been lonely, since Amar and the rest of the freshmen had been moved into new housing at the campus apartments or the dragon canyon. Jamie would be moving over the weekend.

Normally Jamie would have chosen the canyon just so he could see it, but Scott lived in the apartments and Jamie wanted to be as close to him as possible. Amar lived in the apartments as well and Jamie longed to see him; it seemed like ages since he'd seen his friend and former roommate. But until then he was stuck in the dorms, all by himself. A nurse had stayed with him in case he needed anything, but it was one of the lonelier nights in his life. Not even Marisol could be nearby: she had slept with Narné at Scott's apartment as she had since her hatching, even though she was getting too large. She would have her own apartment soon enough, he thought.

Today, though, he was back in class and bored again. Only this time, he had a dragon waiting for him and it wasn't Mr. Ferrin teaching, it was a woman who was substituting while Mr. Ferrin remained at the hospital with the remaining boy who had been attacked. Another boy who had been hospitalized was back in class with two missing fingers and a missing eye, and no one felt comfortable looking at him. That could have happened to any of them, if they had been careless and their dragons had been slightly more aggressive.

Jamie heard their stories from the hatching and had decided that his experience was easy in comparison – he hadn't fought Marisol, after all, only laid there and took her blows. The others had fought back and tamed their dragons into submission. Jamie had been the one to submit in their relationship. He hadn't told anyone that; when he told his story, he only told about finding the island and the egg. He didn't say what happened afterward, leaving it to the imaginations of the other students.

They could see his injuries, after all, and many of them had seen him carried in by Narné near death so their imaginations no doubt painted a vivid and heroic portrait that Jamie didn't want to spoil with the truth.

Ever since he had shown up at class that morning, students had come out of the woodwork to check on him: guys he'd chatted with between classes, guys he waved to sometimes but had never spoken to, even a few girls who snuck over from the girls' campus to see if the rumors were true and Jamie was back in classes. He couldn't believe that his presence made such a difference, but apparently everyone had heard about his injuries and more people than he expected seemed to care.

The only people missing were the ones he really cared about: Scott and Amar, who were at their own classes, and Mr. Ferrin, who had been at his side when he woke up and was now taking care of the remaining boy in the hospital, who rumor said wasn't going to make it despite the doctor's best efforts.

That could have been me, Jamie thought with a chill.

Never, Marisol piped up. She was taking lessons as well, but that didn't seem to stop her from chatting. He suspected her classes were a lot more flexible than his. *You had me to give you strength. This other boy does not have a good bond with his dragon. They cannot even speak.*

What happens to the dragon if the boy dies?

Marisol was silent but Jamie saw a flash of a dragon screaming in agony, surrounded by humans who slowly approached. Jamie flinched as one of the humans in the vision took a spear and expertly pierced the dragon's jugular. The dragon went still almost immediately.

You couldn't have seen this! Jamie was horrified at the thought of his precious Marisol witnessing such a scene.

No, I saw it in Eraxes' mind. It is what happens when a human dies. We cannot live without our humans. That is why I will take good care of you!

Another vision filled Jamie's mind, this time Marisol wrapped around Jamie so that only his head was visible. She was practically purring in pleasure and he had a goofy grin that he hoped never crossed his face in the real world. Jamie smiled at the image and sent her a wave of love. Sometimes emotions and images worked better than words to express their emotions.

And sometimes words were enough, he thought, remembering Scott's confession of love yesterday. It still warmed his heart and made him as giddy as a schoolgirl and Marisol shared in his excitement and delight for a moment, magnifying it until it reached proportions he couldn't contain and he longed to jump out of his desk and start dancing. He took a deep breath and repeated Ashton's words for keeping himself grounded, and soon Marisol's emotions were back where they belonged and he was in control once more.

When Jamie looked around, he noticed a couple of students staring at him with strange expressions on their face. He hoped he hadn't done anything stupid. When he felt Marisol's emotions so strongly, he couldn't always tell what his body was doing. When he was thinking of Scott on top of that, who knew what had happened? But the teacher was nonplussed, even though she was staring at Jamie as well. Something had happened, he decided, but since the teacher didn't seem bothered, it must be a normal dragon thing.

Still, he longed for Mr. Ferrin to be teaching them. Mr. Ferrin would be able to explain what had happened, and perhaps he would have a better strategy of keeping his mind in the real world. It wasn't Marisol's fault that Jamie kept slipping into her mind, after all. It usually started with a strong emotion of Jamie's that Marisol enjoyed and tried to imitate, but her imitations were too powerful and Jamie got swept up in them. Mr. Ferrin would have an answer and Jamie decided to talk to the teacher the first chance he got.

He settled back in to listen to the lecture. They had picked up where Mr. Ferrin left off, finishing up talking about the Tarragon tribe and moving on to other tribes that worshipped mythical creatures but weren't widely known. This was a survey course, so they were covering a lot of tribes briefly and then the students could choose their particular specialty later. Jamie knew he should learn more about the Tarragon tribe, since he, and everyone in the room, was now a member, but he was more interested in the other tribes. Did they still exist, like the Tarragon tribe? More importantly, did their creatures still exist? He raised his hand.

"If dragons are real, then does that mean that the mystical creatures worshipped by other groups are real, too?"

The teacher smiled indulgently and the class tittered as if he had asked something ridiculous, but Jamie knew it was a legitimate question.

"I mean," he continued, "If no one outside our tribe knows about dragons, then wouldn't it stand to reason that no one outside of their tribes would know the truth about them, either?"

"We humans might not know," the teacher answered, "but the dragons would know. They are aware of much more than they share with us but if there were other creatures like them, we would know by now."

Jamie slunk back in his seat, unsatisfied by the answer. The teacher had as good as admitted that they had no way of knowing: as humans, plenty of things could be hidden from them and as the teacher said, even if the dragons knew they might hide that information to shield the other creatures. It seemed the height of arrogance to assume that only the Tarragon tribe worshipped a real creature, but if that's what would be on the test, then Jamie would learn it. He would learn it and find the truth out on his own. Other dragons might keep secrets from their owners, but he and Marisol had a different kind of bond.

He wouldn't ask right now, though. Right now Marisol was learning how to swim, and her delight at splashing around in the swimming pool before she was allowed in the lake was infectious. Jamie kept finding himself grinning and his feet moving, and he had to keep repeating Ashton's words to regain balance within his mind. His teacher said nothing – she knew what was going on – but the other students were beginning to regard him oddly.

This question didn't help, as it was clearly something no one else in the class had considered. He wished again that Amar were here, and resolved to ask Ashton if he could be transferred into Amar's class. Ashton could get it done, he knew. Ashton could get anything done.

Amar had been moved to a different class because he was ready to go back to school immediately after the hatching. The students in Jamie's class had all been injured, in shock, or just not prepared to return to school until two days ago. Jamie had been put with them so he would miss less class time, but he would rather work with the teacher to catch up than be in a class with no real friends. He glanced at the clock and brightened when he saw that class was just about over.

The teacher kept talking right up until they were supposed to leave, unlike Mr. Ferrin who sometimes let them out a minute or two early. She dismissed them promptly on time after reminding them of the readings due on Monday. Jamie realized that it must be Friday and was grateful that he didn't have any more classes for a few days. He could spend them with Scott. As he was leaving, the teacher gestured for him to come to the front of the room and he obeyed.

She was a kind-looking woman with short dark hair that curled around her oval face and large dark eyes. She didn't wear make-up but if she did, he thought she would probably be considered beautiful. Without make-up, though, her perfect lips got lost in her face and her skin looked too pale. Not that he could really comment on pale skin, since his skin was like porcelain. She had a few worry lines on her face, but the laugh lines were deeply etched even at her young age and he immediately liked her, even though he had been skeptical of her while she had been teaching. She seemed like a genuinely nice person and she hadn't even spoken yet.

"Jamie, I wanted to make sure you knew about your next class."

"What class? I already went to my philosophy class this morning and my other two classes meet Tuesday and Thursday."

She sighed. "Now that you have a dragon, you've been automatically enrolled in a class on dragon care. Everyone is. It's a one-credit, ungraded class but it meets every day during the week at five o'clock. I thought someone would have mentioned it to you, but I guess with everything else going on it slipped peoples' minds."

"What else is going on?"

She shook her head and patted him on the shoulder. "It's just the first time in a long time that we've had a Queen dragon, that's all. Nothing for you to worry about. Your class meets in the field and you can be on time if you hurry."

Jamie thanked her and started heading to the field. Inside, he was grumbling. He knew that Marisol had started taking classes but he hadn't expected that he would have to take extra classes too. Four classes were hard enough, even if they were somewhat similar in content and he had already passed the final exam. He wondered if the new class met over the winter break. Probably. Students weren't allowed to go home their first year over winter break, which Jamie had considered a bonus. He had never questioned why the school would have such a peculiar rule but it made sense now that he knew about dragons. The school needed to make sure the students could take care of their dragons before they risked letting the students travel, and the dragons needed to learn how to camouflage themselves and get by in modern society.

For Jamie it meant that he wouldn't have to see his aunt, if she would even let him visit. It was always a gamble with her, a balance between her dislike of him and her need for babysitters and handymen. When she needed something from him, he was treated like a guest and sometimes she had even invited him to eat with the family. When she didn't, he was tossed aside like garbage, forbidden from the kitchen, locked out of the house so often he had learned how to break in without alerting anyone. Sometimes he wondered why his father had left him with her, but he knew there were no other options. And his aunt could be pleasant when she wanted. Jamie's father likely never knew her true self; he only saw the beautiful façade she presented during family get-togethers. She was Jamie's mother's sister, after all. Maybe Jamie's mother had neglected to mention what a bitch the woman could be.

Jamie took a deep breath and tried to release his stress. He didn't want to worry Marisol. Not when she was having so much fun swimming around and splashing her instructors. A little smile worked its way across his lips as he allowed his mind to dip into hers. She was having the time of her life. She wanted to be in a larger body of water, since the pool was only big enough for one dragon and she wanted to wrestle, but she was loving the water. She could easily hold her breath for long periods of time. How long, no one was sure; blue dragons could hold their breath for up to six hours, green dragons only one hour, and her instructors guessed that she ranged somewhere in between.

Marisol most enjoyed holding her body underwater and floating with just her eyes and snout showing, like a crocodile except that her skull structure was nothing like a crocodile's. She could, with effort, change the color of her scales just slightly so that she looked like a floating log instead of a crimson dragon. Jamie could feel her excitement at the trick and her longing to try it someday. She wanted to hide and then burst out of the water, shocking some innocent bystander who had mistaken her for a fallen branch. Jamie tried to tell her that she probably wouldn't be allowed to reveal herself to people who didn't have dragons, and he could feel her teeth bared in a grin.

I want to shock the people with dragons, she said. *The people who think they know better.*

Jamie laughed, then covered his mouth. He was approaching the field and didn't want anyone to hear him laughing to himself. They would think he was crazy for sure, with all of his movement during class, his strange question, and then his random laughter. How could the rest of the students be adapting so well? He tried to remind himself that they had been with their dragons for a week now while he was in a coma, but it didn't help. They acted like they had never seen behavior such as his but surely they had acted the same way at first.

Amar was sitting with the large group gathered at the field and Jamie realized that all of the freshmen must take the class together. It still wasn't a large class, only about a hundred students or so. Jamie had been honored to be accepted into such an exclusive academy, although now he knew that he was accepted for other reasons. He slid through the crowd until he was behind Amar and then he grabbed his friend's shoulders. Amar jumped. Perhaps some of Marisol's mischievousness was rubbing off on him, Jamie thought.

Amar grinned when he saw who it was, and swept Jamie up in a painfully tight hug. Jamie didn't protest even though his injuries ached; he was too glad to see his friend again.

"Jamie! I didn't expect to see you until next week."

"Yeah, I guess they thought I needed something to distract me from my dragon."

Amar looked around and his voice dropped. "Do you get caught up in your dragon, too? No one else seems to. The new instructor says only a few dragons can talk to their partners the way I can but it's hard to imagine having a dragon and not talking to him all the time."

Something inside Jamie relaxed, a part he hadn't even known was tense. Amar understood him. He had a friend in this bizarre experience.

"Yeah," Jamie said. "It's really hard to stay grounded, you know? What's your dragon's name? Mine is Marisol," he added with more than a touch of pride.

"Tephis. He's a blue dragon, far prettier than the others. Even the other dragons say he's the most beautiful they've seen," Amar added.

"You can hear the other dragons too?"

"No," Amar said after a pause. "I just know what their partners tell me. Can you hear other dragons besides Marisol?"

"Yeah," Jamie said. He was a little disappointed that he couldn't relate to Amar on this issue, but a little thrilled that he did have a unique ability as Scott had indicated. "Marisol is a Queen dragon, whatever that means."

"It means a lot, I think," Amar said. "We're all signed up for a class in Tarragon hierarchy next semester – remember how we thought it was weird that that we couldn't register for classes until after the final exam? Now we know why; everyone is required to take certain classes but they couldn't exactly tell us the names of the classes without giving away the game. Anyway, I think we'll learn about Queens and all that after the break."

"I hope that's soon enough," Jamie said, thinking of Marisol's first mating flight. He wanted to understand what it would be like before he went through it, and he needed to figure out why both Ashton and Scott had seemed so intent on talking to him about it.

"Oh, class is starting. You'll like this class. It's actually useful. Today we're supposed to talk about water safety."

"The same day the dragons learn to swim? Good timing."

"Yeah," Amar laughed. "I guess they don't want us trying any crazy tricks with our little dragons. Not that Tephis would mind. He's already come up with various ways for me to surf on his back while he skims under the water."

Jamie laughed, briefly touching Marisol's mind to share the idea with her. She rejected the notion with a dignified snort, then began plotting her own method of surfing. He smiled. He adored the way she was so independent and refused to take ideas from anyone else, even when she secretly admired those ideas. It was a lot like him, he realized. He always had to do things his way, even if meant reinventing the wheel every time he did something. Still, he felt that he learned more and enjoyed himself more when he did things his way instead of following other people's commands.

The class got started and the instructor put up a powerpoint. The first slide said "Do Not Surf on Your Dragon" and showed a looped video of a person being flipped in the air while trying to do exactly what Amar had suggested. Jamie and Amar broke into giggles and exchanged knowing glances as they shared the image with their dragons. Marisol grumbled, but obediently began plotting other ways to have fun in the water. Jamie was a little surprised she was so obedient, but she countered by saying that if Jamie learned it in class, then it must be true. Jamie smiled as he leaned back to take in the rest of the class. He could already tell that this would indeed be the most useful class he took.

CHAPTER TWENTY-THREE

Live for the Present

Jamie hummed with pleasure as he finished packing his clothes for the move into the campus apartments. Scott loved him! Scott's words kept ringing through his head even though over a day had passed since Scott had uttered them. The rest of today had gone well, too: he and Amar were reunited and Marisol was enjoying herself in her new classes and her new home in the apartment. She had already arrived and was waiting for Jamie to collect his things and join her. Smiling, Jamie spread out his favorite shirt and neatly folded it.

He would miss having a human roommate at the apartments, but according to the teacher who explained his living options, each apartment was designed for a single dragon. He would still be in the same building as Scott and Amar, however, and he planned on visiting both of them regularly. In the canyon, there were multi-dragon suites but Jamie didn't want to risk rooming with someone he didn't know. He had lucked out with Amar, and that was enough. Besides, he hoped to be spending time with Scott.

His smile faded slightly as he remembered what Amar had said before they parted after class. Amar had gotten uncomfortable and asked if they could talk about Scott sometime. Jamie didn't understand why, but he couldn't help but remember Ashton's warnings about Scott and think that they were related. Was Scott keeping something from him? He and Amar had made plans to have dinner tonight – pizza – and talk about everything Jamie had missed while he was in a coma, and Jamie tried to focus on getting his apartment ready rather than worrying about what Amar had to say.

Jamie folded his shirts and remembered how uncomfortable he had felt in the apartments before. He understood now why Scott's apartment had seemed strange before, and why he had felt uncomfortable when he visited. The dragons had excellent camouflage and all of the rooms were designed for dragons to come and go silently, so Jamie had probably been seeing or hearing Narné padding around the apartment when he was visiting. Without knowing where the noise and unusual shadows came from, it had seemed like a strange, unfriendly place at times. Now that he knew about dragons, however, he suspected the apartment would feel warm and friendly.

Jamie packed up the last of his clothes and shut the box. Everything he owned was back in a box, only four months after he had unpacked for his first semester at the school. But this second move would be more permanent: he planned on staying in the same apartment for the rest of his time at Tarragon Academy. Some of the teachers lived in the apartments as well, although most of them had rooms in the dragon canyon. Jamie sighed. He would have to get Scott to show him the canyon. It sounded beautiful.

Jamie stood up and went to his door, where a nurse stood and kept an eye on him to make sure he didn't overexert himself. She was friendly enough, but he would have rather had Scott. Scott was busy loading Jamie's boxes into a golf cart and driving them over to the apartment. He would be back any minute for the second and last batch. Jamie didn't have too many things, but it was amazing how much he had accumulated and how much he had brought. It didn't seem possible that everything was his, but Amar had packed up his things and moved days before.

He heard footsteps drawing near and a beloved scent reached his nose, drawing Jamie into the hallway where Scott was just exiting the stairs. Jamie flew towards him and enveloped him in a hug. His happiness spilled over into Marisol and he grew dizzy for a moment as she leapt into the air in response. But he remembered Ashton's advice for staying grounded in his own mind and soon Marisol and he were separate minds again.

With the nurse scrutinizing their every move, Scott and Jamie didn't say much. They smiled shyly at each other as Scott lifted the heavy boxes onto the dolly and Jamie picked up the few remaining items. The nurse followed them down the hallway, down the stairs, and stopped beside the golf cart. She drew Jamie to one side and glared at Scott as if warning him away.

"Jamie, you're still injured so I want you to promise that you won't engage in any strenuous activity until a doctor has cleared you. Do you understand?"

"Yes, ma'am," he said.

"Any activity," she added, raising her eyebrows and glancing at Scott.

Jamie grew hot and knew he was blushing. She was trying to tell him not to have sex! He glanced at the ground in embarrassment and rubbed his hands against his thighs nervously. Once, the very idea of sex would have been the farthest thing from his mind and her warning would have been laughable. But with Scott in the picture, it was something he actually had to consider.

"Yes, ma'am," he repeated in a mumble.

She seemed satisfied. She reminded him to check in with the doctor at the end of the day and left them alone. He would be checking in with the doctor twice a day until his injuries healed, but the hospital was next to the academic buildings so it would only be a short hike for him. There were no cars allowed on campus other than the little golf carts reserved for special occasions like moving, when wheels were needed.

Scott helped him into the golf cart and they began driving to the apartment building on the other side of campus. Jamie had a box of trinkets in his lap or else he would have reached over and held Scott's hand, but he gave a shy smile at the man who had confessed his love just a day ago. Scott smiled back, but there was a weariness in his eyes that couldn't come from the relatively easy task of moving.

"Is something wrong?"

Scott sighed and his smile vanished. "I guess we can talk now. No one's nearby. We need to do it soon. Jamie, about your mating flight-"

"I really don't want to talk about that," Jamie interrupted.

"I know, love. But we have to. I've made a decision that will affect you. A lot. It'll affect me too, but you need to know about it. You need to know what happened."

"I'm listening."

"Marisol's mate will have a lot of power on campus. He'll be equal to the council. So the council has decided to limit who can chase her. They've decided that Narné and I won't be allowed to participate."

Jamie frowned. It had to be a misunderstanding. But a flutter of pure panic began worming its way through Jamie's heart. "That doesn't make sense. You're the only one I'm going to be with. They know it. Ashton knows it."

"Ashton's the one who made the decision, love."

Jamie remembered the anger Scott had displayed when he found Ashton and Jamie together earlier. If Scott thought Ashton was preventing him from being with Jamie, it was no wonder he was angry. He nervously fingered the edges of the box in his lap. Ashton had tried to warn Jamie about Scott, but why? Jamie couldn't imagine the man deliberately preventing them from seeing each other. After all, he had left them alone and he seemed like such a nice father-figure. Maybe he was just a father-figure who was protective of his child, Jamie thought, and he wanted to make sure Scott was good enough for Jamie. No, it didn't make sense. None of it made sense. Ashton was a good person and would never do what Scott was saying.

"Well, I'll just explain to Ashton that I only want you," Jamie said. "He must not realize that we're together the way we are. He didn't seem to have much of an opinion of committed relationships," Jamie added, remembering the man's comments about Mike.

"You shouldn't do that," Scott said. "Jamie, if I participate in the mating flight, the council is going to harm Narné and I can't risk that. I can't let anything happen to Narné."

Jamie was silent. It really didn't make sense now, but he could tell that Scott was telling the truth. The panic was beginning to blossom but he wouldn't give in to fear. He would stay in control. He couldn't get over the feeling that Scott didn't understand the situation. Surely Ashton wouldn't do something like this. He reached out to Marisol.

It is true, Marisol said sadly. *All of the dragons have been told. Only eight dragons will fly with me and Narné is not one of them.*

Who decided this? Jamie demanded. *No one except us should get a say in the matter!*

The highest dragons decided. Narné is not mature enough yet.

Well, Scott is, and he's the only one I want. I refuse to participate if Scott isn't there.

He felt Marisol hiss in surprised displeasure. *You would leave me to fly alone?*

No, of course not, Jamie assured her. It was true; he would never leave Marisol alone. Couldn't leave her alone, for the most part. They were inextricably bound and her experiences were his, and vice versa. But he was surprised that she didn't share his outrage and longing to be with Scott. If she felt his emotions as deeply as he felt hers when she was flying sometimes, how could she act so calm about the situation?

It is only once, Marisol said in answer to his unasked question. *We will obey the council and after this first time, Scott will be allowed. I can tolerate another dragon once. It is not worth risking Narné.*

They wouldn't really hurt a dragon, would they?

Marisol was silent, but Jamie could feel untold depths of sadness within her. She was remembering something terrible, something she had seen or heard or perhaps something the other dragons had told her, he couldn't tell. But she didn't want to frighten him, so she was keeping it to herself. All he could feel was infinite sadness and the shocking assurance that yes, the council would not hesitate to harm a dragon.

"We're here," Scott said, cutting through his thoughts abruptly.

Jamie jolted and Scott grabbed the box on his lap before it tumbled to the ground from the sudden movement. Jamie smiled sheepishly and took the box back. Scott squeezed his shoulder and looked as if he wanted to speak, but he said nothing. Really, there was nothing to say. Jamie would have to sleep with someone besides the man who loved him, and Scott would have to allow it or risk his dragon. It was a horrible situation, but he couldn't see any solutions. It felt utterly unreal.

Jamie carried his little box up to his new apartment feeling like a hollowed out piece of wood. Any minute now, he knew he was about to burst into tears. He just had to get up the steps and inside the doorway to his new home, next to the man who loved him but wouldn't be able to make love to him during Marisol's first mating flight. There had to be an answer, some way to defy the council.

The thought of a stranger's hand upon his body gave him chills and he nearly dropped his box, but he made it to his room safely. Scott was a few feet behind with the dolly. As soon as the boxes were set down, Jamie stretched out his arms to Scott, who embraced him readily.

"I'm so sorry, love," he whispered.

Jamie said nothing, only tucked his head under Scott's and breathed in the scent of honey and dandelions. A tear escaped, then another. He sniffled, not wanting to get tears on Scott's shirt, but Scott refused to let go of him. Jamie glanced to make sure that Scott had closed the door to the apartment after him – he had – and then he relaxed and let the tears start to flow.

Crying was not something that came easily to Jamie. He avoided it at all costs and he was terribly out of practice as he tried to let himself escape through tears. They were supposed to be cathartic, he knew. A good cry could make you feel better. But it never worked for him, probably because he never really let himself cry. A few tears, that strange hiccupping gulp that prevented him from talking, that was it. No release from whatever was paining him.

It was like cutting, in a way, because it was supposed to give him release but it didn't. Only tears left no permanent tracks. He clutched Scott tightly and felt the man's body shudder beneath his hands. He glanced up through his tears just enough to see that Scott, too, was crying. He held Scott closer and his tears began to dry. Scott needed him to be strong. As long as Jamie could accept his fate, Scott could manage as well. It was only one time with a stranger, Jamie told himself. One time with strange hands running along his body and penetrating him. He shuddered. He was still essentially a virgin and the thought of losing his virginity to anyone besides Scott was unimaginable.

Which meant he and Scott needed to have sex before Marisol's mating flight. Jamie felt his cock twitch and cursed his treacherous body. He was in mourning and shouldn't be turned on right now. But the thought of sleeping with Scott, no matter the reason, was enough to stir a little interest in his groin and he didn't want Scott to feel it and misconstrue the movement. His mind whirled towards more pleasant thoughts as he stroked Scott's back and found himself murmuring reassuring words.

Marisol wouldn't mate for weeks, maybe even months. That was such a long time. He and Scott had only been dating for around a week, maybe more. He was still a little hazy on dates because of his coma. It felt like days, but he knew he had been unconscious for nearly a week. Still, the point remained that the mating flight wouldn't happen for a long time, so why worry about it? Maybe they would find a solution before then. But he didn't want to spend the next few weeks in mourning. He wanted to spend them cuddling with his beautiful boyfriend and enjoying every moment.

The two of them separated and Jamie lowered his eyes and looked up at Scott through his lashes.

"I know the future looks bleak, but right now looks pretty good," he said, gesturing around. "I'm in a new place with Marisol, and I'm right next to you. Can't we just enjoy the present and worry about the future later?"

Scott's face shone with tears, but his lips quirked into a smile. "You are amazing."

Jamie grinned and placed his hands on Scott's shoulders. "Not half as amazing as you."

They kissed and lightning sparked between them again. Jamie moaned into the kiss, longing to feel Scott caress his body. He remembered the feel of Scott's mouth on his penis and ached for a repeat, but he remembered the nurse's warning. Even though he felt fine, he had just woken up from a week-long coma yesterday and needed rest, not excitement. Scott must have felt the same way because after a few more addicting kisses, he stroked Jamie's hair and pulled away.

"You must be exhausted," he said. "Your bed is all made up and ready for you. Why don't you rest while I finish unpacking, and then we'll see how you're feeling."

"Okay," Jamie said. A wave of sleep hit him and he knew sleep was the best strategy, even though he wanted to stay and kiss Scott some more. Marisol prodded him to go to sleep as well, letting him know that she was about to take a nap and both of them would sleep sounder if they coordinated the sleeping effort.

Just as Scott had said, his bed was already set up and made in his bedroom, even though everything else was in boxes. Scott helped him with his shoes, but Jamie waved him off before he could take the rest of his clothes off. He didn't feel like seeing the bandages or the scars and it wouldn't be the first time he'd been so tired he slept in his clothes. At his aunt's house, he'd often slept in his clothes because he never knew when she would barge in his room and demand that he help her with some chore or activity. But here, with Scott in the other room and Marisol asleep in the second bedroom, he knew he would sleep soundly.

He shut his eyes and tried to ignore the panic he still felt about the mating flight, and his fears and discomfort about moving to a new place. Amar would be over soon for dinner, Scott was here now, everything was fine, he told himself. He took a deep breath. By the time he finished releasing it, Scott had appeared at his side. He sat up, wondering what was wrong as Scott looked at him with a crazed look in his eyes.

"Jamie," he said breathlessly. "I have a plan."

CHAPTER TWENTY-FOUR

Killing

Mike held the boy's hand as he slipped into death. Tears rimmed his eyes even though he knew he ought to be proud. Only five casualties in a class of one hundred. It was a record, but knowing that didn't make the pain any easier. After Eraxes had rescued Marisol and Jamie at the final exam, he had traveled to the other boys, the ones who hadn't made it. Mike, Eraxes, and a group of select council members and upperclassmen had been forced to surround the infant dragons who were in agony from the death of their human. Mike had been forced to kill the dragons to prevent any further agony. Dragons could not exist without a human; it was part of the bond that sustained the Tarragon tribe.

Now that this boy was dead, he would have to kill another young dragon. It was the most painful part of the job, and not one that he had thought of when he volunteered. His goal had been to curry favor with the council and he had thought being in charge of the first year exam meant making sure that the students were prepared, and then guiding them through their first days afterwards. He knew some of his students would die, but he had foolishly thought that he wouldn't be attached to them. He thought they would be blank faces, not real people whose lives had depended on him. He had failed them, all five of them, and while he was grateful it wasn't more than five, it shouldn't have been that many.

Nick, Spencer, John, Blake, and now Sammy. Gone forever. He

was the one who had to make the phone calls to the parents and tell the lies about various accidents. The council had an entire list of lies to use depending on the student's personality and activities. Football accident, drinking accident, suicide, all horrific in different ways and Mike knew that his call changed the lives of the people on the other side of the call forever, in ways he couldn't possibly imagine. They were taking his lies and changing their lives based on them.

A few families were already members of the Tarragon tribe and those were almost a relief: he could tell the truth. Sammy's parents were in the tribe; this phone call would not be as painful as the others. But Mike knew he would have nightmares about it just as he had been having nightmares about all the other calls, and the other boys. He tried to push the memories aside whenever possible, but the only time he had ever felt at peace since the first year exam was when he was straddling Ashton.

Mike flushed. He shouldn't be thinking of sex at a time like this, but he couldn't help it. He wanted Ashton. Not the sex; he was too traumatized by the boy's death and the thought of killing the young dragon and making the phone call. He wanted Ashton to be at his side and be a support for him. He wanted that sense of completion that had swept over him when Ashton came, that sense that he was treasured and special. But he knew it would never happen, because Ashton didn't care about him. He was just one more fuck, and there was nothing he could do about it.

A tear broke loose as one of the doctors pulled him away from the bed.

"He's gone," the doctor said. "Don't you need to take care of his dragon?"

"Yeah," Mike muttered. The doctor looked mildly sympathetic, but mostly impatient. How could a healer not understand the pain that went into taking a life, even if you were sparing that life from agony?

Mike went to the corral outside where the small dragon was being kept. Normally injured dragons were also here, but they had been cleared away today because everyone knew the boy would die. No injured dragon needed to see an infant killed. Two council members were already standing by. The baby dragon was in a little room similar to a horse stable and they stood guard outside. The baby's screams of pain were audible from the doors of the hospital hundreds of feet away, and they grew louder and more chilling as Mike drew near. He didn't look at the council members, just reached for the spear that would kill the infant. He grabbed it, but the council member holding it didn't let go. He finally looked up. It was Ashton.

"Let me take this one," Ashton said quietly.

The other council member looked surprised, then glanced at the baby and nodded. "It's harder on babies," she said. "You have to hit them just right for a painless death."

Mike gratefully released the spear and moved into position behind Ashton, to catch the baby if it tried to escape. But the baby was in too much pain and lay on the floor, writhing and kicking wildly. Ashton hefted the spear, tossed it up and down in his hand once, and then threw it with a force and precision that shocked Mike. The baby lay motionless and blood seeped from where the spear had pierced it. He took a deep breath and tried not to vomit, as he had after killing the first dragon.

The first dragon had been horrific. It was out at the breeding grounds, surrounded by eggs and the promise of new life. The body of the boy lay nearby, stiff with death and surrounded by a pool of blood. The baby dragon kept clawing at the body as if trying to wake up the boy, but there was no more waking for him. The screams were terrible to hear, and the confusion and fear from the dragon had been contagious. The two men with Mike had handed him a spear and he had done his best to kill the dragon with a single blow, as Ashton had done, but he was inexperienced and it had taken three tries before the baby was killed. Three agonizing blows that were surely as painful for Mike as they were for the baby.

Afterward he had stumbled to the brush and vomited for a long time, long after everything in his belly had come up. He heard the others taking care of the bodies but he didn't care anymore. There was blood on his hands that would never be cleansed. The council had marked him as their own, and because of them, he was a killer.

Ashton turned away from the baby he had just killed without looking at Mike.

"I believe you have a phone call to make," he said, pulling the sleeves of his robe taut. Ashton strode out of the corral without another word, leaving him and the other council member to load the infant's body onto the cart and carry it to the burial grounds.

No words were said in memorial as the baby was buried in the ground – no words were ever said over a dragon who hadn't had a chance to live – but Mike silently prayed that the little dragon had lived a life with more good in it than bad, and that the dragon had experienced love at least once. Probably not, he reflected sadly. The dragon's partner had been in the hospital the entire time and the two couldn't speak telepathically, so the little dragon had never had a chance to feel the bond between dragon and human.

Another tear threatened to fall but he willed it back, not wanting to look weak in front of the council member. She was a tall woman with red hair that perhaps at one time shone like fire, but now lay limply in a ponytail like a fox's pelt. Her eyes were merciless and he wondered if he would eventually lose his sympathy in these dreadful events. Would he eventually become numb to the horror of losing a child and a dragon? Would he eventually think like her, not caring about the loss of life and only caring about the most pragmatic way to kill? He shuddered slightly.

"Ashton has taken a liking to you," she said suddenly, unexpectedly.

Mike scoffed. "I doubt it."

She examined him and he shrunk under her emotionless, analytical gaze.

"Perhaps you are too close to see. It is not always pleasant being the subject of his attention," she added.

Mike thought of the spanking and blushed. Had Ashton done that to other people? It seemed so intimate and personal, but it had also seemed like he had a lot of experience. And even though it was meant as punishment, Mike couldn't help but view it as pleasure now that it was over. It had hurt like hell at the time, and he still couldn't sit down without wincing, but it had made the sex so much more incredible. It had sensitized him in a way he had never expected.

"I don't know what you mean," Mike said stiffly, hoping it would end the discussion.

It did. They walked back from the burial grounds in complete silence, only now her expression was a little amused. She didn't say goodbye but rather vanished down one of the paths towards the dragon canyon, leaving him to continue alone. He headed straight for his rooms. He would make the call there.

At the thought of the call, his heart sank. Thoughts of Ashton had briefly rescued him from the heaviness of his job, but he couldn't put off the call. As soon as he was alone in his room, he called the parents. Sammy's mother answered and she knew immediately what had happened.

"Mr. Ferrin? What's wrong? Is it the exam? Oh God!"

"Mrs. Gordan, I'm sorry to inform you that Sammy died during the first year exam. The thoughts and prayers of the entire academy are with you in this time of mourning."

The last was a lie, but one he always felt he had to add. He knew his predecessors didn't say anything like it; if anything, the man right before Mike had seemed to delight in making the phone calls and destroying people's lives. But Mike would never be that callous, and he knew that there were some people on campus who cared. Sammy's friends cared, even if the academy as a whole never stopped to pay tribute to the boys who didn't survive the exam. Maybe Mike could institute a moment of silence for them. That would assuage some of the grief he felt.

He talked to the mother a little longer, and then talked to the father. It was painful, agonizing, and he was amazed that no council members stopped by to spear him. He was in just as much agony as the little dragon had been, only unlike the little dragon, he would survive this. This would become just one more memory, one more incident in his life. He would get past it.

By the time he got off the phone he was emotionally and physically drained. He went to his bedroom and collapsed. He was just about to drift into a no doubt nightmare-laden sleep when something on his desk caught his eye. It glinted golden in the light. He stood up and stared. There was a note from Ashton that read only: *To my pet.* Mike stared at what must be a gift and realized what it was. He stared in disbelief and lifted it in the air.

It couldn't be.

CHAPTER TWENTY-FIVE

The Plan

Jamie leaned forward in anticipation as Scott sat beside him on the bed to explain his plan.

"I wasn't thinking clearly before," Scott said, shaking his head. "But Jamie, the Queen's mate has the same power as the council. That means that if Narné and I mate with you and Marisol, the council can't touch us."

Jamie hesitated, remembering how Marisol had grown silent when he asked if the council would harm another dragon. If the council didn't care about the welfare of the dragons, would they respect their own laws? He tried asking Marisol, but she was thinking about swimming and on the brink of sleep. Her mind was difficult to predict at times and reminded him of a child's. He was a little annoyed, but mostly grateful because it meant that she was nowhere near ready for the mating flight.

"Jamie, you can speak to all of the dragons, right?"

He nodded.

"That means you can set up a distraction. The other dragons will listen to you because you rule them. I checked with Narné – the other dragons are enthralled by you. Many of the dragons can't speak to their own partners, so they're fascinated by you. All we have to is figure out a strategy for distracting the other dragons in the chase while Narné swoops in to claim Marisol."

"You think that would work? What kind of distraction do you mean?"

"Open the chase. Invite the other dragons to join and there

will be complete chaos. The eight council members will have to get rid of the other dragons before the chase can continue, and while they're busy, Narné will act."

Jamie pursed his lips. The thought of inviting other people into the mating flight was terrifying, almost as terrifying as the mating flight itself. What if one of the others succeeded? What if the distraction proved too successful and Narné came too late? He longed to tell Marisol but he didn't want to trouble her. She hadn't been upset with the original situation anyway, so perhaps she wouldn't want to help him.

He glanced at the other room where Marisol was sleeping. What if she didn't help him? What if he was on his own? He shivered. Scott wrapped his arm around Jamie.

"Don't worry, love. We'll work it out. We'll talk about it more and figure it all out so that everything goes according to plan. We'll make sure there's no chance you get hurt. We've got time, after all."

"Won't I get in trouble for doing that?"

"If we time it right, they'll think you did it on accident. Everything is so chaotic anyway during the mating flight. It wouldn't be the first time that someone accidentally called on other dragons, although usually the dragon is doing the calling and not the human."

"What is it like? The mating flight, I mean."

Scott sighed and stroked Jamie's hand. "When it starts, you'll feel a flush of heat like arousal. You'll see the world the way Marisol does and lose control of your body. The others in the mating flight will be near you and they'll come to your side. Depending on how deep inside Marisol you are, you may not even feel anything besides her experience."

"Then how will I know to summon the other dragons?"

"It will take self-restraint on your part so you don't get completely lost before you call them, but I believe in you. You have a strong will. You partnered with a queen, after all. And we'll practice so you know exactly what to do."

Jamie nodded. "What does Narné think?"

"Well," Scott said slowly, then he paused. His eyes grew distant and Jamie realized he must be talking to his dragon. "Narné says that if we can successfully distract Arion and Eraxes, the plan will probably work."

"But will the distraction work? Can we distract them?"

"That's up to us," Scott said. "Narné can see some things in the future, but not everything. Do you think you're up for it?"

Jamie shut his eyes. It would be a challenge, but they had time. Narné's assurance gave him confidence as well. But still, it felt like Scott was asking him to open the flight without a guarantee that he would be the one to win, and Jamie was frightened at the thought of everyone on campus chasing after him. He still didn't even know how the mating flight worked for him; he knew that Marisol would be flying with the dragons chasing, but he didn't what he would be doing. Scott's explanation didn't help much, and no one else had really explained what he would be doing during the mating chase, except to say that when Marisol had sex, he would also be having sex. If he invited everyone on campus to the mating flight, was that the same as asking everyone to have sex with him?

He flushed. There were so many questions, but there was time. He tried to reassure himself that Scott would never encourage him to do anything against his best interests. Everything Scott did, he told himself, Scott did to protect him. Scott loved him, after all. He smiled and opened his eyes. Scott's brow was creased with worry and Jamie could almost see the concern and love pouring out from him. Jamie's sharpened sense of smell picked up the emotions clearly and he ran a hand across Scott's face. The scent dissolved into Scott's ordinary honey scent and Jamie smiled.

"I trust you, Scott," he said. He tilted his head to kiss Scott, but a knock at the door interrupted them.

Jamie moaned. Amar. He had nearly forgotten that his friend was coming over for a late dinner. Scott looked confused and defensive, as if he thought the council were closing in around him for even mentioning a plan. Jamie was grateful Amar hadn't come earlier, because there was no way they could work on the plan with Amar present.

"It's Amar. Can you get the door?"

Relief washed over Scott's face and he sprang to his feet, hesitating briefly before leaving the room. "This has to remain a secret, especially from the council."

Jamie nodded in agreement. If Narné was worried especially about Arion and Eraxes, then he would have to make sure to keep it not just from the council, but from Ashton and Mr. Ferrin in particular. If either of them or their dragons found out about the plan, then the distraction would fail and someone besides Scott would win the chase.

Scott vanished into the living room just as another knock sounded on the door. Jamie heard the door open and the two men greet each other. He reluctantly sat up, wincing as his side began to ache. He still had to check in with the doctor, he remembered. Maybe he could just call. Surely they didn't expect him to walk to the hospital this late at night. It was already dark, after all. Scott came back in his room and gave him a kiss.

"I'll let you two talk. I'm in 301 if you want to talk to me later, but you should probably go straight to sleep. I'll see you tomorrow, okay?"

"Okay," Jamie said. "I'll call you when I get up. Maybe you can walk to the doctor with me."

"Of course," Scott said, leaning down to kiss him one more time before leaving.

Jamie stood up and went into the living room. His things were still mostly in boxes and Amar was making himself at home looking through the boxes marked 'Kitchen'. An extra large pizza from his favorite pizza delivery place was on the counter. Jamie laughed.

"What are you looking for?"

Amar straightened, looking slightly guilty. "I didn't mean to go through your stuff."

"But you are," Jamie pointed out.

"It's just I didn't pack very well and I left all the plates and

stuff, so I figure you packed them and they're around somewhere."

"I wondered why I had so much stuff," Jamie said. "Half of it
must be yours!"

"Well," Amar said, "I didn't want you coming back to an
empty dorm. Yup, it looks like this whole box is dishes my mom
sent me last month. You can keep them, of course, you know,
until you get your own."

"No," Jamie said. "They're yours."

Inwardly he was surprised he hadn't noticed that he was
packing his roommate's things. They had shared everything so
everything had been vaguely familiar. But of course he wouldn't
have had that many things just for himself. He had come to
college with everything he owned, since his aunt wouldn't store
anything for him, but even so his computer was the largest
thing he brought. His computer was already set up on a desk,
he noticed. He was extremely proud of it and had worked hard
to get the money for it. Scott must have set it up, he thought
warmly.

Amar gave him a plate and offered him some pizza, and the
two of them settled on the floor and leaned against the boxes.
The one thing Jamie didn't have was furniture. The academy
would provide him with furniture but he had to request it and
the requests took at least three business days, so he was limited
to a bed and a desk until the form went through. He would
definitely be spending time at Scott's place.

"So how have you been?" Jamie asked between a mouthful of
gooey cheese and pepperoni.

"Okay, I guess," Amar said. He set his pizza down and showed
Jamie a deep scar across the side of his face. "I was in the hospital for just a few hours. It's amazing how quickly we heal now."

He picked his pizza back up and hesitated before taking a
bite. "Jamie, I've heard some things from the upperclassmen
that make me wonder about Scott. They talk to us now," he
added. "Not like before when they just acted all superior. I guess
we're worth talking to now."

"Scott told me," Jamie said, lifting a hand to indicate that he didn't want to talk about it.

He still had a cold pit of fear in his belly at the thought of someone else sleeping with him at Marisol's first mating flight, but Scott had a plan and Jamie trusted him. It would be a good plan. They would somehow make it work, even if it meant lying to the council. To Ashton, who had seemed so nice, and to Mr. Ferrin, who had been there when Jamie woke up. He thought about Ashton and Mr. Ferrin being in the mating flight and ducked his head self-consciously. It was strange knowing that eight people were hoping to have sex with him and he wondered if they were looking forward to it or just getting it over with, as Marisol seemed content to do.

He thought about sleeping with Ashton and shivered. As much as he respected the man, he did not want to go to bed with him. Ashton was decades older and reminded Jamie too strongly of his father. It would be utterly wrong to sleep with him. Mr. Ferrin was a little better, but sleeping with a teacher was still something he didn't want to do. No, he and Scott would have to work out how to invite the other dragons to the mating flight so that Scott was the only one in Jamie's bed. It was the only thing Jamie could possibly tolerate; the only way Jamie would be able to live with himself afterward. Sleeping with anyone else would shatter him in a way that could never be repaired, he knew.

Amar looked shocked that Scott had told him and Jamie wondered if everyone on campus knew about the mating flight. If they knew, would they even want to join in? Scott said the other dragons were enthralled by him, but did that mean they would obey him? Would they obey their queen when she was so young and inexperienced? He needed to ask Scott about it as soon as possible. If they couldn't recruit other dragons to join in and distract Arion and Eraxes, then Jamie suspected their odds of success plummeted. Narné hadn't said if they would succeed if Arion and Eraxes weren't properly distracted, after all.

Amar cleared his throat and opened his mouth, then hesitated. Then he seemed to gather his courage to speak.

"He told you he was assigned to seduce you?" Amar asked in a tone of total disbelief. "Wow, that's pretty bold. And you forgave him?"

Jamie opened his mouth to say that of course he forgave Scott when Amar's words hit him. Assigned to seduce him? Assigned? Jamie was an assignment to Scott? Jamie felt as though the ground dropped out from under him and he watched rather than felt the piece of pizza in his suddenly numb hand fall onto his plate.

"He was what?"

CHAPTER TWENTY-SIX

Betrayal

Amar stared at the ground uncomfortably as Jamie reeled from the news. Had he heard correctly? Had Amar really just said that Scott had been assigned to seduce Jamie?

"I heard the upperclassmen talking about it," Amar said. "About you. How you were a difficult case and that's why Scott was assigned to you."

"What do you mean a difficult case?"

"Apparently, virgins can't bond with dragons, so the upperclassmen are assigned to the freshmen to make sure they aren't, you know, virgins. But you were different."

Jamie touched his lips in shock. He remembered the boy in the locker room exposing himself; what Jamie had assumed was a prank. He remembered Mr. Ferrin asking if he needed anything, touching him in a way no teacher should. He remembered all of the girls who had approached him when he went out with Amar, girl after girl, always upperclassmen, always interested in him and no one else. Sure, a few had ended up with Amar, but they had always been after him and he had always deflected them. And he remembered Scott and how persistent he had been, how Scott had carefully woven himself into Jamie's life and then quickly escalated their relationship.

Jamie had told Ashton that he had been the one to initiate the intimacy in their relationship, but only because Scott had laid the groundwork. Scott had seduced him perfectly, but Jamie had assumed it was out of love. Scott had even confessed his love just the other day! Why was Scott keeping up the façade if it was all an act? Perhaps Scott was too afraid to tell Jamie that it wasn't real, and that was why Scott had agreed to the mating flight. Perhaps Scott wasn't upset about having someone else sleep with Jamie but he was instead relieved. Perhaps that was the real reason Scott wanted to open up the mating flight!

Each kiss that Scott had left along Jamie's shoulder the previous day tingled, and Jamie remembered the shock and horror he had felt when Scott had seen his scars. Scott had accepted them and everything that they represented, but did he really care about Jamie or was Jamie just a means to an end? The cold fear that had been in the pit of his belly since hearing about the mating flight erupted into full-fledged panic as he realized that Scott might only be using him to gain power through Marisol. After all, why would anyone love Jamie?

Panic began to course through him and the world became tinted in a crimson wash. His hands trembled and he stood up, not quite knowing what he was doing. He needed to act, to move, to do something to ameliorate the fear and pain in his mind and body. Had Scott betrayed him? Did Scott want other people involved in the mating flight so that he would have a good excuse for not winning? Or, if Scott did want to win, was it for Jamie's sake or because he wanted to have power equal to the council?

Enough, Marisol said with a snarl. His anger and fear had woken her from her nap. She appeared in the living room and knocked several boxes out of the way as she made her way over to him. Amar went white and flattened himself against the floor as if that would save him.

"Is that Marisol?" he asked, his voice a full octave higher than usual.

"Yes," Jamie said. He could only barely speak; he was on the brink of tears. "She won't hurt you."

"I dunno, she looks pissed."

Marisol carefully avoided Amar and instead butted her head into Jamie, hard. He winced and felt one of his bandages unravel under his shirt. He would definitely need to go to the doctor tonight. If only the doctor had an answer for his heart. Had Scott been lying to him this entire time? As he thought about his breaking heart, his real heart started pumping faster and his stomach began to cramp. His vision began to tunnel as his breaths became short and quick. Everything was happening so fast and the panic was overtaking him. What were Scott's intentions? What did Scott want? Was Scott honest when he kissed Jamie's scars and confessed his love, or was it all a ploy to become as powerful as the council? How could he ever trust Scott again when Scott had lied about the basis of their relationship?

Jamie covered his ears with his hands even though it didn't work to drown out his fears. He felt like he was about to faint and he tried to take deep breaths, but he couldn't. His chest felt like it was on fire and he could barely breathe. It felt as though he were going to die and he wondered if people really could die from a broken heart.

You are being a fool, Marisol said. She was angry. He had never felt her angry but he knew it was because he was so upset. She had never felt him upset before and was trying to protect him, but there was no way to protect him from himself. They were both experiencing unusual emotions and their panic, fear, and anger were bouncing off each other and beginning to escalate. Already Jamie could feel himself slipping away from his body but he repeated Ashton's words and held firm to his grip on reality.

He did what he had to do to save you, she said. *You needed to be ready so we could bond.*

"Wait," Jamie said, turning to face Marisol. "Don't tell me you knew about this, too! And you didn't tell me?"

Amar slunk into the kitchen where he would be safe from their argument. Jamie was glad; Marisol's anger was contagious and he could feel it sweeping over him and invading his mind just as her playfulness had earlier in the day. The pain in his side was nothing as he leapt closer to her and slammed his fist into her massive side. He couldn't harm her, but he wanted her to know how angry he was. His body was primed for action and he felt an overwhelming surge of hormones encouraging him to fight and attack the dragon who represented the lies that were causing his pain.

"What kind of partner are you if you keep secrets from me?"

I didn't want to upset you!

She lowered her head and he could feel the anger ebbing from her. She hadn't expected him to react this way, he could tell, but it was too late. He was furious and since Scott wasn't there to receive his anger, Marisol would have to do. He was vaguely aware of Amar making a phone call.

"What else are you hiding from me? What more horrible secrets are there that you think I'm too weak to hear?"

You are not weak, Marisol said, lifting her head on her neck and staring down at him. *A weak human could never bond with me.*

"I didn't bond with you, you bonded with me," Jamie said, thinking of the lake and how he had just laid there passively while she had done all the work. He had done nothing, nothing at all except adapt when she broke into his mind.

You think adapting was an easy task? Marisol asked. *Most humans would die from what you experienced. You saw the world the way I do, felt it and smelled it and sensed it and if you choose, you could do it again. Our world is not a world for humans but you entered it. Perhaps you did not fight like this human did,* and she tossed her head at Amar, who cowered in the kitchen and kept looking at the door as if wondering whether or not to make a break for it, *but you battled yourself and won.*

"Then why don't you trust me?"

Jamie slammed his fist into her side again and burst into tears. Suddenly it was all too much. The lake, the dragons, the mating flight, and now losing Scott on top of everything else; he couldn't bear it anymore and he slid to the ground in tears. His body was out of control and so was his mind, and he couldn't face it. He gasped for breath and his vision cleared as he started taking deeper breaths, but his heart still pounded in his ears and felt as if it were about to explode from his chest. Marisol crooned at him and tried to head butt him gently but he shoved her away. She was part of the problem. She was the reason Scott had lied to him. If Marisol didn't exist, then Scott never would have been assigned to seduce Jamie and maybe they would have met each other naturally and had a nice, normal relationship. If Scott would even be interested in him without Marisol.

Scott wasn't even there when he woke up, Jamie realized. He was taking care of Marisol. The dragon had come first to Scott, so maybe it was true that Scott was after the power of being the queen's mate. Maybe he had been assigned to Jamie and when Jamie partnered with a queen, Scott had kept the illusion going in order to gain even more power. Jamie's entire body trembled with the thought of the betrayal that would entail. It would mean that everything he knew about Scott was a lie, but it was possible. Everything was possible. Scott lied to him, and there was no way of knowing the truth.

A sob broke loose and suddenly Amar's arms were around him and he was weeping into his friend's shoulder.

"I can't do it," Jamie whispered. "I can't keep going on my own."

"You're never on your own, Jamie," Amar said, patting his back and holding him tight. "You've got me, you've got Marisol, you've got the whole school looking out for you."

Jamie shuddered. The whole school. The whole school would literally be after him if he followed Scott's plan. How could he have even considered such a plan? Opening himself to the advances of everyone on campus? Never, he vowed. He would never go through with the plan for a man who only cared about him because he was assigned to care.

"They don't care about me, they care about her," he said with an angry gesture towards Marisol.

Now it was Marisol's turn to cower. She slunk down against the wall and he could feel her confusion and fear, but he didn't feel like comforting her. She was the cause of all of his pain. He wished he could just go back in time and never come to the academy to begin with. Or at least he wished he had touched that other egg, the first egg he had seen on that fateful day at the lake, and gotten a normal dragon and not the queen dragon that everyone was so obsessed with. He just wanted a normal life, with normal relationships. He didn't want some stranger having sex with him just because of a bunch of rules made by people he didn't know. And he didn't want to think of his boyfriend being assigned to seduce him just so he could bond with the dragon easier.

Marisol let out a whine and he could feel her fear mounting. She fluttered her wings and tried to reach out to him with her mind but he ruthlessly cut her off and instead focused on Amar. Amar had always been a true friend. He had never lied, unlike Marisol and Scott. Another sob broke out at the thought of his two supposed friends lying straight to his face. The tears seemed to have a calming effect because in a few minutes his body seemed to return to normal and his heart was no longer beating as loudly, and his lungs were no longer burning with the need for air. He felt calmer, but the rage inside of him was still flaming as he thought of Marisol and Scott united against him.

There was a knock at the door followed by its opening; Jamie flinched at the thought of Scott returning, but when he looked up he saw a different figure in the doorway. It was Mr. Ferrin.

CHAPTER TWENTY-SEVEN

Collared

Mike looked around his bedroom to make sure no one was there, then picked up the large metal chain that Ashton had left on his desk with the note. The chain was just the right size for Mike's neck and he knew without asking that it was a collar. Beautiful, elaborate, and more like a necklace than a traditional collar, but a collar nonetheless. Ashton was leashing his pet.

Mike held the ring up. It looked to be solid gold. Eraxes studied it as well from his vantage point across the room. The ring was in two halves with a latch, so it would snap around his neck and fit snugly. It was thin and would be barely visible when worn, unless the viewer knew what to look for. Most people would mistake it for a necklace, Mike decided. He hoped, at least, because he knew there was no way he could turn down this gift.

He thought of all the things Ashton had done for him, especially helping with the killing of the baby dragon, and knew that Ashton had the right to ask this of him. Ashton could ask anything and he would obey. Eraxes snuffled unhappily and Mike remembered the conversation he wanted to have with the dragon. He needed to make sure that their relationship was still strong. It was unusual for the bond between a dragon and human to weaken after the first critical months, but Mike knew his bond with Eraxes had been strained for too long. He couldn't afford to lose his dragon. But first, the collar.

"Should I wear it?" he asked his dragon.

"Ashton insists, as does Arion," Eraxes replied out loud. They rarely spoke telepathically anymore. Mike hoped to fix that, but not now. He was too emotionally drained from the killing of the baby dragon and the phone call. "It will not hurt you and it will help you achieve your goals."

"My goals?"

For a moment, his mind went blank. Then he remembered the rebellion that he was supposedly a part of. He had forgotten them completely in the rush of the first year exam. But they were the only reason he had volunteered for the exam in the first place – he was trying to get on the council so that they could eventually overthrow Ashton. He felt his mouth turning downwards into a frown at the thought. He despised what Ashton did, but he was starting to crave Ashton – his touch, his help, everything about him. He longed for that sense of completion he had felt when they made love and he knew the only way he could feel it again was to obey Ashton completely and hope to win the man's heart. How could he work towards destroying something that he craved?

He didn't see how getting closer to Ashton would help the rebellion, but he trusted Eraxes so he snapped the collar around his neck. It fit perfectly, just loose enough for comfort but not so loose that it dangled or got in his way. It looked like a strand of gold around his neck and he decided it looked good with his shirt opened a few buttons. Eraxes added his admiration as well.

Mike was just about to unbutton the rest of his shirt and get ready to bed when Eraxes let out a hiss at the same time his phone rang. It was Amar.

"Amar, how are you? Still having problems adapting?"

Amar had been to an older hatching ground and his dragon, Tephis, showed signs of having a special talent, even though no one knew what it was yet. Amar and Tephis were one of only four pairs who could communicate telepathically from this year's batch and as a result they were having difficulties adapting to life together. The first few months were critical to forming the bond between human and dragon and even though the danger of the first year exam was over, if the bond didn't form properly there was still a chance that the student and dragon could lose their bond and die as a result. All of the students were supposed to call Mike or another instructor if they were having problems with their dragons, and idly Mike realized that no one had probably informed Jamie of that.

"It's not me," Amar said breathlessly. "It's Jamie. He's fighting with Marisol. I don't know what's going on but it's not pretty. We're at Jamie's apartment."

Mike felt his hands grow numb and his stomach flipped. "I'll be right over."

An argument with Marisol at this stage of their relationship could be deadly. Mike quickly but carefully slid onto Eraxes's back. Eraxes was already primed to leave, having felt the fight from Marisol's mind. Mike leaned down close on Eraxes as the great beast leapt out of the large, open window designed for dragon exits and headed towards the apartments. Blue dragons were not designed for passengers with their large ridged heads and spikes along their spines, but Mike and Eraxes had long ago figured out a safe way for Mike to nestle between the spikes and he was grateful now. Even running to the apartments wouldn't be fast enough.

Jamie had passed the most important part of joining with a Queen when he bonded with her, but history had taught the academy that bonding was a long process, especially for Queens. The previous Queen's partner had killed himself because he couldn't stand submitting to other men, but if he had been properly bonded to his dragon it never would have happened. If anything happened to damage the bond between Jamie and Marisol, there was a great chance that Jamie would also become suicidal and Marisol would have to be killed. The bond between them was all important and kept both of them alive; as long as it was functioning, they would be able to survive anything but if it failed they would both die.

Mike wondered what had set Jamie off, and whether Scott had told him about the mating flight. He hadn't considered that Jamie and Marisol's bond might not be strong enough to withstand that news yet. Marisol had taken the news of the mating flight restrictions well, and if the bond between them had been functioning properly then her calmness should have rubbed off on Jamie or at least given him hope. But if they were fighting, then perhaps they weren't as well-bonded as Mike had thought.

He arrived outside the apartments and ran up the stairs. The elevator to the sixth floor might have been faster, but the elevators were unreliable and his feet were swift. He reached the door out of breath and knocked once before bursting in.

Marisol huddled in the corner and her confusion was evident. She did not understand why Jamie was upset. Jamie, for his part, was hugging Amar and in tears. Mike approached Jamie slowly. Without knowing what set Jamie off, it was hard to figure out what to say but he could almost feel the bond between human and dragon evaporating as he stood there.

"Jamie," he said quietly, not wanting to frighten the boy. "You need to say something to Marisol."

"She lied to me! Why should I care about her?"

Mike tugged at his lip with his teeth. He had hoped that Jamie would be angry at Scott, or at fate, or at anything besides his dragon. Being angry at Marisol was undoubtedly what was causing their bond to falter and he knew now that it would fail if he couldn't get them back in communication quickly.

"She's a child, Jamie. I know she seems like an adult, but she's not. Whatever she lied about, she did because she didn't know any better."

Jamie lifted his head and looked at Marisol, then shook his head. "She's old enough."

"She's not," Amar said, patting Jamie's back encouragingly. "And she's scared. Look, I barely had the courage to tell you and I'm your best friend. How do you think she felt, knowing about Scott and not knowing whether or not to tell you?"

Mike ran his words over in his mind. What exactly about Scott were they talking about?

Jamie turned to Marisol and it was clear that they were talking. Jamie's face took on the slightly vacant look all humans took on when they spoke to dragons telepathically. It was a good sign if they could still speak. Then Jamie shook his head again.

"She's hidden so much. I thought I could trust her. I thought we were different."

"You will be different," Mike said. "But trust takes time. You two barely know each other. And remember that you're still injured. If she's keeping secrets from you, perhaps it's because she doesn't want to injure you further. She's only been alive a little more than a week and most of that time you were in a coma, after all."

Jamie flushed and looked embarrassed. He fingered his side and Mike could make out a faint red spot. The boy must have reopened one of his wounds, Mike thought with a sigh. It would be back to the doctor for him.

"Look, Jamie, we need to get you to a doctor but first you need to spend some time alone with Marisol. Talk to her, embrace her, understand her. And Marisol, if you have any other secrets, Jamie is strong enough to hear them. You can trust him."

Marisol nodded her head once and looked at Jamie shyly, as if wondering if he would agree to the private talk. Jamie looked reluctant. He was still next to Amar, although no longer embracing the man, and Amar pushed him gently towards the dragon.

"Go on, man. She's important to you and you have to take care of her."

Jamie nodded. "All right. We'll talk. Will you help me get to the doctor after?"

Mike stepped forward. "I'll help. I'll be waiting outside when you're finished."

He took Amar's arm and pulled the boy out into the hallway with him, leaving Jamie and Marisol alone. The mood in the room had changed, though, and he sensed contrition in both parties. As soon as he and Amar were in the hallway, he patted Amar's shoulder in gratitude.

"Thank you for calling. Something very bad almost happened back there."

"Yeah," Amar said. "Tephis was going crazy. He kept saying

Marisol's bond was breaking and you needed to hurry up."

"He knew her bond was breaking? Interesting," Mike said. He wondered if perhaps that was Tephis's strength, the ability to see the bond between dragon and human. "So what exactly set Jamie off?"

Amar blushed and stared at the ground. "Just some rumors from the upperclassmen. Nothing, really, sir."

"Rumors?"

Amar kicked his toe into the ground. "That the upperclassmen were assigned freshmen to seduce and Scott was assigned Jamie. That's not true, though, is it?"

"It's true."

He relished the look of shock on Amar's face at his casual response. It was always refreshing to see someone who was shocked and appalled at the council's decisions. Mike no longer had any qualms about seducing younger men and he had lost his shock at the assigned seductions years ago, but it was good to see someone so surprised. He was willing to bet that within two years Amar would be seducing young women at the council's request. But perhaps Amar was mostly shocked at the homosexual nature of Scott's assignment. For a straight man, it was one thing to be assigned to seduce a girl and something entirely different to find out that a man had been assigned to seduce you.

Amar was still staring at him in shock when the elevator dinged down the hall and a familiar shape got off. Amar and Mike went silent as Scott approached. He glared at Mike and looked at Amar in confusion.

"What's wrong? Is everything okay? Narné said something was wrong with Jamie."

"Did Narné tell you to come up here?" Mike asked.

"No," Scott said. "He said it wouldn't help. But I came anyway. Jamie is my boyfriend, after all."

Amar glared. "Is he?"

Scott looked taken aback, and Mike stepped between them. "Look, it's been a long day for everyone. Amar, why don't you head back to your apartment. I'll take care of things here."

"If Jamie sees him," Amar began, but Mike cut him off.

"I'll make sure he doesn't. Now run along."

"Yes, sir," Amar said grudgingly, then padded down the hallway to the stairs. He was only one story away from Jamie; Scott was three stories away but they were all in the same building.

"What's going on?" Scott asked when Amar was gone.

"Jamie knows about you being assigned to him," Mike said. "He's pissed. He almost lost his bond with Marisol he was so upset. I think for the time being it's probably best if you don't see him. I'll let you know when he's ready to see you again."

Scott went white, then red, an interesting display on his dark face. "He – he knows? Narné didn't mention that. I have to talk to him. I have to explain."

"Not now, not after everything else he's been through. Give him time."

Scott shut his eyes. "So I'm supposed to back off and let you swoop in?"

"You could say that," Mike said with a grin. He had no plans of seducing Jamie, but getting on Jamie's good side now would improve his chances in the mating flight and he *would* win the mating flight, no matter what it took.

"I won't stand for it," Scott said.

"Think of Jamie, and what he's been through these past few days. Don't you think he needs some time to be alone with Marisol, without worrying about you?"

Scott opened his mouth as if to argue, but then he shuddered and shut his mouth with a click. "You're right. I shouldn't intrude tonight. But I won't go away forever. The instant he feels better and he's had a chance to think things through, I'll be at his side."

"I wouldn't expect any different," Mike murmured, wishing for one moment that Ashton felt about him the way Scott felt about Jamie. He felt the collar weighing heavily against his neck and he wondered if it was simply a mark of possession or if it entailed any feelings, romantic or otherwise. He hoped there were feelings attached to it, because he certainly was developing feelings for Ashton at an alarming rate. It was as though not having the man was making him want Ashton even more.

Scott turned and headed back to the elevator after giving Mike a soul-searching stare, and Mike wondered what he saw. Perhaps he saw that Mike was no real threat in terms of stealing Jamie's heart because Mike's heart was elsewhere, or perhaps he simply saw the truth that Jamie was an exhausted boy who needed a break. Either way, Mike was glad Scott left when he did because moments after he vanished, Jamie opened the door. The blood on his side was a little larger and Mike decided they would use the golf cart to drive the boy to the doctor.

Jamie sighed as they waited for the elevator as if knowing that Scott had been there, and he stared at the number three as they rode to the first floor, but he said nothing. The third floor was Scott's floor, Mike thought, and he wondered how Jamie felt about the man now that he knew the truth. He helped Jamie into the golf cart and Jamie leaned into him as they drove to the hospital.

CHAPTER TWENTY-EIGHT

No More Secrets

"**Y**ou could have told me," Jamie said as Marisol sank into a comfortable position.

They were alone together and he almost wished Mr. Ferrin had stayed in the room. He kept his distance from the dragon but his anger had faded. Sometimes it was easy to forget how very young she was, and how inexperienced. Just over a week ago she had attacked him, and instead of being killed, he had been able to enter her world and bond with her. Even though she had lived for centuries in her egg, she had no experience with the outside world and everything was still new to her. It was so easy to forget all of that, Jamie thought. She seemed so mature at times.

I didn't want to upset you and it doesn't change his feelings for you, Marisol said.

"It does, though," Jamie said. "They aren't real feelings. And even if they are, how do I know when he started having real feelings for me? Maybe he loves me now, like he says. But how do I know he loved me when we- when we were together? It was my first time and it was his job. That's not love."

Marisol was silent. She didn't understand, he could tell. He sighed and thought about the mating flight and Scott's plan. He still couldn't figure out Scott's intentions with the plan, but he could only think of negatives. Either Scott wanted to appear to put in a good effort at winning the chase but didn't really want to win, or else Scott wanted to win and gain power. But even so,

Jamie would almost rather go through with the plan than obey the council, who just assumed that they could dictate who Jamie slept with. At least Scott's plan gave him some freedom.

The mating flight will not happen yet, Marisol said. *I am not big enough.*

"Thank god for that," Jamie muttered. Then he stared at Marisol. "Can you see the plan in my mind? What do you think about it?"

I won't be the one inviting the other dragons, she said. *You will have to do that. I will be flying.*

She sounded happy at the thought of flying and for a moment Jamie saw her thoughts and felt the air thread between his toes as he flew through the sky. Then he braced himself and was back in his body.

"But if I do call the other dragons, would you be upset?"

It will not matter, she said. *I do not care about my mate as much as you seem to.*

"No, you don't, but you should," Jamie said. "I feel your feelings all the time since I've woken up, and back at the lake, I had to experience the world the way you do. Why is our relationship so one-sided? Why can't you understand the world the way I do?"

Marisol tilted her head. *I am bigger than you. My mind cannot comprehend the world in your terms.*

"Try," Jamie said. He placed his hands on her side and pressed his forehead against hers. "Just focus on me and let me show you what I see and feel."

She snorted and her breath rippled across his shirt and bandage. Then she shut her large eyes and he heard a buzzing sound like he had heard at the lake shore. His vision grew sharp and everything became super-saturated with color just like at the lake. Marisol's scales were angry crimson and mellow brown mixed together in a kaleidoscope and he shut his eyes to keep from getting dizzy, but the colors were still there.

He pressed his forehead against hers more and tried to focus on what he wanted to show her: the love he had felt for Scott, the betrayal he now felt, and the utter terror at the thought of a mating flight without his loving boyfriend. What was he supposed to do without Scott? He didn't know how to navigate this strange world; he had hoped to rely on Scott to teach him what he needed to know. Who would take Scott's place?

The buzzing grew louder until he slapped his hands against his ears, even though he knew it would make no difference. It wasn't an external sound, it was the sound of Marisol's mind entering his. The colors grew brighter and suddenly the scents of the room grew unbearable – he could smell the pizza that had fallen on the floor and the pizza still in the box, the soda that Amar had been drinking, even the plates had their own china scent that swamped him until all he could do was gasp for breath and hope it would be over soon.

Then Marisol pulled away and the buzzing faded. The colors and scents returned almost to normal, but the world maintained a faint glow and he was intensely aware of the smells in the room and in the entire area. He could smell Mr. Ferrin and Amar outside, and his heart clenched as he smelled that unique combination of cloves, honey, and dandelions that was Scott. He did not want to see or talk to Scott.

Marisol lowered her head and used it to pull Jamie close to her body for a hug. She was gentle with her claws and he hugged her back. Already she was developing spikes along her spine, but he was still able to hug her without any problems.

I understand now, she said. *I see how much he means to you. I will not keep any secrets from you, especially about him.*

"Thank you, Marisol," Jamie said tenderly as he stroked the ridges above her eyes.

I see why secrets make you upset, she said. *Narné and the others keep many secrets from me. I did not think to question them, but now I am curious about what they will not say.*

"Narné keeps secrets?"

He is not talking to me now. He thinks both of us should rest. He thinks we are both confused.

"Maybe he's just upset because I found out the truth."

Yes, Marisol said. *He is upset. He did not want to hurt you.*

"Well, it's too late," Jamie said. He fingered the bandage on his side. He was bleeding. He was hurt in more ways than one, but at least the physical injuries could be taken care of.

"I have to go to the hospital, I think," Jamie said. "Will you be okay here?"

I am with you always, Marisol said firmly. *Even when I am not at your side. We will never have secrets again.*

Jamie smiled and kissed her cheek. Her cheeks turned a slightly darker red in response and he could feel her pleasure. Her emotions didn't spill over into him, however, and he wondered if this second bonding had fixed that problem. It would be nice if he didn't have to constantly worry about slipping into Marisol's mind.

He waited until Scott's scent was gone before he left the room and found Mr. Ferrin waiting for him. Mike, he reminded himself. He needed to start calling the man by his first name, especially since Mike was going to be part of his mating flight. He inwardly squirmed at the thought, but then he remembered Scott's betrayal and reassessed Mike. Mike had been at his side when he woke up and had come here to save his and Marisol's relationship. So far, Mike had been extremely kind to him and appeared to genuinely like him. Would it be so wrong if he ended up with Mike?

Yes, a part of his mind answered, but he squashed that part ruthlessly. He needed to start dealing with the reality of his situation. If Scott didn't love him, then he would have to be with one of the eight council members and at least he knew Mr. Ferrin. He knew Ashton, too, of course, but there was the matter of the age difference. Besides, Ashton was more of a father figure than a lover. No, Mike was the best option. If he couldn't have Scott.

As they rode the elevator he stared at the third floor where he knew Scott was waiting. Did Scott truly love him? He would have to wait to find out, and he wasn't sure how he would be able to tell the truth when he saw Scott again. Scott had lied to him, straight to his face, and seduced him as part of an assignment. How was he ever supposed to trust Scott again?

Mike helped him into the golf cart and Jamie blushed as the man's hands lingered on his arm. He knew Mike was only making sure he got up to the seat safely, but he couldn't help but imagine those hands touching his bare skin. The idea wasn't entirely horrific, but it made him long for Scott. After Mike got in beside him and started driving to the campus hospital, Jamie made the bold move of leaning against him. Mike responded by wrapping his arm around Jamie's shoulder to hold him in place, and for a moment Jamie shut his eyes and imagined that it was Scott holding him. But his heightened sense of smell couldn't be fooled and he found himself shifting uncomfortably. Mike pulled him closer.

"You're injured, just relax," Mike said. "I'll make sure nothing happens to you."

Jamie swallowed hard and nodded. Mike must not even realize the source of Jamie's discomfort: being held by a man who was not Scott. Yet he didn't want to be held by Scott either. It was too confusing. He wanted Scott and he didn't. He wanted to trust and he couldn't. How was he supposed to make sense of everything when people kept piling on more and more? He was still reeling from learning that dragons were real, and that he was bonded to a queen. And now he was also supposed to nurse a broken heart? It was too much for anyone, let alone a kid who had no experience with love. He didn't even want to think about the mating flight; he would worry about that later when it became a more pressing issue.

"What's wrong, Jamie?" Mike asked.

Jamie realized he was crying and hastily wiped the back of his hand across his face to rid himself of the evidence of tears. His nose was stuffy and his eyes were hot. His throat was closed up and it felt like he would never be able to speak it was so tight.

"It's just," he managed, "a lot. Right now."

Mike gripped his shoulder firmly and pulled him into a hug even as they drove.

"I know it's hard," Mike said. "But it'll get better. Everything will look better in the morning, when you've had a chance to sleep."

Sleep did have a strong allure and Jamie was so tired he knew he could fall asleep in Mike's arms if he wasn't careful. Would that really be so bad, he wondered. Falling asleep in Mike's embrace? It wouldn't be betraying his relationship with Scott, because they didn't have a real relationship. But they were boyfriends, and hadn't officially broken up, so even though Scott had no real feelings for him, Jamie thought to himself, he still should honor the bond between them.

The thought of Scott not having feelings cut like a knife in his gut and he doubled over. Mike sped up, a worried look on his face.

"I didn't realize your injuries were so bad," he said, sounding almost guilty.

Jamie nodded and clutched his belly. He didn't want to tell Mike that it wasn't the remnants of Marisol's clawmarks causing him pain but rather the agony of knowing that Scott's confession of love might be fake. No, he told himself firmly. Scott meant what he said. He had to, Jamie thought with a hint of desperation. But there was only one way to tell, and he wasn't ready to face Scott and hear the answer. If Scott said that he was only using Jamie, Jamie didn't know what he would do. He didn't know if he would survive.

Marisol crooned comfortingly in his mind and he shivered. Scott's love was the only thing that had kept him alive during the exam when Marisol had attacked him. It was the only thing that kept him going on the long flight back to the hospital, and it kept him fighting for life even as his heart stopped. Scott's love gave him hope when he heard about the mating flight, and it gave him courage to live for the present and embrace every moment together without fear of the future. He was even willing to open his mating flight to the entire campus to hold onto Scott's love. If Scott's love wasn't real...

We will deal with him, Marisol said. *But you will not give up life because you have me now. We are together, with or without Scott.*

Jamie nodded. Scott had gotten him to where he was, but Jamie couldn't keep relying on him for everything. Jamie needed to form other attachments, and Marisol should be his main concern. Human love came second to dragon love. The thought came from Marisol but Jamie repeated it to himself. Human love came second. But the thought of Scott kissing him, his tongue tracing Jamie's scars, the memory of Scott opening his pants and taking Jamie into his mouth, would not go away. He didn't just love Scott, he wanted Scott sexually and the thought frightened him. He had never wanted anyone the way he wanted Scott and his perfect, dark and handsome body.

"Everything okay?" Mike asked.

Jamie realized he was clutching Mike's shirt. He released it with a start and tried to smooth it out. Then he realized that by smoothing his shirt he was running his hands along Mike's body and he stopped, confused. He knew he was blushing and the feel of Mike's torso felt branded into his palms.

"I- I was talking to Marisol," he said. It was partially the truth, and he didn't feel like talking about Scott.

"Is everything all right between you?"

"Yeah," Jamie said. "It is now. Thanks for making us talk."

"It's important to stay connected to your dragon at all times during the first few months," Mike said.

Jamie nodded, although he hoped Mike didn't mean the kind of connection that caused the buzzing and hurt so much. Probably not, he decided. Mike probably just meant staying in mental contact with Marisol.

"But not too connected, right?" Jamie asked. "Ashton showed me how to get out of her mind when I get stuck. That's okay, isn't it?"

Mike smiled and patted his shoulder. "Yes, you and Marisol have an unusually close connection. You'll have to find your own comfort level where you both can exist separately, but also share your thoughts when you want."

"Are you and Eraxes like that?"

A pained expression crossed Mike's face and Jamie wondered

if something had happened to Eraxes. He still remembered the blue dragon looming over him on the shore of the lake, suggesting that it would be better to give him a quick death than attempt to save him. If Narné hadn't been there, Jamie would have died that day. He didn't hate Eraxes, because he knew the dragon was only trying to do what was best, but he didn't trust the dragon's judgment. He wondered how closely the dragon reflected the human and if Mike's judgment was also suspect. With a shiver, he realized that if Mike won the mating flight, it would mean that Eraxes would mate with Marisol. Even though Jamie would prefer Mike over the other approved council members, he didn't want his dragon stuck with Eraxes. Scott's plan was sounding better and better, even if Scott was lying about loving Jamie.

"Eraxes and I are going through a rough patch," Mike said softly. "It shouldn't have happened. As a result, Eraxes has been a little short-tempered lately. I suppose I have too," Mike added in a reflecting tone. "That is why I don't want you and Marisol to lose the bond between you. It's… painful for the bond to weaken."

Jamie nodded. He tried to reach out to Eraxes but the dragon politely declined to talk to him. Instead he reached to Marisol and asked her what she thought of Eraxes. He could feel Marisol shifting in her massive dragon bed at his apartment as she responded.

He is a good dragon. He rescued me from the lake.

Jamie's brow wrinkled. He had forgotten that Eraxes was the one to carry Marisol after the exam while Narné was carrying Jamie. Perhaps he had good in him after all, as Marisol said. He was considering this idea when the golf cart came to a stop. Mike stepped out and came around to his side to help him out. Jamie tried closing his eyes and pretending it was Scott again, but again his sense of smell foiled him and he knew without question that it was Mike helping him out of the cart and into the hospital.

The nurse at the front tsked when she saw the blood on

Jamie's shirt and bandage, but didn't say anything as she led him back into a private room and asked him to get into a hospital gown. Mike lingered for a few minutes.

"Are you sure you're okay being alone?" he finally asked.

"Yeah, of course," Jamie said.

"If you need anything, call me," Mike said, pressing a piece of paper with a phone number into his hand. "If you lose this, all of the doctors and nurses have my number."

"Thanks," Jamie said, hoping Mike would leave soon. He felt awkward holding the hospital gown to his chest, unwilling to change in front of the other man but wanting to be obedient and change as quickly as possible.

Mike departed and Jamie changed, stacking his clothes in a neat pile on the hospital bed before getting in the bed. He drew a blanket up to his chin. He felt exposed in the gown that only covered his thighs and left his legs exposed. His legs were too white, he thought, and he was embarrassed that someone might see them so he carefully tucked the blanket around him.

No one came in. He shifted and wondered if he was supposed to do something to indicate that he was dressed. Maybe open the door a little. But he was already in the bed and comfortable, and his side was truly aching now. He didn't want to move. Eventually a doctor will knock and come in, he told himself. He wished that Mike were still here to go get a doctor for him. Mike wasn't a bad person, he thought. He thought of Scott and he squirmed. Was Scott a bad person? Which of the two was better? Scott said he loved him, but Mike was the one at his bedside when he woke up, taking him to the doctor in the middle of the night. And surely Mike would never seduce someone because he was assigned to do so.

But Scott wouldn't leave his mind, and as Jamie waited for the doctor he remembered everything he and Scott had done together and decided that there had to be some truth to it. It couldn't all be lies. No one was that good an actor. Scott had to have some feelings for him. The only question was what those feelings were, and when they started. Jamie shifted uncomfortably in his bed and tried to distract himself while he waited, but thoughts of Scott kept dancing through his mind.

CHAPTER TWENTY-NINE

Party

One week passed without sight of Scott, and Jamie tried to reassure himself that it was a good thing. It was now Friday after their last class of the semester, and Amar and his girlfriend were coming over for a small party to celebrate the start of winter vacation. It wouldn't be much of a vacation, however: the dragon training classes would continue through the break, as Jamie had guessed. They would continue to get weekends off, and a few days for the holidays, but they would still be going to class nearly every day. Still, they didn't have homework and all they needed to do was show up and pay attention, so it was easy enough. And the lessons they learned were invaluable.

Jamie had already learned a way to rub Marisol that helped her shed scales faster so that she could reach her full height and weight sooner. He was a little reluctant about it, because the sooner she was full size the sooner he would have to worry about the mating flight, but his instructor assured him that the sooner a dragon reached full size the healthier that dragon would be. Marisol had to be close to full size by now, he thought, imagining her heft in his mind. She had been growing steadily for much of the week but had leveled off the past day or so, and only ate one cow yesterday instead of her usual two. Lessened appetite was a sign that full growth had been reached, according to the instructor.

He tried not to think about the mating flight – tried not to think about a lot of things, really, with Scott being at the top of the list. He knew Scott had tried to see him a few times, but had turned away for some reason. Maybe Scott couldn't face what he had done any more than Jamie could. At night, though, Jamie gave his imagination reign and pretended that Scott really did love him. He imagined Scott straddling him, whispering his love over and over again while kissing his scars, his body, making him feel warm and accepted and loved. Jamie's hands slid over his own body while he imagined but whenever he approached a climax, Amar's words came back to him and even in his fantasies Scott drew away with a smirk and said it was all a lie. Jamie was left feeling shattered, his arousal abruptly doused, yet he knew the next night he would imagine Scott again in hopes of a different ending.

There would be no different ending until he talked to Scott, but if the man wouldn't approach him, he wasn't about to make the first move. It would hurt too much if Jamie extended the olive branch and Scott snapped it in half. No, Scott would have to make the first move, and Jamie wondered what was taking so long.

He brushed Marisol thoroughly to get her ready for the party, but none of her scales fell off. She was definitely either full grown or almost there. Mike had stopped by to see her several times during the week, and he was amazed at her growth but said they didn't really know how quickly queens could grow. The last queen, he said, was partnered to someone who didn't want a queen, so she had grown slowly and in fits and starts. Marisol was different because she and Jamie had a good bond.

And the bond was good, now that they were no longer keeping secrets. He hadn't slipped into her mind a single time because he already was in her mind most of the time, sharing his thoughts and feelings with her, and she shared her experiences back. They were together in a way he had never imagined and it took away some of the sting of losing Scott. With Scott, he could never truly understand what the man was thinking, or if he was being honest. With Marisol, he could just concentrate and know everything she was up to.

"Hello," a voice called. It was Amar, peeking his head in the front door. Jamie had left it unlocked so his friends could come on it, and he called for them to head to the kitchen as he kissed Marisol's scales and headed to the kitchen himself.

Amar and his girlfriend Nikki had brought an entire buffet, it seemed. Two six-packs of Coke, chicken wings, salsa and chips, hummus and pita bread, and a veggie tray that looked as if they had thrown it in as an afterthought – there was no rhyme or reason to the foods, but they all looked delicious.

"Um, you know it's only us, right? I mean, I know I said party but I didn't invite anyone else," Jamie said worriedly. He had never really gone to parties in high school and he considered any gathering of friends a party, and now he wondered if he had misled them about the nature of the night. Worse, he worried that they had invited people and he would be stuck hosting a real party when he really just wanted to hang out with friends.

"Relax," Amar said. "I just thought we might like a variety. Nikki's vegetarian so I wanted to bring something besides chicken wings."

"He's lucky I let him bring them at all," she added with an exaggerated shudder.

"How can you be vegetarian when your dragon eats meat?" Jamie asked.

She laughed. "I do lots of things my dragon doesn't do. But I don't try to inflict my preferences on her, if that's what you mean. No, she's a carnivore and she needs meat, but I'm not. People can live perfectly good lives without meat. But I don't want to preach," she added. "I'm not one of those vegetarians. You eat what you eat and I'll eat what I eat, and we'll all be fine."

Jamie nodded and gestured to the living room. It was newly furnished with furniture from the academy, and the academy had spared no expense. Although Jamie hadn't gotten to choose his furniture and he suspected most of the rooms looked like his, it was incredible what had been accomplished in the for-merly bare room. An interior designer had been called in while he was at class, he had been told, and now he had couches, end tables, a circular coffee table that doubled as a footrest, and a massive television that he never could have afforded in his wildest dreams.

Based on Nikki and Amar's gasps as they entered the living room, their rooms were not as elegantly stocked and Jamie flushed in embarrassment. He wasn't used to having the nice things; he was always the kid who didn't have enough. His entire apartment had been upgraded, though he doubted Amar had noticed the new appliances in the kitchen or the fancy chairs and tables in the entryway.

"Wow," Nikki said. "It pays to be queen."

"Kind of," Jamie said, gesturing to the heavily furnished room. "She can't really get around in the rooms anymore. She's stuck in the bedrooms and the bath."

"Can we meet her?"

"Of course!"

Jamie glowed with pride as he led them out of the living room into the bedroom area. The hallway was enormous and virtually empty so that Marisol could use it, and there were three large doors, one for the bathroom, one for Jamie's room, and one for Marisol's room. He opened the door to Marisol's large chambers and Nikki gasped. Marisol was standing in the center of the room to greet them and she looked far larger than she did when she was curled up in the dragon bed. Her scales glistened crimson in the light and the long spikes on her spine were ivory-white in comparison. She lowered her head and gestured for them to come in. She didn't like to speak aloud, as the other dragons did. Jamie translated.

"Nikki, this is Marisol. Marisol, this is Nikki, and you might remember Amar."

She ducked her head in greeting and extended a claw. Nikki went white but Jamie reached forward to take the claw.

"You're supposed to shake it. She's seen people shaking hands and she likes to greet people this way."

Amar shook her claw but Nikki still looked hesitant. "You're sure she won't attack?"

I am not a child, Marisol growled.

Jamie translated and Nikki apologized profusely. "It's just that some dragons don't have good self-control, even weeks after the exam," she explained. Then she reached forward and shook Marisol's claw.

Jamie could sense Marisol's desire to scratch the girl for doubting her and firmly told Marisol to behave and not prove Nikki right. It wasn't worth it, he told her. She reluctantly obeyed and returned to the dragon bed to sulk.

"Um, I think that's it for Marisol," Jamie said. "Why don't we go back and sample the snacks?"

"Great idea," Amar said. "I have to tell you the crazy thing Tephis did yesterday. Made all the instructors mad, but he was delighted."

As Amar talked, they wandered back to the living room and arranged themselves on the couches. Jamie felt a bit like a third wheel, sitting all alone on the couch while Amar and Nikki sat together on theirs. He helped himself to some hummus and laughed when Amar got to the punchline of his story. He was a little glad that Marisol was so obedient. It sounded like Tephis rarely listened to Amar and never told him what he was doing in advance. It made for some good stories, and undoubtedly it was a relationship that Amar was comfortable with, but Jamie needed more security. He needed a dragon that shared things with him and didn't keep secrets. He needed Marisol and he didn't know what would have happened if he had ended up with anyone else.

"So what's your dragon like?" he asked Nikki, knowing it was a question everyone liked to answer. Everyone at Tarragon Academy was proud of their dragon and Nikki was no exception. A bright smile lit her face as she began to talk.

"She's wonderful. Not as much of a handful as Tephis, thankfully," she added with a laugh. "She's a blue dragon, a deep, sea blue. Her name is Yanna. She's from a traditional breeding ground and I can't talk to her the way both of you can talk to your dragons, but we talk to each other plenty to make up for it."

Jamie wondered if she resented not being able to talk tele-pathically, but her voice didn't have any accusation or anger. He was glad he had ended up at the breeding ground that he had, even though he hadn't known at the time that the island was a breeding ground. Had he known, he might not have gone and he would have missed out on Marisol.

No, Marisol said. *We were destined to be together.*

Destiny, Jamie thought. Once he had thought that he and Scott were destined to be together, but that was before. He took a deep breath. He had vowed not to think about Scott during this get together. If Scott were here, he wouldn't be a third wheel, and with Scott at his side to give him courage, he wouldn't feel so shy about speaking.

He realized with a start that Nikki had been through a mat-ing flight. She knew what it was like and how it would feel, but he didn't know if it was appropriate to bring up in front of Amar. It seemed like girl talk, almost, except he was a guy. But he knew that he had to talk to her about it. She was the only person who could tell him what he needed to know.

"Nikki," he began, and then he stopped. He couldn't do it. Couldn't ask about the mating flight with Amar in the room.

Amar and Nikki exchanged a glance and Amar stood up. "I think I'll see how well-stocked your bathroom is," Amar said be-fore vanishing into the apartment.

Jamie blushed. Had they known all along that he would ask? It hadn't even occurred to him to ask until just now. Or was Amar just being his usual diplomatic self and he realized that whatever Jamie wanted to ask was for Nikki only?

"Um, Nikki," he continued. "Can I ask about the mating flight?"

"Sure," she said. "I've been through a lot."

"How often do they happen?"

"A lot. For most women it's once a month, but for some it's only once a year," she said. "It might be different for a queen."

"What- what is it like?"

Nikki hesitated and a blissful expression crossed her face.

"There's a sudden feeling of warmth. That's the only sign it's starting. You'll learn about it, I'm sure. You lose control of your body, but you're still in your body. It's strange, but not frightening. It's like you're inside the dragon and yourself at once. But maybe you feel this way already."

He nodded. "Sometimes I get lost in her mind, but not lately."

"Then it won't be frightening for you," she said. "It is for some. Not for me. For me it was… a revelation. And then the mating begins. Dragons chasing you for control. And when one catches you, you feel it twice, in the dragon and in yourself. It's incredible."

She blushed. "Was that too much information?"

"No," he assured her. "That was what I wanted to know. Everyone keeps talking about the mating flight but no one has ever told me what it will be like. Did you get to choose who you mated with?"

"When you're in a relationship, that dragon usually wins," she said. "Otherwise it's random."

"Does Amar know?" Jamie asked with a laugh. She sounded so calm about it, perhaps it wasn't something to worry about.

"It's fine if he does," she said. "And in my next flight, I hope it's Tephis who wins."

"Hope," Jamie repeated. "You hope, but you don't know for sure?"

"There's always a chance someone else could swoop in," she said. "But everyone is kind. No one would ever dream of hurting the dragon or the person getting chased."

Jamie kept his mouth shut, but he thought of Marisol's silence on the subject of hurting dragons. He hadn't asked her to explain that silence and he didn't want to. There were some things he didn't want to know. But still, her calmness and acceptance of the mating flight were extremely reassuring. And there would be good people in Jamie's flight, even if Scott wouldn't be there. Part of him wanted to open the flight and hope that Scott would come and rescue him, but he tried to tell himself that Scott no longer loved him. If Scott loved him, then why had he waited a full week to come and see him? And Scott had come close, Jamie knew. He could smell the trace of honey in the hallway sometimes and he knew that Scott had been standing outside his door, but why didn't Scott knock and come in?

Jamie sighed as Amar came back in the room. He was together with his friends and his dragon, but the person he really wanted was three floors away and didn't want to see him. What was he going to do?

CHAPTER THIRTY

Blocked

When Scott went to visit Jamie the Saturday after Jamie was taken to the hospital, there was once again a bouncer guarding the hospital door preventing him from getting in. Scott tried back several times, but there was always someone there to stop him. Sunday was the same. If he wanted to talk to Jamie, it seemed that Scott would have to go back to his old habit of hanging around after Jamie's classes as he had before they started dating.

On Monday he waited after Jamie's first class but Jamie never showed. When he asked another student, the student shrugged and said Jamie wasn't in class. Scott immediately fell into doubt and self-loathing. Jamie's injuries must have been more serious than he had expected, and they were all his fault. Everything was his fault, in fact. If it weren't for him and his seduction, Jamie would be healthy and happy right now, busy in his classes.

Or he would be dead, a more practical voice said. Without the sexual experience Scott had been able to give Jamie, the boy likely would have died during the bonding. And as painful as it was to know that Jamie hated him, he was just grateful that Jamie was alive. Even if Jamie hated him for the rest of his life, he would never undo his actions. If it hadn't been Scott, it would have been someone else, someone who didn't love Jamie, someone who would hurt Jamie the way Mike had hurt Scott. What Jamie didn't understand was that Scott had told the truth – he had started falling in love with the boy long before the assignment. In fact, the only reason he had requested Jamie as an assignment was to protect the boy and keep him away from sleazebags like Mike. If only he could explain it to Jamie, but Jamie was nowhere to be found.

Tuesday arrived and Scott heard that Jamie was finally back in classes. But when Scott showed up after class, he found Amar waiting.

"Jamie told me you might be here," Amar said. "He doesn't want to see you."

"What did you tell him?"

"The truth," Amar said, holding his head up as if trying to look proud. "That you don't really care about him."

"I care about him more than you know. Do you have any idea what I sacrificed to be with him?"

Scott shivered as he thought of his promise to sleep with other men. Ashton had said the promise would be enforced, and Scott believed it now that he knew more about the council. That was something he would need to explain to Jamie as well, but not now. He would wait until it happened, until the council called on him to sleep with someone other than his boyfriend.

"I know he was nothing more than an assignment to you," Amar snapped. "But he's my roommate, and my friend. I won't let you hurt him."

"If he doesn't want to see me, then I'll leave, but you have to try to understand how much I love him."

"You shouldn't throw that word around so lightly," Amar said. "Jamie might just believe you."

"He should," Scott said. He was getting angry and he didn't want to appear angry if Jamie showed up. "I don't use that word lightly. He's the first and only person that I love, and I don't care if you don't see it. I just want him to see it."

Amar sniffed and turned his back as if to indicate that he had nothing more to say. Scott thought about staying and hoping to talk to Jamie, but with Amar there as well the conversation would be poisoned. He needed to get Jamie alone. He would visit Jamie's apartment that night, he decided. When Jamie would be alone and ready to talk. Scott returned to his own classes and stared at his watch as the hours passed.

Almost before he knew it, it was evening. Jamie's dragon training class had ended and all of the freshmen were back in their rooms. There were no parties the first few weeks after the exam: students were too exhausted from taking care of their dragons. He went to Jamie's door but as he got off the elevator he saw the same bouncer from the hospital standing guard outside. The bouncer acknowledged him for once and waved him over.

"Look," the man said. "The kid doesn't want to see you. I'm here to see that it happens. If I see you hanging around anymore, you're in for a pounding."

"Did he say he doesn't want to see me?"

"Those are my orders," the bouncer replied.

Scott wondered if there was anything besides orders in the man's fat, thick head. He tried to contain his anger but he couldn't. He was about to shout Jamie's name when a fist slammed into his gut. Gasping for breath, tears rimming his eyes, he crouched over the injury as the bouncer rubbed his hand.

"Stay away from him," the bouncer repeated.

The bouncer grabbed Scott by the collar of his shirt and dragged him to the stairs. For a moment he was terrified that the bouncer would throw him down the stairs, but the bouncer only pushed him slightly and told him to get off the floor. Scott obeyed, his gut vibrating with agony.

He tried again the next day and received a black eye for his trouble, and the third day he sent someone else up instead to see if the bouncer was still there. He was. Scott needed to talk to Jamie, but it looked to be impossible with Amar guarding him during the day and the bouncer guarding him every other minute. He would have to wait for one of them to slip up.

It was the first Sunday of winter break when Scott noticed the bouncer leave the building. Over a week since he had last seen Jamie. Scott raced to the stairwell and was at Jamie's door in moments. He glanced at his watch – noon, not too early to visit someone. He knocked on the door and prayed that Jamie opened it before the bouncer came back. He had never seen the bouncer leave before and he didn't know why he had, but it was surely temporary.

Scott knocked on the door again. He heard a sigh on the other side, and then Jamie opened it and gestured for Scott to come in. Scott entered with a little more haste than usual and closed the door firmly behind him so the bouncer wouldn't suspect anything. He took a deep breath. He knew he looked flustered and out of breath, and there was just the faintest bruise left from the black eye. He had been so focused on getting here that he hadn't planned what he would say. But Jamie started before Scott had a chance to talk.

"I don't know what you can say to change anything, Scott," he said. "No matter what you say, things are just so rough right now I really don't want to deal with it. I think it's best if you just leave me alone for a while. I need to sort things out and get my priorities straight, and I can't do that with you here."

Scott opened his mouth and was cut off.

"I don't want to hear anything from you," Jamie said. "Nothing you say can help. I just- I just want you to leave."

"I think you want to hear me," Scott said. "Just let me say one thing."

Jamie's face contorted as if he were struggling with an interior battle and finally he nodded. But he turned his back to Scott as if he couldn't bear to face him. Scott wondered what he thought Scott could possibly say. His heart went out to Jamie, not for the first time, as he wondered what Jamie's life was like that he automatically expected rejection. The thought of anyone hurting Jamie filled him with rage and it was with perhaps a little too much force that he reached out to grab Jamie's arm.

"I love you, damn it," Scott said as he yanked Jamie around to face him.

Jamie's mouth opened and shut as his face registered anger and shock.

"Whatever you've heard, I did it all because I love you and I couldn't bear to let anyone else have you, so yes, I requested to be assigned to you. I wanted you and I wanted to protect you and I love you more than you can possibly know."

"But-" Jamie stopped, looking around as if for a reason to reject him. Scott wouldn't allow it. He loved Jamie passionately and the only way to convince Jamie was to show it.

Scott pulled Jamie into a kiss. He resisted at first, but when Scott ran his tongue along Jamie's lips he moaned, opened his mouth to the kiss, and melted in his arms. Scott held him up as he mapped Jamie's mouth with his tongue, tracing every surface and claiming it as his. Jamie's hands hesitantly moved up along Scott's biceps to his shoulders, then one of his hands tangled in Scott's hair while the other moved to his back. The boy's tongue began to dance with his own and it felt as though lightning were passing between them.

Scott let his hands drift downward to the soft curves of Jamie's buttocks. The boy whined and pressed into the kiss, his hand tightening in Scott's hair. Everything felt right and he knew Jamie was experiencing the same sense of rightness. They broke away from the kiss to gasp for air and Jamie rested his head again Scott's chest. Scott kissed the top of his head.

"Why didn't you come sooner?" Jamie asked.

"You're very well guarded," Scott replied. "That bouncer outside wouldn't let me near."

"What bouncer?"

"Guard, whatever you want to call him."

Jamie pulled away and shook his head. "There's no one outside. Who are you talking about?"

Scott paused. "You really didn't know you were being guarded?"

"I would know. I can sense people and smell them because of Marisol and there is no one outside."

Scott reached out to Narné and asked him about the bouncer. The answer astonished him. "Wow," he said. "Apparently that's his dragon's special talent. He's only visible to people he wants to see him, and no one else can even sense that he's there."

Jamie's face took on a vacant look as he no doubt checked Scott's information with Marisol. A brief flash of anger crossed his features.

"Marisol knew I was being watched, but she didn't say anything because Arion told her it was my request. How could she not know he was lying?"

"Children don't expect adults to lie," Scott said. He wasn't surprised by Arion's involvement; the dragon was just as manipulative as his partner.

"She's not a child anymore," Jamie said, and fear appeared in his eyes. "She's full grown."

Scott's heart stopped for a moment. Full grown. The mating flight would be soon, much sooner than he had anticipated. Jamie's fear was more than understandable. They needed to focus on the plan, but he still didn't even know if Jamie forgave him.

"You know, Jamie," he said. "I've told you that I love you, but you haven't said the same to me."

Jamie laughed. "Are you worried? How could I not love you? Even if you lied to me, it doesn't change my feelings. I don't know if I can trust you, but," he hesitated and looked up at Scott through his lashes. "I do love you."

It was all Scott needed to hear. Plans for the mating flight could wait. Right now, he needed to make sure his Jamie understood the depth of his love. He scooped Jamie up as the boy laughingly protested, and carried him over to the bed. He laid Jamie down gently and kissed his forehead, his cheeks, his nose, and finally his lips. He was going to give Jamie everything the beautiful boy deserved.

CHAPTER THIRTY-ONE

Accidental Flight

Jamie laughed as Scott set him down on the bed. Scott's confession of love rang through his body with far more conviction than the last time the man had admitted to loving him, because now Jamie knew the full extent of his love. It was everything Jamie had hoped: Scott loved him from the first and the assignment came second. So what if Scott had been assigned to seduce him, Jamie thought. Now he knew for sure that it didn't affect Scott's feelings for him. Scott loved him, and that was that. Nothing else should matter.

Scott kissed him fiercely, possessively, in a way that made Jamie melt inside and out. Scott was claiming him with his kisses and Jamie adored the feeling of being protected and cherished. He had thought that Marisol was enough, but now he knew that he needed Scott as well. He belonged with Scott, and nothing would ever pull them apart. Scott's hands reached to unbutton his shirt and Jamie hesitated for a second out of habit. He was still ashamed of his scars, even though Scott had seen and accepted them.

"I love you, Jamie," Scott said between kisses. "All of you."

Jamie smiled and tousled his boyfriend's hair playfully. "I love you, too, Scott. All of you."

"Even the part of me that seduced you?"

Jamie's smile faded. "Why did you do it?"

"I was in love with you from the moment I saw you," Scott said. "When I heard that the Council was assigning someone to seduce you, I couldn't let it be anyone else. I had to have you. I love you."

"Have you seduced anyone else?"

"I've had sex before," Scott said. "But not at anyone's command."

Jamie touched Narné's mind and saw that it was the truth. Cautiously, he kissed Scott.

"I accept all of you, and I'm glad you were assigned to me. But would we still have ended up together without your assignment?"

"Yes," Scott said firmly. "It may have taken longer, but we would still be together."

Something inside Jamie relaxed and he took a deep breath. He wasn't just an assignment to Scott, he was a true boyfriend. He ran his hands through Scott's hair and kissed him. Scott began unbuttoning Jamie's shirt and Jamie became aware that Marisol was watching the scene with a great deal of interest. She was tucked up in her dragon bed but as Scott and Jamie kissed, he felt her stretching out. She was hot, he realized, and trying to cool off.

He was hot too; on fire with Scott's caresses as his shirt was pulled off completely. He kicked off his shoes and peeled off his socks as Scott did the same. He took a deep breath, trying to still his rapidly beating heart. He was getting naked with Scott, and he could imagine where this would lead. He was going to lose his virginity, and the thought of being pinned beneath Scott while the other man penetrated him and whispered sweet words in his ear was making him hard already.

Jamie and Marisol moaned in unison as Scott grabbed the band of Jamie's pants and started to pull them off slowly as he nibbled his way along Jamie's collarbone. He and Marisol were filled with an inner fire that could only be quenched by having Scott deep inside and Jamie squirmed in an attempt to get his pants off faster. Sweat dripped down from his hairline as he scrabbled at Scott's chest in an attempt to get the other man's shirt off so he could feel skin against skin. He needed physical contact. He needed to be close to someone, anyone. He needed touch.

"Jamie, are you alright?"

The question didn't make sense. Of course he was alright, or he would be once Scott's bare body was pressed against his own. He pulled uselessly at Scott's pants, too hot and flustered to be able to unbutton the jeans.

"Jamie, say something."

"Touch me," Jamie begged.

His entire body felt like it was on fire and he needed Scott. Why was Scott pulling away? He heard the door open and smelled another man walk in. He barely recognized Mike. Everyone just blurred together; he could barely tell the difference between Mike and Scott except for their different scents, and even that was starting to blur. He didn't care who touched him, as long as he got the physical contact he craved.

"He's going into the mating flight," Mike said. "You need to get out of here, Scott."

"No," Scott said. Jamie heard a note of terror in his voice. "We have to stop him. He's not ready."

Jamie was ready, ready to be touched and caressed and penetrated. He needed someone and it didn't matter who. He just needed someone. Marisol was still in her room, but she was writhing in her dragon bed, struggling to subdue the arousal taking over her senses. Soon she would take to the air and summon the other dragons to chase her, and the winner would claim his place with Marisol and with Jamie.

"There's no way to stop him," Mike said.

"There has to be. What if he cuts his link to Marisol?"

"I doubt he would want to, or even be able to. This is happening, Scott, and as soon as Marisol leaves his apartment the other dragons will see her and their humans will be in this room for their chance to claim him. If you're here when they show up…"

"I know," Scott said. "But we have to do something. We have to at least try to pull him out. He doesn't want it, I know."

Jamie arched his back. He did want it. He wanted hands and

tongues and cocks on his body, caressing him, filling him. He knew that was the only way to cool him down and if the fire remained in his veins much longer, he feared he would roast alive.

"Look, Scott, we don't have much time. You have to get out of here. I'm trying to help you."

Scott sighed and leaned over Jamie. Jamie grabbed his head and tried to kiss him, but Scott's mouth moved to his ear instead. Scott sucked on his earlobe, then whispered, "Call the others. Open the flight. It's our only chance now."

Open the flight. Once that had filled him with fear, but now it filled him with excitement. His Marisol would have her pick of every dragon on the campus, not just the ones chosen by the Council. She would have freedom to quench the heat that was filling her.

He felt Marisol leap out the exit of the apartment, no longer able to stand being still. The cool breeze helped calm her. Almost instantly eight dragons were after her and Jamie grimaced. They were probably strong dragons, but were they the best? He would find out.

Jamie was practically vibrating with lust and he sent his lust into the minds of every dragon he could find, male and female, commanding them to chase his Marisol. It seemed as though the entire campus took to the air and through Marisol's eyes he saw the original eight dragons surrounded in a chaos of wings and fire. But what about him, Jamie thought. He needed release as well, and Scott was no longer touching him.

There were others in the room now, other men, but he couldn't distinguish who was who. Someone touched his shoulder and he curled into the touch. Another hand was on his other shoulder, and then hands appeared everywhere. Wherever someone touched him, the heat became less and he could breathe easier.

"Follow Marisol," a voice told him. It might have been Scott, but he couldn't tell anything except that it was male. "Be one with Marisol."

He shut his eyes against the shapeless male figures and focused on Marisol.

Marisol soared so high in the sky that none of the others could follow her. She peered down at them and wondered if any of them could possibly be worthy of her. She was so hot and she needed to feel another creature beside her, but she wouldn't let just anyone touch her. They had to be worthy. She dove down into range of the dragons to tease them and nine dragons surged into the sky towards her. With a snort, she returned to the higher altitude. Those were her potentials, she decided. The dozens of other dragons chasing her were desperate for her, but they wouldn't stand a chance.

She circled back and watched the nine competitors mingle with the other dragons. Two of her competitors crashed into other dragons and fell to the ground in the chaos. She dipped down again to see what would happen and the entire mass of dragons lifted towards her. Snorting again, she watched her competitors struggle through the morass of dragons wings and sheer chaos that was her mating flight. Then she began flying as fast as she could away from them. She would choose based on speed, she decided. If anyone could keep up with her, then they would be worthy to touch her.

Only two dragons were clever enough to extricate themselves from the jumble and dash after her, their wings pumping madly as they fought to catch up. A green and a blue, she saw. Both were medium-sized, which no doubt helped them escape the chaos. The other, larger dragons had been easily trapped due to their vast wingspan.

There was nothing wrong with being smaller, she decided. After all, she was barely full grown herself. And even the largest dragon was smaller than her, so it would be a size mismatch no matter what. She flew as quickly as she could, then returned to the high altitude and paused while the two dragons caught up. She was starting to get tired, and she was so desperate for the touch of another dragon. She flew lower and hummed in puzzlement. There was only the blue dragon following her. The green dragon seemed to have vanished. Well, she would mate with the blue dragon. He was handsome and strong, and had earned his place.

Two claws dug into her back and she shrieked. The green dragon was behind her! He scooted close to her back and latched on tightly to prevent her from escaping. Unable to use her wings fully, Marisol started to fall but the smaller green dragon held them aloft as he prepared to enter her. Marisol screamed in protest even while she craved his touch. She had been tricked.

Without warning Jamie was back in his own body and a man was over him, whispering for him to relax. Something large was pressing against his opening and he shouted in fear. There was incredible pain and then the man was inside him. Who was it? Jamie's eyes were glued shut, he couldn't open them, and there were so many people's scents surrounding him that he couldn't tell who this was. Scott, please let it be Scott, he silently begged.

"Hush, Jamie, relax," the man said, and Jamie tried to obey.

The man leaned so close that his breath tickled Jamie's ear. "It's me, sweetie. You did it."

Jamie's body melted at that, and the man was able to enter him fully. It was painful, but now that he knew it was Scott, it didn't hurt nearly as much. He trusted Scott. Scott would never hurt him.

Scott was inside him now, and as he started moving Jamie cried out in pained pleasure. He had never imagined it would feel so good. He felt Marisol crying out in pleasure as well and the doubled pleasure swamped his senses until nothing else mattered but the rhythm between them. Jamie threw his head back and grabbed Scott, begging him to go deeper. Scott obliged as much as he was able, and then the rhythm between dragon and man matched and it felt as though Jamie's entire soul was being lovingly penetrated. He saw into Scott's mind clearly and he knew Scott could see him as well. Marisol and Narne were just a thought away and Jamie gasped as he saw his own face through Scott's eyes and knew Scott was feeling everything Jamie was feeling.

The sex became rougher and Scott let out a sound of astonishment and joy. Jamie opened himself fully to Scott and felt Scott do the same. They were bonding, Jamie realized, remembering how it had happened between him and Marisol. Would he be able to speak to Scott the way he spoke to Marisol? He didn't know; all he knew was that this was the most magical moment of his life and he wanted it to last forever.

But it couldn't last forever, nor could it last much longer. He and Scott were both so sensitive and aroused that they wouldn't last, and it was almost with disappointment that Jamie felt his balls tighten in preparation for his orgasm. But when his orgasm hit, he realized his fears were misplaced. The initial wave of pleasure hit him and Marisol at the same time and it was so powerful that he nearly blacked out. The second wave left him boneless and limp, and the third wave sent shivers through his body as his body finally finished expelling his pleasure. He could feel Scott experiencing the same waves at the same time and that only heightened both of their pleasure.

When they were finished, Jamie lay limply on the bed, barely aware of anything except Scott above him. Scott pulled out slowly and it barely hurt at all. Once Scott was out, the link between them vanished and Jamie was Jamie again, with no connection to Scott. But he knew that every time they had sex, that link would still be there. He felt Marisol sinking into a hot spring with Narné and knew she would soon fly back to the apartment for a very long nap. He was exhausted himself and wanted to sink into sleep, but he could hear angry voices and knew he needed to get up. With a sigh, he opened his eyes and faced the consequences of the mating flight.

CHAPTER THIRTY-TWO

New Life

Scott tried to argue with Mike, to find some way to pull Jamie out of the mating flight, but he knew it was too late. Jamie was in too deep. He should have known better. Most mating flights started when the human partner experienced great arousal, and Jamie had even warned him that Marisol was full-grown. But he had needed Jamie to know how much he loved him, and he hadn't considered the consequences. Jamie writhed in the bed, sweating profusely. He seemed completely unaware of the world around him.

"Look, Scott," Mike said. "We don't have much time. You have to get out of here. I'm trying to help you."

Scott sighed and leaned over Jamie. Jamie grabbed his head and tried to kiss him, but Scott's mouth moved to his ear instead. Scott sucked on his earlobe, then whispered, "Call the others. Open the flight. It's our only chance now."

Jamie moaned and Scott hoped he understood the words. Jamie was so far gone he may not have even heard what Scott had said. Then a wave of lust hit him and he gasped. It was coming from Narné. Narné shot out of his dragon bed and took to the skies immediately, filled with a foreign lust and only one way to satiate himself: mating with Marisol. Jamie had summoned the dragons but if Narné's response was any indication, he might have done too good a job. There would be a lot of aroused, unfulfilled dragons at the end of the chase and Scott hoped other females would offer themselves to those males.

Mike grabbed his arm and led him to the door. The door opened from the other side and Scott was face to face with Ashton. Ashton grimaced at the sight of him, then grabbed him by the back of the neck. The older man glared at Mike, who fingered a gold chain around his neck nervously.

"You shouldn't be here, Scott," Ashton said.

"He was just leaving," Mike said.

"Quiet."

Mike shivered and backed up, physically removing himself from the conversation.

"You know what the punishment for interfering with the mating flight is," Ashton said.

"It hasn't started yet," Scott said, trying to sound defiant. "And there wouldn't be a mating flight if it weren't for me."

Ashton blinked as he processed those words and seemed to realize what had triggered the mating flight.

"I see," he said. "Well, your role is over."

Mike went to Jamie and laid a hand on the boy's shoulder. Jamie wrapped himself around his hand.

"Ashton," Mike said. "He's too deep in it. He needs contact so he can connect to Marisol."

Ashton went to Jamie and placed a hand on his other shoulder. The other six council members circled Jamie and each reached out to touch him. Scott bristled. How dare they touch his boyfriend in front of him? But he knew how important touch was during the mating flight, and none of them were touching him inappropriately. They were just taking some of the heat from the boy's body so he could safely transfer into Marisol's mind for the flight.

There was a knock at the door and suddenly people started pouring in the room. Amar was at the front and he had a dazed look on his face. Scott tried to block them from entering the bedroom, but they swarmed past him in their efforts to reach Jamie. He hadn't counted on the human partners showing up when he had suggested opening the flight, but here they were. There would be more than just disappointed dragons, he realized.

Then everyone turned to Marisol's bedroom in unison as she flew out and the chase began. People tried to get close enough to touch Jamie and the eight council members had to fight to keep their place. Scott snuck forward and managed to get a hand on Jamie's hair. The council members were too busy to notice him.

He shut his eyes and connected to Narné. His dragon was doing well, he was pleased to see, but a dragon and rider combined was the only sure way to win. The other dragons, including Arion and Eraxes, were on their own because their human partners were so distracted. He and Narné operated as a team. Surely it would give them an advantage. Marisol began flying swiftly away from the chaos and Narné and Eraxes were the only two who managed to follow her. Scott spotted a cloud coming up and urged Narné to hide inside of it.

Marisol zoomed past them, then flew back casually, as if seeing what had happened to her pursuers. She cocked her head consideringly at Eraxes, struggling to backtrack and catch up with her, and right when it looked like she was going to fly to him and complete the mating, Narné popped out of the cloud and grabbed her.

Back in Jamie's room, Scott stood and shoved everyone else away from his prize. He was still heavily in Narné's mind, just as the others in the room were in their dragons' minds. The seven council members and Mike backed off and allowed him to mount Jamie. Jamie whimpered as Scott kissed him and pushed against his opening. He didn't want to hurt Jamie but the lust was all-consuming and he couldn't go slow, as Jamie deserved for his first time. He needed to be inside Jamie, needed it the same way Narné needed to be in Marisol.

Jamie was stiff as a board until Scott kissed him. "Hush, Jamie, relax. It's me, sweetie. You did it."

He barely managed to speak, the pleasure was so intense, and it only grew. By the time he reached his orgasm, he and Jamie were in total harmony with each other in a way he had never known could exist between two humans. Afterwards, he felt limp and satiated. But he knew his problems were only beginning, so he pulled out of Jamie and stood up to face the consequences of his actions. Ordinarily he would have been embarrassed by his nudity, but not after a mating flight. It was one of the few times when nudity was expected and even encouraged.

Ashton faced him with arms crossed and a scowl on his face.

"I didn't mean for that to happen," Scott lied. "I didn't tell Narné to join the chase."

"No," Ashton said. "Everyone joined the chase. A perfect excuse, if you ask me. Do you have any idea how much trouble you're in?"

Scott straightened. "I'm the Queen's mate. Do you really think you can threaten me?"

The other council members in the room went silent. Everyone else started murmuring. There were at least two dozen people crammed in Jamie's bedroom, and he was willing to bet there were more outside. He needed to establish his position in front of as many people as possible to gain legitimacy. He heard whispers leaving the room, carrying with them his words.

"You are still in training," Ashton said. "The Queen's mate must undergo training like any other position."

Scott winced. It was a perfectly fair requirement, but it would give Ashton complete control over him. There had to be some way out of this. Ashton might not be able to kill him or Narné, but he could make their lives hell with whatever training he came up with.

"I'll train him," a familiar voice said, and Scott was surprised to see Mike step forward. "After all, I'm a teacher."

Scott wasn't sure which would be worse: Ashton and the certain threat of physical harm, or being forced to spend time with the man who raped him.

"I will consider your offer," Ashton said. "Now I must ask everyone to leave. Scott and I have certain things to discuss."

The room was quickly cleared and Scott noticed many of the people pairing up as they went home. They would have experienced the same searing lust he had felt, only they hadn't gotten any satisfaction. It was fairly common for the losers of a mating flight to pair up with each other and this flight was no exception. He tried to see if Amar paired up with anyone, but the crowd was too thick. Then Scott was alone with Jamie and Ashton, and Jamie was just sitting up in the bed.

"Jamie, I'm glad you're awake," Ashton said. "It's time we had a talk about your future. Both of your futures."

Jamie seemed to realize he was naked because he pulled some blankets to cover himself before scooting to the edge of the bed and gesturing for Scott to join him. But Ashton prevented Scott from sitting.

"Scott will need to complete basic training before the two of you are allowed to be together again. It will take about a month."

"But why?" Jamie asked, clearly not understand how much trouble they were in.

"The eight dragons assigned to your flight were well-trained and qualified to be your mate," Ashton said with just a hint of anger in his voice. "But Narné and Scott have no idea what to do. Until I feel that they are ready to take up their responsibilities, they will not be allowed at your side. You may say your good-byes now."

Scott glared at Ashton. On the one hand, a month was nothing. But what if Ashton kept saying that he wasn't ready yet, and that month turned into months or even years without seeing Jamie? Still, there was nothing he could do to fight it. He tried reaching out to Narné for help but his dragon was in a sex coma and completely nonresponsive.

Jamie reached out to Scott and Scott was at his side in a moment, kissing him tenderly all over his face so that his lips would remember that beloved face as well as his eyes did.

"Why is this happening?" Jamie whispered. "Why can't I be with you?"

"We will be together, I promise," Scott replied. "Don't be afraid, love. This is just a temporary delay in our lives together."

"But you just came back."

"Absence makes the heart grow fonder," Scott said, knowing

that he needed to be strong for Jamie but feeling tears forming in his eyes. "One last kiss," he said, half-asking and half-
commanding.

Jamie wrapped his hands in Scott's hair and pulled him
forward into a slow, passionate kiss that reached deep into his
mind until he could feel both of them at once, the same way
he could feel Narné's thoughts sometimes. He felt Jamie's fear
and also his love, and he tried to strengthen the latter. He knew
Jamie was feeling his emotions as well and he filled his mind
with the pure passion bursting from his heart as their tongues
danced together. It was a perfect kiss, but even perfect kisses
end and soon they broke apart to gasp for breath.

"This is temporary," Scott said. "Soon, we'll begin our new
life together."

As he followed Ashton out of the room, hope swelled in his
heart. Ashton could try to tear them apart, but their love was
true and it would always win in the end. Whatever training he
had to undergo was nothing if it meant getting back to Jamie's
side. He took a deep breath and prepared himself for the start of
his new life as the Queen's mate.

ABOUT THE AUTHOR

Elizabeth James

Elizabeth James hails from Portland, Oregon and spent many hours of her childhood tucked away in the Gold Room of Powell's Books, reading science fiction and fantasy masterpieces and hidden treasures. She writes romance with strong elements of science fiction and fantasy as a result, focusing on LGBT characters.

THRALL OF DARKNESS

Thrall of Darkness was founded because there is a shortage of good, quality literature featuring gay protagonists that does not reduce gay characters to stereotypes or dismiss them as secondary characters. Every story seeks to challenge the status quo by focusing on gay characters and combining drama, action, and sex into an addicting blend of fun-filled narrative.

You can find more information on Thrall of Darkness novels and short stories at **thrallofdarkness.com.**

BOOKS BY THIS AUTHOR

Demon Season

Taylor just wanted to bond with a regular demon during his first demon season, but instead he ends up with the prince of demons, an incubus! He fights through his fears of intimacy while battling past enemies as he and his demon come to a new understanding.

A Vampire's Desire

Kairos takes a job in an ancient vampire house knowing nothing about them and their society, and immediately falls in love with his boss, a powerful but cold vampire. As he tries to get closer, threats from a rival house threaten to tear them apart.

Dragon Tamer

Luke has heard dragons all his life and when a dragon summons him to raise her dragonlings, he runs away to help her. But the world he enters is fraught with danger and he knows little of the outside world. As the dragons begin dying off and dragon tamers like him become scarce, a rival tribe kidnaps him and everything he knows is thrown into question.

Sagent

Gabriel is a sagent, a sex agent, at the start of his career, but he is already scarred by his previous agency. When he is sent on a dangerous mission to the underbelly of Destiny, everything starts to fall apart. Isolated from his agency and not knowing where to go, Gabriel must choose between returning to safety and Destiny, or staying and forging his own path.

First Prince

Wren is the beautiful yet rebellious first prince of Fontain, forced to move to the Imperial Palace as part of a treaty. Upon arriving, he receives a frigid welcome and realizes his stay will be fraught with danger. When he finds romance in an unexpected place, he realizes that his life may not be as dire as he imagined and pleasure can be found where it is least expected.

Prisoner Of Love

When Prince Tristan is captured in battle, he fully expects to be tortured and killed. But the torture turns to erotic pleasure as he learns that his enemy, Prince Ryan, is in love with him and has been planning his capture with meticulous care for years. Will Tristan hold firm to his principles, or will Ryan's forceful seduction overpower his senses?

Dark Offering

Nightmares are a nightly occurrence on the planet of Ylse, and they're strong enough to lure humans to be fed on by the creatures who haunt the night. Jarl is charged with risking the night to feed the colony. He comes across one of the creatures offering peace. Is the creature sincere or is this just a new way to lure the humans to their deaths on this inhospitable planet?

Bride Of Albis

Sam and his small crew of space-faring traders have their usual routine permanently shattered when they are kidnapped by pirates. Sam makes a deal with the head of the pirates: he will be sold as a slave in exchange for the freedom of his crew. But when he discovers that the pirate lied and sold his crew as well, he vows vengeance.

Seeking More

Seeking More is a collection of eight contemporary gay romance stories that range from the deeply emotional to action-packed, from hapless MFA students to couples on the brink of a new relationship. Each story is focused not only on steamy romance, of which there is plenty, but also on character development and an emotional connection between reader and character.

Eve Of Eternity

Sabine is a young woman searching for her identity while fleeing the powerful man trying to steal her heart and mind. She's almost under his control when she is kidnapped by a man with conflicting loyalties and a mysterious past who claims to kidnap her in order to rescue her. Will she break free from the men around her?

Treacherous A Dragon's Love

In the middle of the final battle against the great dragon Arostrath, a woman appears bound in golden chains. The King claims her as his reward but the youngest son has an unusual fondness for her that could cast the kingdom into ruin. Will his love for the beautiful and strange woman destroy the kingdom, or does her mystery hide the answer to all of their prayers?

Made in United States
Orlando, FL
27 April 2022